OUR
STOLEN
YEARS

OUR
STOLEN
YEARS

Wartime diary and letters of a Liverpool couple

Compiled
and
presented
by

Martin Salter-Smith

CENTRAL PUBLISHING LIMITED
West Yorkshire

Paperback ISBN 1 903970 72 5

**Published
by**

Central Publishing Limited
Royd Street Offices
Milnsbridge
Huddersfield
West Yorkshire
HD3 4QY

www.centralpublishing.co.uk

Dedication

For my parents, to whom I wish I'd talked more.

Acknowledgements

Mike, for his critical eye; Owen, for his soldier's view; Peter, for his wartime reminiscences; and Gill, for her inspiration and support.

FOREWORD

By Major General AH Boyle CB, Chairman, Royal Signals Association

The term 'the man on the Clapham omnibus' was, in time gone by, used to denote the ordinary man. Mr Leslie Smith, he with a common name and perhaps more aptly described as ' the man on the Liverpool tram', was to outward appearances an unremarkable citizen. Yet he was no ordinary man of his time. A policeman who did not enjoy that role so became a GPO switchboard operator, and someone with an interest in the French language, he became one of the many whose lives were caught up and radically changed by the Second World War.

Through the medium of his wartime letters to his wife Grace, and from her early diaries, their younger son, Martin, charts a chapter in the social history of a Liverpool family. Leslie joined the Royal Corps of Signals in July 1942 and saw service in England, France, Belgium, Holland and Germany until September 1946, with but a couple of brief spells of leave with his family. His letters speak of a religious man with cultural instincts; he clearly enjoys architecture and music. No extrovert, Mr Smith nevertheless uses and improves his French to make friends in the newly liberated France and Belgium. Above all, his letters speak of his yearning to be with his wife and newly born son, a message that will strike a chord for any soldier today.

However, the soldier of today is rarely required to be separated from his loved ones for longer than a year at a time, and he volunteers to be a professional soldier. Leslie Smith did not, but took his civil occupation to war for over four years. During that time his letters provide a contemporary view of history as it was being written, while revealing the routine life (and diet) of a signalman, day by day.

In editing his father's letters and his mother's sporadic diary entries, Martin Salter-Smith provides both a glimpse of family life separated by war, and a tribute to outwardly unremarkable, but otherwise very special, parents.

AHB

CONTENTS

Introduction

War is the thief of normality; it takes its toll in many ways. Not just in death and devastation, fear and havoc, but in a stealthier, more subtle fashion. The two World Wars of the last century robbed whole generations of their youth through conscription, separation, postponed marriages and broken relationships. Many children grew up scarcely knowing their fathers – those strange men in khaki, with worn kitbags on their shoulders, who called once or twice a year.

What follows is the story of two ordinary people caught up in the greatest conflict the world has ever seen, and whose lives and attitudes were changed forever by their wartime experiences. They were part of no great personal drama and saw no front-line action, and in that they were no different from most of the population of Britain. Yet when the guns finally stopped in 1945, the pre-war world of the thirties had been swept away, and the British people stepped uncertainly into the nervous peace of a new era, where the international landscape was re-defined. The United States had assumed the pre-eminence which we now take for granted; Germany and Japan were smoking ruins, and Russia was perceived as the great threat to future peace. Britain had lost much of its status as a world power, and the Churchill coalition, so redolent of the bulldog spirit of defiance, was replaced by the Labour government with its agenda of social change, voted in by the newly assertive working class.

But the wartime years affected individuals profoundly. When we look back at the courage and stoicism displayed by our parents, we question whether we would be able to show the same qualities today. "Every man thinks meanly of himself for not having been a soldier" was Dr Johnson's perceptive judgement, and generations have grown up treasuring the gift of peace, yet wondering secretly whether they could have matched the wartime achievements of their parents' generation. The ordinary folk who personified the spirit of the Blitz, and of Dunkirk; the young men joking as they fought and died in the skies above southern England; the nerveless agents dropped into occupied France; the conscripted soldiers leaping from landing craft onto foreign beaches, braving the bullets of the unseen enemy: could we equal their selfless bravery today? Could we have coped with the freezing tedium and danger of the Atlantic convoys, or the privations of jungle warfare? We pray we will never know.

But even in those dark days, not everyone was called upon to show individual heroism. For most people the Second World War was a time of danger and discomfort, largely to be endured. At the height of an air raid, or in its aftermath, there was often nothing to be done but to put up with it, to clear up afterwards and to share a nice hot cup of tea with family or neighbours. On the other hand, young men who had never dreamed of soldiering as a career found themselves called up and often spent years in training, learning the Army's way, moving from billet to billet, making friends briefly here and there, becoming close to the men of their own unit. And when they travelled abroad with the Allied armies, meeting servicemen from America, Australia, France, Belgium, Poland, and many other countries, it opened their eyes to a new world and new possibilities.

Even those who lost friends, or were wounded themselves, can sometimes balance the memory of comradeship and acts of great bravery against the evil legacy of the time, and certainly those who were not in the front line, who did not face combat and see their comrades die, often remember the war years as the greatest experience of their lives, albeit one that they would happily have done without.

My own parents were typical of many thousands of ordinary Liverpool couples of the times. Both left school at fourteen, with little formal education. My mother worked as a shorthand typist, although to judge from her responsibilities and the reliance placed on her by her boss, would probably nowadays describe herself as a Personal Assistant. My father was by turns office boy, clerk, policeman, GPO telephonist, and after the war, Clerical Officer and finally Executive Officer in the DHSS. They both, however, enjoyed reading and, my mother in particular, loved classical music. She was an enthusiastic if erratic piano player, and my first memories of Chopin came from our slightly out-of-tune upright. Sometimes, when I was small, she would sit me on her knee and tell me stories to go with the music of Rachmaninov or Tchaikovsky, weaving webs of magic in the mind of a sleepy child, while preludes and piano concertos poured from the grooves of scratchy but atmospheric 78s.

My mother followed the politics of the time with great interest, and wrote frequent letters to the papers and to Members of Parliament concerning the Polish and Irish questions. Unfortunately her uncompromising and argumentative nature would often bring her into conflict with others, even, it seems, on more than one occasion, to the extent of losing friends. My father was much more easy-going and forgiving. But both of them knew how to turn a phrase, and it comes as no surprise that their war diaries and letters are filled with fascinating detail.

The house in which I grew up, and in which my parents were living during the war, had no central heating, no shower, fridge, washing machine or telephone. There was no television or stereo system, although we did have a wind-up gramophone. There was, of course, no car, and no foreign holidays. In all this there was no difference from the home of the average working-class person, and my parents would not have considered themselves poor. They were fed and clothed; they were able to go to the cinema, to a dance or out for the occasional drink, and they enjoyed an evening reading by the fire.

Our house in Smithdown Road was rented, and it was partly over a sweet shop, the living room and kitchen being on the ground floor at the back and reached by a long narrow hallway. Through the wall, when we were young, we could hear the tantalising sound of sweets being tipped into the scales and then poured into paper bags. The front door opened directly onto the street, while at the back there was a small yard in which my father built a knee-high brick enclosure, filled it with soil and planted climbing roses in it.

When my father moved into the house in 1941, after marrying my mother, he joined a household which consisted of my grandfather and grandmother, neither of whom were in good health, my mother, her older sister Nina and her younger brother George, who was a conductor on the trams. My father did not own his own house until the 1970s, and throughout his life never lived just with his wife and children, since Nina always shared the house with them.

So, at the start of the Second World War, my parents were an ordinary young couple, worrying about jobs and money and thinking about marrying and starting a family. They were probably not considering that soon my father would wearing the khaki battle-dress of the British Army, that they would be effectively parted for four years, that my father would hardly see his first child until he was over two years old, or that he would travel abroad for the first time in more dramatic circumstances than most young people do nowadays. He had already taken the trouble to learn quite a lot of French at evening classes, but he did not at that time realise how useful it was going to be.

Prologue

Normandy, October 1989

"Are you going to sign the visitor's book?"

As I passed it to him I ran my eyes over the names of the recent additions to the Livre d'Or at the Café Gondrée, many of them obviously veterans of the Battle of Normandy – infantrymen, engineers, gunners, commandos, drivers and all the other soldiers and sailors who were involved in the greatest amphibious operation the world has seen.

"How can I sign it?" My father's reply astonished me. "I was only a Signalman. I never fought in the front line."

"I know, but you were there! You waded ashore on Gold Beach in June 1944. You helped to keep the lines of communication going for the British Army from your conscription in 1942 until 1946. You were a trained soldier!"

"Yes, but I wasn't in the infantry. They took all the risks. They were the ones who got killed and wounded. The Royal Corps of Signals were just the back-up. We were quite safe really."

"Safe!" I stifled a snort. "You spent part of the war in England, working at a switchboard with a glass roof, with bombs dropping all around you while others were in the shelters. Then when you landed in Normandy you were still part of it all. Anyway, what's "safe" got to do with it? You gave some of the best years of your life to the war effort. You didn't see your son properly until he was two and a half years old. Look! Some of the signatures in the book are just from holidaymakers. If you won't write anything in it, I'll do it for you!"

Angry at my father's self-effacement, I scribbled something in the book about our current visit and my father's first visit to Normandy in very different circumstances forty-five years earlier.

The Café Gondrée

The Café Gondrée is situated next to Pegasus Bridge, and was the first building on French soil to be liberated in the early hours of June 6th 1944 by men of the Oxfordshire and Buckinghamshire Light Infantry, fighting under Major John Howard as part of the 6th Airborne Division. They landed by glider and secured the bridges over the Orne and its canal in an operation described by Air Chief Marshal Sir Trafford Leigh-Mallory as the finest piece of airmanship of the war. Later that day the remaining Germans watched open-mouthed as Lord Lovat's 6th Commando marched up to the bridge to rendezvous with the other British troops, openly contemptuous of danger and led by the skirling bagpipes of Piper Bill Millin. Since then it has become something of a place of pilgrimage included in tours of the invasion beaches.

Now, on this sunny autumn day so many years later, it was a peaceful place to pause and drink coffee, and to muse on the cataclysm of violence which was the Second World War, a catastrophe for European society and for families and individuals; but which had brought out so many instances of fortitude, stoicism and heroism such as our generation have rarely been called upon to display. And when people of our generation or our children's generation do display those qualities, it is often splashed across the tabloids, they are offered counselling, and they become, perhaps rightly, media celebrities.

But my father's generation was different. Not only were so many called upon to play their part in the world wide fight against the evils of Nazism and Fascism, but they did it in the days when trauma counselling consisted in having a smoke and a chat and a joke at their own expense. They were part of the generation who knew their place, who believed that the authorities "must know what they're doing", who respected their leaders, accepted hardship and had a dismissive and self-deprecating attitude to their own contribution. By now, the stories of the fighter aces and the secret agents have been told, and the commandos and paratroops monopolised the pages of my childhood comics. But who cares to tell the tale of the ordinary enlisted man and his family left to fend for themselves back home? I determined there and then that I would try to find my own way of doing so, but at that moment I didn't know how.

We emerged from the café into the sunshine, where the ripples on the river Orne shone like beaten silver, and the woods glowed with the incandescent reds and golds of autumn. Normandy, with its lush green farmland and grazing black and white cattle, streamed past the car windows as we headed west, like a summation of all that is peaceful and rural, just as it was during the caricature of peace that preceded the irruption of the Allied Armies onto its sweeping golden sands. The deep-set lanes and hedges of the *bocage,* such a barrier to tank and troop

3

movements in 1944, were a maze of quietness, and the ancient timbered farmhouses dozed amid the long October shadows.

We had finally persuaded my father to return to Normandy to revisit the places he had first seen as a young man in 1944. We had talked about it many times in a desultory sort of way, but this time he took us up on it. Perhaps, at 75, he was suddenly conscious of the passing of time; and we knew that he had already discussed such a trip with one of his wartime comrades. So we took the ferry to Ouistreham, arriving on a morning of dispiriting rain. To pass the time and cheer ourselves up we drove to Trouville, and on to Monet's favourite port of Honfleur, where we explored the craft shops and St Catherine's wooden church. As we walked around the enclosed harbour, admiring the jumble of picturesque houses, the sun broke through and the pavements began to dry. Our spirits lifting, we headed back to begin our tour of the beaches with a first stop at Benouville and the Orne Bridges, just as the British troops had begun forty-five years earlier.

That evening, in our hotel at Langrune, my father sprang his surprise.

"Do you mind if we call on someone tomorrow?"

"Of course not" – my voice betrayed my puzzlement – " but who do you know in Normandy?"

"Well, do you remember me telling you about making friends with a family near Bayeux when I was here in 44?"

I did, vaguely, but was not prepared for what was coming.

"When we decided we were visiting Normandy, I wanted to find out if they were still alive – they were about my age – so I phoned International Directory Enquiries and got their number. I had their address, and it turns out that they're still living there! So I phoned them, and they've invited us to call."

Apparently, not having spoken French for forty years, my father had casually picked up the phone (but then he was a

4

former telephone operator), rung Monsieur and Madame Sophie – friends from four decades before – and got us invited round for tea at four o'clock the next day.

Somewhere, the next morning, near Ver-sur-Mer, on a stretch of undistinguished beach-side road, my father asked me to stop the car.
"This is it. This is where I came ashore."

The landing beach at Ver-sur-Mer

We walked down to the water's edge, sand and pebbles mixed under our feet with scrunching shells. It looked like any other section of beach, tiny wavelets rippling lazily in on one side, anonymous houses and bungalows gazing inscrutably seawards on the other.
"Are you sure this is it? It just looks like anywhere else." I wondered how he was so certain.

5

"This is it." His eyes were half closed, searching his memory for that mass of shipping crowding in from the Channel, the shouted orders, the bustle, the chaos, the sound of engines, the rumble of gunfire somewhere inland. The men of his unit assembling after the long night-time passage from England, marching inland along dusty roads ... how could you forget that?

"We marched inland ... we met the rest of the unit in a village ... I think it was called Creully. We were tired and it was hot. We were carrying all our equipment. Then we got a lift in a truck. I don't know whether we should have done ... they took us to Bayeux ... maybe we were supposed to walk..."

It sounded as though, even with the passage of time, my father was still worrying about his moral right to accept a lift from a passing truck. Would anyone even give such a thing a second thought nowadays?

We quietly got back in the car and continued on our way. The Museum at Arromanches was our next stop. It has fascinating mock-ups of the artificial Mulberry Harbours which were towed across from England and used to unload many thousands of tons of supplies and nearly a quarter of a million men. The wrecks of these harbours can still be seen offshore to this day. But it is the darkened room with its diorama of the D-Day landings that brings a tear to the eye, showing the troops bundling ashore as the front of the landing craft goes down, some – too many – dying on the beaches; then pressing inland, men and women cheering and handing flowers to the young soldiers as they go forward to give battle to the retreating enemy. Not professional soldiers, but men like us, swept up in the net of conscription and pushed into the front line, many of them never to return.

Later that afternoon we arrived at the village of Saint Martin des Entrées, on the outskirts of Bayeux, once on the main route to Caen, but now thankfully bypassed by the new road. We parked the car and tapped on the door, reassuring each other that we didn't need to stay long if it seemed not to be appropriate. We should not have worried. My father was welcomed by Monsieur and Madame Sophie as an old friend, and as his son and daughter-in-law we were fussed over as well. Coffee and tea and patisseries were offered, and the conversation flowed easily. The afternoon faded into early evening, and drinks were brought out. Soon I was asking if I could phone our next hotel, in Tilly-sur-Seulles, to let them know that we would not be there for an evening meal. The Sophie's daughter, Françoise – a child of two when my father last saw her – arrived with her husband and son, and a little later we were eating dinner with them.

After dinner I phoned the hotel again to warn them we would be late, and at midnight I had to ring once more to enquire what time the door would be locked. By now my father's French was slipping away and I was having to translate more and more of the conversation for him. He was obviously very happy that the reunion had gone so well, but also very tired. We arranged to call again the next day, and M. Sophie then got his car out and guided us all the way to Tilly and our hotel.

The next morning we called again at the Sophies', and Monsieur gave us a tour of the garden, then took us a little way down the road to show us the house where my father had been billeted, and the pump where they had drawn water, such a long time ago. Later, when we had said our goodbyes, we went into Bayeux, crossing the ring road whose prototype was the military road built by the British for their transport vehicles, too large for the medieval streets of the town. We went into the cool hushed shade of the cathedral, wandering amongst its soaring arches and pillars, where my father had attended a Mass of Thanksgiving in 1944. In Bayeux, the first major French town to be liberated, General de Gaulle, hero of the Free French, had addressed the citizens on the 14th June, and they had followed him through the streets giving an impromptu rendition of the *Marseillaise*.

As we drove away from Bayeux and the landing beaches, and left behind my father's friends from long ago, I was still thinking about the millions of soldiers and civilians whose war was difficult, uncomfortable and potentially dangerous, and yet unremarkable; and wondering how to celebrate their experience. A year later, my father was dead of cancer before he could fulfil his wish to revisit Normandy with some of his wartime comrades.

It was then that his letters to my mother came into my possession, along with my mother's wartime diary. This diary tells of the everyday life and hopes of people living through the threat of Hitler, the continual fear of air raids, and the pounding taken by the city of Liverpool. My father's letters contain the minutiae of Army life, from Basic Training through all the postings and movements to the War's end in far off Hamburg; yet through it all their love for each other shines through. Everyone who has experienced Service life or the pain of separation will identify with their situation. This is their story.

Chapter One

Pre-War

Liverpool before the Second World War was a proud place, a great seaport with one of the most instantly recognisable skylines in the world, where the Liver Building, the Cunard Building and the Dock Board Offices presided grandly over the bustle of the waterfront. The great River Mersey, whose thirty-foot tides scour its narrow mouth twice a day, gave a safe harbour to even the largest vessels, and over thirty ocean-going ships a day passed through its labyrinthine dock system.

From here, up to the end of the nineteenth century, untold numbers of emigrants with the exotic clothing and impenetrable languages of Eastern Europe had taken ship for the Americas, and in still earlier times a flood of Irish families fleeing the Great Famine of 1845 had come the other way to enrich the life of Liverpool. During the War, the port would become the Allies' access to the Western Approaches, a safe haven where the Atlantic convoys came to unload their precious cargoes.

In the 1930s, Liverpool was suffering, like everywhere else, the effects of the Great Depression. But evidence of its successful commercial past was all around. Tate and Lyle, the great sugar importers and founders of the Tate Gallery, were in full production, and had long since shaken off their connection with the slave trade. The city was England's chief flour-milling port, and the leading world market for cotton, so many a man found work in the great Corn and Cotton Exchanges of

Liverpool. Thousands of others swarmed every morning to the dockside, bending their backs each day to the labour of loading and unloading the great ships from around the world, while the giant cranes wheeled above them and the scent of spices drifted from the cavernous holds. And Cammell Laird's, over the water in Birkenhead, still gave employment to the shipwrights who built the great ocean-going liners.

In 1939 two great buildings were rising in the City of Liverpool: the huge sandstone Anglican Cathedral, designed by Sir Giles Gilbert Scott and founded by Edward VII in 1904, and the grotesquely ambitious Catholic Cathedral, brainchild of Sir Edwin Lutyens, founded in 1933 but destined never to be completed in its original form. The acoustically perfect Philharmonic Hall, where Paderewski used to play, had been rebuilt after the fire of 1933, and these landmarks were to take their places alongside St. George's Hall, the Walker Art Gallery, the great libraries and University buildings, and all the other architectural tributes to the success of this unique city.

Nominally part of the County of Lancashire, Liverpool had always stood apart, looking seawards to the great trade routes rather than inland. A cosmopolitan city, it had the oldest Chinese community in England and a high proportion of people of Irish descent, whose surnames still sprinkle the telephone directory. Sailors of all nationalities came and went, people of different ethnic groups stayed and settled, and all contributed to the rich diversity of life in Liverpool.

The local inhabitants were marked out by their unique nasal accent, which contains strong traces of Irish, and was in those days limited more or less to the city boundaries – the totally different Lancashire accent took over before you got to Widnes or St. Helens – and by their ironic sense of humour, which would be tested to the full in the years to come. Spiky and clannish, the ordinary people of Liverpool were largely working-class, but proudly so, and not necessarily lacking education, despite the preponderance of flat caps and well-worn overcoats in the town centre crowds. Saturday afternoons saw many thousands of them at the football grounds of Anfield, or Goodison Park where Everton's Dixie Dean wove his magic for a workman's wages; and weekend evenings were a time for the "pictures", the pub, or a sing-song around the piano.

The ordinary Scouser in those days, like most people across the country, lived in conditions which today would be considered spartan. No central heating, and a bath once a week. No electrical devices to make housework easy. Little access to recorded music or entertainment – although my father sang, my mother played the piano (Chopin, Rachmaninov's 2nd and, later, Addinsell's 'Warsaw' Concerto were her particular favourites) and her sister Nina performed in productions of Gilbert and Sullivan operettas. There were no supermarkets, and because of the lack of refrigeration most people would buy meat or fish for the evening meal only on the day they meant to use it. "Doing the messages" was a common chore for children when they got home from school – running to the local shops for food for the family's tea. Most people had a set of clothes for work, and one for best; men wore detachable collars, clothes were darned and mended, and the cobblers did a good trade

There were still a good many horses in the town. Dust-carts, rag-and-bone dealers, milk floats and many other small businesses still made use of horse power, and the trams (and for the dockers, the Overhead Railway) provided public transport. Where the University Halls of Residence now sprawl at the bottom end of Penny Lane there was a farm, and the cows would cross the bridge over the railway line as they came for milking to the dairy. Parts of the present-day city, such as Woolton and Childwall, were still "out in the country", and families would stroll out on a Sunday, down the lanes between the flower-filled hedgerows, to take the air and have a pot of tea at one of the small tea-rooms. In many ways it was a harder life in the nineteen thirties, but a simpler one than that we know today.

Against this background, across which the activities of Hitler and his National Socialist Party were already casting a long shadow, my parents went about their business. My mother, Grace Farmer, the offspring of a family of Irish Catholics, had grown up in a terraced house in Standale Road, in the Wavertree area. A keen netball player at school, she had trained as a shorthand typist and worked in a variety of offices in the city. By the time she met my father, the family had moved to rented accommodation in Smithdown Road, nearer to the more middle-class address of Allerton. My father, Leslie Smith, had grown up in Neston on the Wirral, and had come to Liverpool to find work as an office boy when his family moved to the city, settling in Portman Road, off Smithdown Road.

Their simple story begins shortly after they met in 1938, when peace was fragile and rumours of war already abounded.

Grace Smith

Diary of Grace Smith

I am commencing this – dare I call it autobiography? – just about the time I met Leslie, because all that went before doesn't matter very much.

When we met, Leslie was working in a cotton office and was in receipt of a microscopic salary. He was also a member – if that is the correct description – of the Church of England, and had all the usual mistrust of the Catholic Church which seems to characterise non-Catholics. He was not, however, in the least bit bigoted. The only other blot – a very small one though, was that he was three years younger than me.

Now it has always seemed to me that whereas to some people these obstacles might have discouraged them right from the start, we immediately set about getting rid of them as fast as possible.

Being the most important, we took the question of religion first, and I must say that I thoroughly enjoyed the period of questioning and discussion which ensued. I did my best to enlighten Leslie's darkness as regards the Catholic faith and with some success. The top and bottom of it was that he eventually decided he would like to take instruction. We found a Father Conroy at Bishop Eton *(a Catholic church in Woolton Road)* and it was arranged that Leslie should attend two or three times a week. They seemed to like each other immediately and I am quite sure that Leslie quite enjoyed his visits at Bishop Eton. I used to go and meet him and several times I went with him to visit Father Conroy.

I well remember the period because it was one of the many "crises" that always seemed to be popping up. *(Austria was annexed by Hitler's Germany in March 1938)* But this seemed

15

to be serious because we were issued with gas masks. I remember Father Conroy telling us about the nuns having difficulty with their headgear and the gas masks.

Intermingled with this Catholic instruction business was also the desire to get another job – what I mean to say is that just about the same time we decided that something must be done about it. The only thing we could think of at the time was the Police force. This appeared to us to have all the advantages – of course, we didn't know very much about it. We thought Leslie was just about right in build and so on, and the upshot was that he obtained an application form, filled it in and waited until he was called for an examination. He eventually had this – physical and mental – and we waited with almost bated breath for the result. The result was that he passed and was put on probation.

It didn't take us very long to realise that the job was not what we had believed it to be. In the first place Leslie was posted to one of the filthiest and lowest districts in Liverpool 8 *(Toxteth)* and, to my mind, this probably made all the difference between his sticking it and not. In the second place it would seem that one has to be very hard-hearted to be a Policeman, and it was only with the greatest reluctance could he bring himself to summons people. Notwithstanding, he had several cases as he was being constantly nagged at by his Sergeant and he had to try and justify his existence.

When Leslie eventually went on the road – or should I say, on the beat – we thought that unless he did anything very terrible he would probably be settled for life, and we therefore decided that we might now start thinking about becoming engaged. We thought it would be a good idea to let this occasion coincide with my birthday, which was on the 18th June, and so we went to Watson's in Dale Street and looked at rings. Oh boy!

What a job it was. Eventually, however, I found one I liked – it was expensive enough anyway – and we bought it and took it home, where it was to repose in its little box until my birthday.

Now my birthday that year – 1938 – fell on a Saturday and as it happened it was the day of the Police Sports. We therefore sallied forth in the afternoon – Leslie, Nina and I – and watched husky men running races – having tugs-o'-war etc., and proud indeed was I of the lovely sparkle of my ring.

Very soon after that too, Leslie was received into the Church, Father and Walter being his godparents – I'm sure that isn't the right word but I can't think of anything else. It was a very nice day and I remember standing in the grounds afterwards with Father Conroy and he saw my ring and congratulated us on our engagement.

Leslie's father was very peeved about Leslie becoming a Catholic and was rather nasty to him for a time. His mother was quite sweet about it.

For some time after all these important happenings things went on fairly peacefully. I don't think Leslie was ever happy in the job. He knew the law perhaps better than lots of other policemen, but he really didn't like the feeling of having to be on the lookout all the time for people doing things they didn't oughter. Of course, the money made a big difference to us. We were able to get about a lot more than we had been able to do before and we also had both started saving.

That summer when we had our holidays we went about a lot on day trips here and there. We went to Blackpool one day and went on the things in the fairground. We went to Llandudno another day, by boat and returning by motor coach. That was lovely and we had gorgeous weather. Chester another day, up the

17

Dee in a rowing boat with poor Leslie rowing miles and miles. Then the Christmas of that year Leslie was able to spend more money than before and he bought me a nice little gold wristlet watch – which, alas, was doomed to be lost.

That winter I decided to join a Cookery class at the Technical School. I think I actually started some time toward the end of September. It was rather fun in a way but I can't say I learned an awful lot. It was just round about this time, I think, that the Munich crisis was on. Hitler started making a nuisance of himself over Czechoslovakia* and it looked like business this time.

It really was a terribly worrying time. Everybody thought that a war could not possibly be averted. Every day the papers had glaring headlines that Hitler said this or Hitler said that. It was round about this time that everybody was fitted with gas masks. I remember going with Nina to Our Lady's School where they were working furiously to fit everyone out. Nina and I stood in the schoolyard talking to Mrs. Riley. There was a sort of subdued feeling over us. We couldn't really believe that we were on the threshold of another war and yet there was every appearance that such was the case. Then one evening coming out of the cookery class to meet Leslie I heard marching feet and a contingent of soldiers went tramping past. That night when I was going to bed for a long time I heard those feet tramp, tramp, tramping along. Lorries with soldiers in them rumbling past – where they were

---

* *The German-speaking Sudetenland region of Czechoslovakia was ceded to Germany in September 1938 by an agreement signed by Germany, Italy, France and Great Britain, but not Czechoslovakia itself. Germany occupied the rest of Czechoslovakia in March 1939.*

going I don't know.

About this time, too, they were putting guns up on the buildings in town – very little guns they seemed. I don't think anybody had much faith in them or, in fact, in any of the preparations that were going forward.

Then, suddenly, we heard that Mr. Chamberlain was going to fly to Munich to see Hitler. He went, came back, went again, came back and the situation became gloomier. At last, one afternoon in the House of Commons, Mr. Chamberlain began to tell to a packed house the story of his mission and the result. It wasn't a very cheerful tale. He had done his best but Hitler had raved and ranted and not given way and the situation indeed seemed hopeless. It seemed that this, then, was the eve of war. But no; suddenly there is a stir in the House and a messenger pushes his way to the Prime Minister. Mr. Chamberlain reads the message and then to a hushed crowd he says "This is a message from Herr Hitler. He asks me to go and see him once again and he says this time he will meet me half-way." A last minute reprieve! The Members rise to their feet and cheer their heads off – and once again the country settles down to suspense – a thing by now they ought to be very used to.

Mr. Chamberlain once again flies to Germany. He sees the Führer and he comes back with a pact – that so much of Czechoslovakia shall be handed over to Germany and that they and we will never go to war upon each other. Nobody places much faith in Hitler's word, but we all hope fervently that now perhaps he has got what he wanted.

I shall never forget the evening that Mr. Chamberlain returned to his house in London. The streets were thronged with "grateful" people all cheering themselves hoarse. We listen to it on the wireless and it all sounds very marvellous. Mr.

Chamberlain reaches his home, he comes out and waves to the crowd and they all sing "For he's a jolly good fellow." They don't want to go away. Mr. Chamberlain appears in floodlight on the balcony of Buckingham Palace with the King and Queen and is again acclaimed. We say "Thank God," and wonder how long it will be before the next crisis.

❧

The year 1939 started rather unpromisingly in more ways than one. Leslie wasn't feeling too happy in his job but was trying terribly hard to settle down to it. Also there was more uncertainty regarding international affairs. Apparently Hitler was not really satisfied with the Munich agreement and he was starting to cause trouble again.

Anyway, we drifted on till March 1939, and then Germany marched into the whole of Czech-o-Slovakia. Soon after this they started ranting about Poland. We seemed to be hearing nothing but "Danzig, Danzig"* all the time.

As the year went on it became obvious that Leslie wasn't going to stick the Police Force. It wasn't that he didn't get many cases or that he hadn't as much knowledge as some of the other fellows. It just seemed to be a case of not being suited to the job – and when the finish eventually came it was as much of a relief

---

* *This city, now part of Poland and known as Gdansk, was historically one of the Germanic Free Ports of the Hanseatic League. After World War I it was demilitarised and a strip of land with a coastline was granted to Poland to safeguard their access to the sea. This was known as the Polish Corridor, but the presence of a German-speaking majority encouraged Hitler in his claims to have the city re-unified with Germany.*

as anything else.

That year also we went to our beloved Llandudno and had another lovely day. We also went to Blackpool and several other places – we were determined to have a good time before settling down to looking out for something else for Leslie.

Well, we had our good time and then, in a remarkably short time Leslie got another job. Not a very good job but better than none at all. This was Night Telephonist for the Post Office and as regards hours, not very much of an improvement on the Police. Still, we were glad of it.

At this time tension was growing regarding Danzig and the Corridor – places we had never even heard of up till now. There was great excitement in Berlin. Our poor Ambassador there was constantly seeing Hitler and trying to make him see sense – an obviously impossible task. Germany was using all her usual dirty tricks to foment trouble in Danzig. Planting agents there to cause trouble. There were constant stories of Polish atrocities towards the German minority and equally constant protests from the Polish Government that these stories were untrue. But it was really all too obviously manufactured, and the world had by now become accustomed to activities of this nature by the Germans.

Meanwhile Stalin and the Russians changed their attitude towards Hitler, and decided to sign a pact of non-aggression. So Ribbentrop flew to Moscow and signed the pact with Molotov, which seemed to mean that Russia would no longer support us. This was the signal for Germany to get cracking and I clearly remember the morning in the office when Miss Pitt came in and said "it says on the placards that Germany has invaded Poland." We knew what that meant for some little time previously we had given our word to Poland* that if she was attacked we would declare war.

Our Government sent a note to the German Government stating that if they did not withdraw their troops from Poland within twenty-four hours we would have no option but to regard ourselves at war with Germany. This was, of course, ignored and on Sunday morning, the 3ʳᵈ day of September 1939, Mr. Chamberlain pronounced those fateful words "We are at war with Germany." Nina and I were having breakfast, having just returned from church, and we were both nearly in tears. Although the thing had been hanging over us for so long, now that it had really come it seemed dreadful.

---

* *In March, Neville Chamberlain, in a complete about-face from previously declared policy, had pledged to support Poland against "any action which threatened Polish independence, and which the Polish Government accordingly considered it vital to resist". This offer, impossible to fulfil without help from Stalin (and any hope of this was quashed by the signing of the unexpected pact of non-aggression between Germany and the Soviet Union) linked Britain's destiny, and the rush to war, with the fate of Germany's neighbour.*

Chapter Two

War-time in Liverpool

I think it was on the Monday evening following the declaration of war that we came home to find that Mother had bought all sorts of "first aid" things – bandages, cotton wool, sal volatile and so on. This seemed to bring things even nearer. I think everyone was expecting immediate heavy air raids – although no one had the faintest idea of what they would be like. We used to have visions of having to pick our way to work over rubble and debris and so on. Actually when it did come it was nothing like that, but more of that anon.

Time passed and nothing much happened. This was the period of the "Phoney War", at least as far as we were concerned. But at the same time there was a hideous battle going on in little Finland*. Russia, taking a leaf out of Germany's book, had made demands on Finland which had been refused and they therefore immediately attacked Finland. We would go

---

* *In November 1939, Finland having rejected Soviet claims to border revisions in the Karelian Isthmus, Soviet troops invaded the country. The fiercely fought Winter War, during which the Soviet forces suffered astonishing reverses, ended in March 1940 with a peace treaty that ceded 16,000 square miles of Finnish territory to the Soviet Union. The Finns lost 25,000 men, while the Soviets endured the loss of 200,000 men, 700 planes and 1,600 tanks. These figures led to a drastic miscalculation on Hitler's part as to the fighting capacity of the Red Army when he invaded their homeland a year later.*

to the pictures and see terrible pictures of people being bombed, women cowering behind trees trying to get a bit of shelter – sights that seemed frightful to our eyes, and which we certainly couldn't imagine ever happening to us.

Then all of a sudden the unequal battle ended. Finland probably realising that they couldn't go on for ever keeping the Russians off – although they had put up a truly magnificent fight – eventually agreed to make terms with their attackers and so that episode ended.

At the beginning of 1940 it looked very much as though Leslie would have to go in the Army or something pretty soon, so we decided that if we were to have a holiday at all it had better be early. I managed to arrange to be off in May. We hadn't the faintest idea what to do or where to go and after racking our brains for hours we decided to chance going to Mrs. Lumsden's place at Bodfari, near Denbigh. We duly made the necessary arrangements and eventually arrived there safely.

The country round about is absolutely lovely. Mrs. Lumsden's house is a huge mansion-house which has been allowed to get into a terribly dilapidated condition. What on earth one woman with only a husband to look after, should want a house that size for I do not know. Of course, she does appear to take in quite a few people, but she doesn't seem to mind whether she has guests or not. She is a real character. I didn't care for the food much but that was really the only snag, except also that I was petrified with cold practically all the time I was in the house.

Leslie and I on two or three occasions started out soon after breakfast, taking sandwiches with us, and tramped all over the place. The weather was, fortunately, lovely, even quite hot at times. We would come back to the house about four or five and have tea or a sort of dinner then we would go down to the little village, if it can be called that, returning about nine p.m. Most evenings we spent yarning with the natives. There were two fellows there, Ted and Bill, who greatly entertained us with their stories of poaching etc. The Welsh accent fascinated us and when Mrs. Lumsden joined in the fun and started chortling it really was funny.

It was whilst we were at Bodfari that the news broke that Germany had marched into Holland and Belgium.* I remember

---

The Blitzkrieg: This started in earnest on the 10th May, when Panzer divisions, ignoring the heavily armoured Maginot Line which was built to protect the French Border, pushed North and West through the wooded hills of the Ardennes and crossed the River Meuse. Meanwhile, German paratroops and glider troops seized Dutch river crossings and the great Belgian fort of Eben Emael.

The lightning German tank attack had begun, and the French and British Armies reeled before the onslaught, spearheaded as it was by the leadership of Guderian, von Runstedt, and Rommel. Belgium surrendered on the 28th May, Paris fell on the 14th June, and Petain signed the Armistice with Germany at Compiegne on the 22nd, ironically and at Hitler's request, in the same railway carriage used for the Armistice of 1918. Meanwhile, between the 26th May and the 4th June, nearly 350,000 men were famously evacuated from the beaches of Dunkirk, to preserve the nucleus of a trained British Army.

From now on, although many observers considered that Germany had already won the war, Britain stood alone, doggedly determined under Churchill's leadership to resist Hitler and to win the ultimate struggle. With hindsight and the knowledge of the eventual outcome of the War, it is easy to underestimate how perilous the situation was at that time. Yet people who lived through it often maintain that they were never in any doubt that Britain would prevail.

My mother mentions none of these fateful happenings in her diary; but as she explains, she had other concerns closer to home at that time.

the morning distinctly. Mr. and Mrs. Lumsden had taken us into Denbigh in the car and all the way along Mrs. Lumsden was talking about the war situation with great gusto. When we arrived at Denbigh Leslie and I went up to see the ruins of the Castle and as we were returning we passed down a little alleyway and heard the one o'clock news being broadcast. We stood there and listened to the announcer telling about the invasion of Holland and Belgium and I felt terribly worried.

When we got back to the car Mrs. Lumsden settled herself down comfortably and started to give us the works. "You mustn't go back to Liverpool yet," she said. "I believe all the people are wandering up and down Lord Street not knowing what to do." She seemed to be thoroughly enjoying herself and it really made me feel we should rush home straight away. However, I managed to control myself until we had rung Nina up and she was very calm and cool about it. She didn't see why we should come home so we stayed until the Sunday.

Mother hadn't been at all well during the previous few months, blood pressure was supposed to be the trouble. She had been visiting the Heart Hospital as an out-patient and the Doctor had asked her if she would be willing to go in for a month. She was rather keen as she thought it would do her a lot of good and so it was arranged.

Nothing at all seemed to happen to her except that she lay there and rested all the time – which I suppose was all right. The place itself was terrible. The beds all sagged right down in the middle, the sheets were full of holes and the food was awful. It looked like a broken down boarding-house. Mother seemed to be doing all right, however, but after she had been there about three weeks she began to want to come home. It was eventually arranged that she would come out on a Saturday afternoon and Nina and Leslie went to fetch her. Auntie Mary was at the house and had brought cakes, and we had had the house cleaned practically from top to bottom – Beattie doing most of the work. It looked lovely. Father, Mary, George and I just sat and waited and it seemed ages. Every time we heard a car we thought it was a taxi outside the door and we would all rush about. However, at about four o'clock or thereabouts we heard a key in the door. Nina walked in and we could see instantly that there was something wrong. It seemed that on the previous Thursday night Mother had an attack of ague or something like it – she was shaking uncontrollably and was very ill indeed. We knew nothing of this at all. She actually had the Last Sacrament and we still didn't know. It was not until Nina actually got there to take Mother home that she was told and it was a terrible shock to her.

Nina and I went down on the Sunday afternoon and we bought some rum or brandy. I forget which. We put this in a drinking cup and had to practically pour it down Mother's throat as she couldn't even hold the cup to her mouth. She looked terrible. Her lips were covered with little sores and her eyes were sunken in. I thought it was all up. We had a terribly anxious time for about a fortnight with not much change and then she began to take a turn for the better. We thought we had best try and get her home as she was unhappy there and we brought her in a taxi and put her into bed downstairs.

She was very weak for a long, long time and another thing we had to contend with at the time was the air-raids which we were just beginning to have. Nothing ever happened, of course, but the siren would go and we would all troop downstairs, always expecting the worst. Of course in those days we didn't really know what to expect.

(From about this time, instead of recalling past events, my mother starts keeping a day-to-day diary. There is some overlap.)

24th June 1940

Had our first air raid tonight.* Nina and Father had gone to bed and I was waiting up for George. He came about 12.15 and had his supper. I was sitting – dead tired – waiting for him when the siren sounded. Went up to Father who was remarkably calm. Helped him to dress then we all went to the living room and sat for about an hour when the "all clear" went. We all trooped to bed and hoped for a night's rest – which, fortunately, we got. For a rehearsal it went off quite well. Thank God it was no worse.

25th June 1940

Everybody full of talk about Raid. Wondering whether anything will happen tonight. Nina phoned Hospital – was told all patients quite calm.

---

* *From July to September 1940 the Battle of Britain raged in the skies above southern England as the Luftwaffe attempted to destroy the RAF in preparation for the invasion of Britain. On 17th September, with the RAF stretched to the limit but still undefeated, Hitler decided to postpone the invasion indefinitely. Instead, he and the Luftwaffe's Hermann Goering turned their attention to the bombing of British cities.*

There had been spasmodic bombing on Merseyside throughout August, and the first casualty was a domestic servant in Prenton on the Wirral, killed on the 9th – the first of 3,875 victims in the area. From the end of August, however, air-raids became a much more regular feature of Liverpool life.

26th June 1940

Well, no air raid last night. Thank Heaven! Mother says she was very frightened but they didn't go down to the cellar. I wish she was home.

27th June 1940

No Raid last night. Our lives are beginning to be governed by one thing. Will there be a raid tonight. It isn't that people are frightened but they resent having to get up out of bed. I suppose that is a very slight inconvenience compared to what we will have to face in the coming days. Lot of French sailors wandering about & Polish & French soldiers. The town is most interesting.

28th June 1940

All quiet last night.

It was one evening in September that I had my first really unpleasant experience of an air-raid. I met Leslie in town and had a bit of tea and went for a drink in a place in Renshaw Street. At about 7.30 p.m. we thought we could hear a siren but it was so ridiculous that it should go at that hour that we couldn't believe our ears. Everybody looked flabbergasted. Anyway, as Leslie had to leave me to go to work, and as we could hear gunfire, I thought it best to just pop into the underground shelter across the road until things quietened down. Incidentally, at this time the trams were all ceasing to run as soon as the siren sounded. Since that time this practice has been discontinued. I couldn't get over it that there was actually a raid on in broad daylight. There was quite a lot of gunfire and although, had the trams been running, I might have chanced getting home, I didn't fancy having to walk.

Well it would be about 9.20 when we eventually got the "All Clear" and by this time, of course, it was quite dark. I found it impossible to get on the tram in Renshaw St. as everyone else had the same idea – to get home as quickly as possible. Anyway, in the end I jumped on to a tram going to the Pier Head, thinking that it would be best in the long run to stay on and come back. All the time I was praying like anything that I should get home before the siren went again. I seemed to be quite sure that it would go again.

Well we got along beautifully without anything happening until we reached Hartington Road – so near and yet so far – and then we heard the wail. The driver seemed rather keen to continue his journey but opinion seemed divided. Anyway he did drive on furiously as far as Portman Road, where there was a shelter. Here everyone had to get off and most, I think, went into the shelter. I, of course, had to try and be smart. I thought I might be able to get home by running before anything happened. I started off along the now deserted road, feeling very forlorn, but I hadn't got to the end of the Hospital walls when the guns opened up.

I had never seen the effect before and now I was terribly frightened. The sky seemed to be pink and full of crashes and bangs. I was stumbling along thinking a bomb was going to land on me any minute and I thought I had better take shelter somewhere. I suddenly remembered that there was a shelter at the bottom of Ullet Road somewhere and I made for it. When I got there I couldn't find it at first it was so dark, but after flopping round a bit I got it. I could hear voices inside but as it was pitch dark I couldn't see a thing. I dived in and stood there panting. I was trembling like a leaf and whether or not my panic conveyed itself in the dark to the others I don't know, but a voice suddenly asked me if I was scared and we began to talk. I discovered there were two young men with me and nobody else in that big shelter.

They gave me a cigarette and after a while I calmed down. Then when it went a bit quieter one of the lads and I decided to make a dash for it. He escorted me as far as Penny Lane and I gratefully reached the haven of my own home, where everyone was in a state of great anxiety on my behalf... All's well that ends well.*

On the night of Friday the 20th December Nina and I decided to go to the Plaza to see "The Mortal Storm". ** I rushed home and had a cup of milk and we dashed off. We went early in case of a raid and we expected to be home before seven p.m.

The programme was nearly at an end, the time being about

---

* *On the 6th September a bomb fell on a Children's Convalescent Home in Birkenhead, and this, together with the apparently indiscriminate bombing of hospitals, churches and schools, aroused the anger and resolve of the populace. It was around this time that someone chalked on his window:* Beware Hitler there will come another day...

Five days before Christmas 1940, after a raidless respite of three weeks, the bombs were unleashed again, and nearly 800 people lost their lives in a few days.

** *A film typical of the time, about a German family in the 1930s split by Nazism. It caused Josef Goebbels to ban the showing of MGM films in all German territories.*

6.25 p.m. when we heard the wailing of the siren. I didn't feel too happy about it as I don't like being out in a raid, but Nina didn't seem to feel perturbed so we stayed on till the show finished.

We then went out into the foyer where we met a girl we know. The gunfire was very heavy and the doorman would not let anyone go out, so we just settled down on the edge of the fishpond – which was very cold – and waited for the "All clear" to sound. This we expected, very optimistically, would not be long. However, we were doomed to disappointment. There appeared to be no cessation in the sound of gunfire and planes, even after we had been there a couple of hours.

I was by this time becoming very hungry, but unfortunately the café was closed and there was nothing available to eat or drink.

At 9 p.m. when the show finished altogether the fireman came and told us to go inside the cinema again and sit under the balcony in the three back rows. There we sat until about 11 p.m. Still very hungry and rather tired.

We occasionally went to the door, but the verdict was always the same. "It isn't safe to go yet. The planes are overhead". Anyway at about twelve we were thoroughly fed up and as there was a lull, which might last possibly long enough to let us get home, we decided to make a dash for it. We collected two elderly ladies and a girl and darted out. We had no sooner traversed a few hundred yards when we heard a plane very loud and saw the flashes which meant the guns were at it again.

We all started to run, Nina being rather handicapped by the elderly lady she was with. We managed to get to a shelter at the top of Queens Drive and we dashed in there. There weren't many in it and it was bitterly cold. Added to this, I never feel at all safe in these shelters and my one ambition was to make another break and get home. This we decided to do after about half an hour, and we eventually reached the house safely. We could see the flames from what appeared to be a huge fire over in the direction of the docks. We first had something to eat and then the gunfire commenced again and went on more or less without stopping until about four a.m. when we trooped off to bed. The fire still appeared to be burning.♣

I went to the Hospital to visit Leslie *(My father at this time was suffering from quite a serious skin complaint)* on Saturday afternoon – the 21ˢᵗ December. I bought fish and chips for my tea and had hardly finished when the siren sounded.

George was at work and Nina, Mother, Father and I took our accustomed places under the stairs. The gunfire was extremely heavy and non-stop and the roar of the planes was very loud and they were obviously coming in waves every second.

We said our prayers as usual and then settled ourselves to wait for the "All Clear". I went upstairs once and on looking out could see what appeared to be a huge fire over in the direction of the docks, pretty much in the same place as the night before. It seemed to us that they must be following their usual procedure, dropping incendiaries first and then coming back to drop H.E. bombs.

All went well until about 11.30 p.m. Father had gone out to lie on the sofa and Nina, Mother and I were still sitting under the stairs. The gunfire was terrific and Mother called to Father once to tell him to come inside but he didn't. Then suddenly we heard the horrible swishing of a bomb. I instinctively ducked forward

---

♣ *In the course of this raid, the Liver Building and Dock Board Offices were damaged, as was the Adelphi Hotel, where, in the dust-laden confusion of the darkened dining-room, the orchestra led the singing of* There'll always be an England.

and the next instant there was the most frightful crash and the sound of breaking glass and we were all choked by dust. Mother leapt into the living room and called to Father to come in which he did. Then when we had pulled ourselves together a bit Father and I went to the front door. I saw ambulances dashing past and there were some trams standing outside, but, of course, we had no idea where the bomb had dropped, except that it must be fairly near. We had to put the fire out, of course, on account of the blackout. Then we got back under the stairs and waited.

We were petrified with cold and fear. Each plane that came over seemed, we thought, about to drop something else right on us. Actually, after about another hour or so there was a second crash but this time not so near. We all felt that it would never stop. I kept asking Father all the time "What time is it?" and the hours seemed to be crawling past. We fully expected that it would go on until four or five a.m. as it had the night before, and I, for one, felt that I simply could not bear it any longer. But there being nothing else to do, we just had to stick it out. It must have been somewhere round about four a.m. when the first lull came, and then I decided that I would try and get the window fixed up in order that the fire might be lighted. Whilst I was struggling with the window Nina made tea and it was not very long before we had the window fairly satisfactorily fixed up and a lovely fire and nice hot tea.

Nina and I went out into the street to see if we could find where the bomb was and, lo and behold, just around the corner in Calton Avenue, about one hundred yards away, there were three or four houses in ruins. It was a miracle that we escaped.

The "All Clear" went at about 5.30, by which time we had managed to get the living room fairly tidied up. Then George came in and told us about his adventures. There was another siren about half an hour later but by that time nobody seemed to care. As it happened the "All Clear" went soon after.

We were unable to go to bed because there wasn't a room in the house with any windows in. The back-kitchen door was blown off its hinges and the front door lock broken. Plaster was all over the place. We merely sat around until it was time to go to church then Nina and I sallied forth and oh! my hat! The sight that greeted our eyes was indeed strange to behold. The gown shop across the road had no windows and there were dresses lying on the pavement. Outside Pugh's there were bottles of perfume etc. strewn about. Just around the corner outside the greengrocers there was a lovely pile of oranges and apples. It was bitterly cold and we walked to church and back again. When we got home we tried to clear things up a bit more, but mostly we just huddled round the fire trying to keep warm.*

That night Nina and Father went to stop with a Mrs. Hutton from Nina's office. Mother, George and I were left alone. I went to the Hospital to see Leslie. When I got to Edge Hill church I found the car was going no further as the track was covered with rubble caused by a bombed shop on the corner of Kinglake Street. What a mess. I tripped down the hill seeing evidence on all sides of the "blitz", broken windows, streets with ropes across denoting the presence of a "Time" bomb etc.

---

* *In this raid the northern docks took a beating, as did the warehouses and markets, where, apparently, a delicious smell rose from the fires as many families' Christmas turkeys were prematurely roasted. St George's Hall was only just rescued by the Civil Defence from the effects of a shower of incendiary bombs.*

I got to the "Royal" and walked in. I had only taken a few steps along the entrance passage when I saw a sight that made my heart jump into my throat. A bomb had evidently fallen right on the passage and we had to make a detour. There were nurses rushing about and men carrying stretchers and the whole atmosphere was one of urgency. I went up the stairs feeling very anxious and when I got to Leslie's ward I found it closed and two or three beds stuck in the little passage. There was no sign of Leslie and I was beginning to think the worst had happened when a boy out of No. 12 ward shouted to me that Leslie was all right. I soon found him and he was in a state of shock, having received the full force of the blast from a bomb which had fallen across from his ward. He was waiting to be taken to another Hospital. I felt very upset.

When I got home I sat and had a little rest and then Hilda Devlin and her Mother came to see if we were still alive. Immediately after they went we started to get tea ready, and hardly had we sat down than the siren went. Mother and I scuttled under the stairs with cups of tea and mince pies and George fixed up the gas fire just outside the door. I felt absolutely terribly tired but I read for some time. The gunfire was heavy and planes going over every minute. We thought we were in for a repetition of the previous night. I must have fallen asleep from sheer fatigue – nothing else would induce me to sleep during a raid – and the next thing I knew Mother was calling me and it was eleven-thirty p.m. I thought the "All Clear" had gone but Mother merely wanted me to have my supper. I could hardly crawl across the room I was so tired. However, I had a bite and then I got into the little bed and went to sleep immediately.

I got up very late next morning and sallied forth to the office

– having to walk from the top of Bold Street. As I walked down I saw two lovely big shops burnt out and, in fact, in one window the remains of what looked like an oil bomb was reposing.

At the bottom of Bold Street I found that a cord was drawn across the road and I made a detour round the little back streets, from where I could see that the block of shops previously housing Jay's, Phillip Son & Nephew, Robinson & Cleaver's etc., was absolutely burned out. The firemen were still there with their hoses. I saw several other damaged buildings round the back streets and then I emerged into Lord Street and found that the corner of South John Street – Church House – also had been badly damaged.

I arrived at the office about 11 a.m. and found that Mr. Lawrence and Crichton had left for our house to see if I was all right.

That night Crichton took Miss Pitt and me home. The traffic was terrific, Lord Street and Church Street being closed. It took us about twenty minutes to go from Castle Street to Byrom Street. We also picked up Crichton's brother who works at the docks and he had some terrible tales to tell. I felt that the world had practically come to and end.

We discovered that on the previous night, Sunday, Manchester had had a big raid – some people said worse than ours – which I don't believe, so that is where the planes that we heard were going.

Monday 6th January 1941

Leslie called in the evening. Just like old times. He had been to the Hospital and got some ointment and stuff.

Bardia has fallen at last. Nice work. Our troops will now push on to Tobruk. Heard Pre. Roosevelt giving his speech to

Congress. Very heartening. "We must give all aid to our friends who are putting up a tremendous and heroic resistance to the Aggressors which will go down in history" or words to that effect, at which we all stick our chests out. No raid.*

Tuesday 7th January 1941

Leslie came. Had a gayish evening. Nothing much to report. No raid.

Wednesday 8th January 1941

Did a lot of washing in the evening. Then read and ate chocs. No raid. Lots of rumours of German invasion of Bulgaria. Have no doubt it will happen sooner or later.

Thursday 9th January 1941

Lovely day, but terribly cold. Should be a good night for our visitors, if any. Leslie came, brought some books, one an old war book. We were busy looking through it when the siren went. Quite a lot of gunfire. Spent most of the time under the stairs. All clear about 1.30 a.m.

Bardia: This town, on the North African coast in Libya, was captured from the Italians by the 7th Armoured Brigade (the 'Desert Rats'), spearheaded by the 7th Royal Tank Regiment. They continued to Tobruk, which fell on 22nd January, and Benghazi, captured on 7th February. At this point, unfortunately, with the way to Tripoli open before them, the advance was halted due to Churchill's insistence on diverting troops for the landings in Greece.

Friday 10th January 1941

Heard that they did quite a good deal of damage last night. Bibby's was hit and some working class flats and so on. Nothing much to report on the raid question.

Saturday 11th January 1941

Went to office. Finished about 12.15. Rushed home for lunch then to Rialto. Saw "Foreign Correspondent".* Very good indeed, and very topical. Went for a coffee then walked home. Leslie went for fish and chips for our tea. Had slight air activity – very slight.

Sunday 12th January 1941

Nothing to report on the war front. Had usual siren but nothing much else.

Monday 13th January 1941

Leslie came. Had warning and heard a spot of gunfire but nothing much. All clear about 11.15 p.m.

Tuesday 14th January 1941

No raid. Leslie visited Hospital. Worse if anything. Mother

---

* *A Hitchcock film starring Joel McCrea. Full of impressive set pieces, it was a propaganda piece, indicting the Nazi regime. Goebbels recognised it as "a first-class production which no doubt will make a certain impression on the broad masses of the people in enemy countries."*

has a bit of a cold.

Wednesday 15th January 1941

Mother stayed in bed all day. Has very bad cough. Think it is a touch of bronchitis. Leslie came and we read. Siren went about 9.30. Soon got the "All clear". Another siren about an hour later. I heard another about 2 a.m. but took no notice.

Thursday 16th January 1941

Mother had Doctor. Has to stay in bed. Leslie visited Hospital. Looks a good deal better. No raid. Big R.A.F. raid last night on Wilmshaven. Snowing.

Friday 17th January 1941

It is very cold. No raid.

Saturday 18th January 1941

Morning off. Nina off also. Got up late. Went messages. Snowing all the time. Getting pretty deep. Man in the house tramping all over the place putting the windows in. Leslie came in afternoon. Looks a lot better. Doctor came out to see Mother. No raid.

Sunday 19th January 1941

Went to church through knee deep snow. Very cold. Horrible

day, everybody shouting, especially Father. Nina cleared snow in yard and Father did the front. Snow is still falling, however, so it seems a waste of time. Had fire upstairs in evening. *(In the sitting-room)* Went to bed late. No raid.

Monday 20th January 1941

Very tired. Lousy out. All sloppy. Beginning to thaw. Floods all over the place. No raid.

Wednesday 22nd January 1941

Snow all gone, thank Heaven. Sun actually shining. Silly Doctor came to see Mother. Didn't say a thing. Acting as locum for our own Doctor. Went for Mother's medicine. Raining. Leslie came. We read. No raid.

19.2.41.

I am afraid I have been rather slack over this so-called diary lately, chiefly, I suppose, because nothing much seems to have been happening.

We have been free from blitzes for about seven weeks or so now – that is to say we have not had any terrific raids, although we have had one or two minor ones. How long this state of affairs will last we do not, of course, know. Oh! That it could go on for ever!

There is much talk now about invasion. It seems to have become more a concrete thing than it used to be. Also many warnings have been issued that GAS will be used probably at any time now, and everyone is exhorted to carry his or her gasmask about. I keep meaning to look for mine but haven't done so yet.

Mother had a three week do with bronchitis and we were very busy.

Mr. Wendell Wilkie came over from America to "see for himself". I hope he was satisfied.

The Lease and Lend Bill* is still dragging on its weary way to fulfilment. Let's hope the war will not be over by the time America decides to help us all the way.

More recently there has been great excitement in Japan. A war would appear to be imminent between that so and so nation and America – probably at the instigation of our old pals the Nazis – but whether it will come to anything remains to be seen.

General Wavell is still carrying all before him in the East. Here's to him and his lads and may he carry on the good work ad infinitum.

The latest surprise on the map is a declaration or some such thing just signed by Turkey and Bulgaria, a sort of non-aggression Pact. We don't know yet whether this is a blow or otherwise. It doesn't really seem to alter things much, but I suppose we'll soon find out about this. Anyway we are so used to being let down now that another country one way or the other doesn't seem to matter much.

---

* *The Lend-Lease statute, finally passed on 11th March, gave President Roosevelt powers to lend equipment to countries on whom the defence of the United States depended. Britain eventually received $31 billion in aid.*

Haw-Haw[*] continually plugs into us the frightful things that are going to happen when Mr. Hitler is ready to tackle us. We are awaiting that gentleman's pleasure – but whether it will be a pleasure for him when he eventually decides to come here is a matter of conjecture – not much doubt about it really as far as we are concerned. We hope to have the opportunity to deliver what we think will be a coup-de-grace to him for ever more, and I guess we are ready when he is – sez me.

20th Feb. 1941

Nothing much to report except that it is snowing, and has been apparently since early this morning. Nobody objects very much because it is commonly thought that it keeps the Nastys away.

Headline this morning – "America tells Japan to leave the Axis or else!" Refuse to have anything to do with them so long as they claim to be partners with Musso and Itler. Evidently the U.S.A. believes in letting Japan know that they are not frightened of them.

7th March 1941

I find that it is a fortnight since I did any diary so I'll try and remedy the matter now.

---

[*] *William Joyce, known as Lord Haw-Haw from his way of speaking, was a British Fascist and broadcaster who worked for Goebbels Propaganda Ministry, making regular radio broadcasts to try to weaken the British people's resolve. He was hanged at Wandsworth Prison in 1946.*

We are beginning to find it really difficult to get certain foods – such as meat, jams etc., while as for sweets, chocolate or anything in that line, it is hopeless. It is bad enough as it is but it seems to be getting worse all the time. We are smoking all sorts of most peculiar things.

Monday 10th March 1941

I don't know where I was up to when I last did some of this diary so I'll just carry on from where I think I should be up to.

For the past fortnight or so all interest has been centred on the Balkans. First of all Rumania went down to Germany – that is to say they just allowed the Germans to do what they liked and Rumania is occupied by Germans now. Then there was a lot of excitement about Bulgaria. Would they or wouldn't they? Well, of course, they did, and the position now is that Germany is just where she wants to be to get at Greece.

There is, of course, Turkey still to be dealt with. Which way will they jump? Nothing would be a shock to us now I don't think, and although Turkey is still full of brave sayings and so on I wouldn't be at all surprised if they decided to sit back and do nothing.

Apart from all this there has been little else of importance happening. We are still progressing well in Libya and just recently we landed troops at Lofoten* in Norway and blew up oil refineries

---

* *Not only did British commandos destroy German factories producing glycerine in the raid on the Norwegian Lofoten islands; they also captured a German armed trawler and two weather-ships, and found the current settings for the ENIGMA code machine. This enabled the Code and Cypher School at Bletchley Park to break the ENIGMA codes for that period.*

etc., with very little interference from the Germans. Nice work.

The Lease and Lend Bill has at long last been passed by the American Senate and all that now remains is for the long promised help to be received.

London had a "blitz" on Saturday night – the first for some weeks. We here had a siren at about 9.30 p.m. yesterday, the All Clear going about half an hour afterwards. Then at about 1.25 we had another siren, a certain amount of gunfire and the All Clear about 3 a.m. – so I believe. It looks as though things in that direction are about to recommence.

We did well last night – 10th. About 12.15 a.m. the siren went – complete silence followed for about three-quarters of an hour then the All Clear. I believe there was another siren later on but I was deep in sleep.

Today in the office the siren went at about 12 noon. The All Clear sounded about half an hour afterwards and immediately, without a pause hardly, the siren went again. Looks as if they are working up to a grand finale.

Mr. Lawrence hasn't turned up at the office today. Believe he was fire-watching last night. Must have exhausted him.

Am going to the dentist at five o'clock. Hope he doesn't hurt!

Wednesday 12th March 1941

Went to dentist last night. Pretty horrible. Anyway have got the worst part over. Going next Thursday for the final stage.

Thursday 13th March 1941

We had a raid last night. Leslie called on his way to work

and at about 7.20 the siren sounded. Naturally, in view of past experience, we thought we were "for it" and I hustled Leslie off so as to make sure he got there all right. Then we rushed around getting things ready. Judge our astonishment when the "All Clear" sounded a few minutes later. We didn't, however, feel at all easy about it and our feelings proved to be quite right for at about twenty five to nine the siren sounded once more.

There was a period of about half an hour quite quiet and then it started. Plane after plane, incessantly, but, strangely enough, very little gunfire. We couldn't quite make this out. It was a glorious night. Full moon and as light almost as day. We heard one or two thuds but nothing very close. It just went on and on and on. Eventually I went to sleep under the stairs and the rest of the family scattered over the living room. I think the "All Clear" went about 4 a.m. Felt horrible, but still alive, thank God.

It was not until I reached town this morning that I realised that any damage had been done. Lord Street was full of glass and South John Street, South Castle Street and James Street were roped off. As the day wore on we began to hear various reports. A large block of office buildings and commercial properties stretching from South John Street to South Castle Street were on fire. We also heard reports that Birkenhead and Wallasey had had a very bad "do".

Friday 14th March 1941

Leslie was off last night and we went out for a while and then made a fire upstairs and had hardly sat down when the Siren went. We waited until we heard some rather loud gunfire and then trooped downstairs. We made several journeys up and down but eventually gave it up as a bad job and settled down – downstairs – to wait for the "All Clear". It is rather amusing the way, early on in a raid, Nina, Mother, Father and I all huddle under the stairs and feel petrified every time we hear a plane. By the time it gets to somewhere around midnight we all seem to be wandering round the kitchen or lying around, taking no notice of the planes and guns. It is as though one gets so used to it, or fed up with it or something like that, that it ceases to make an impression. Rather foolish really, and yet it is far more nerve-wracking to sit under the stairs and tremble every time a plane approaches. The "All Clear" went somewhere around two a.m.

Saturday 15th March 1941

Was off this morning so stayed in bed until about 11.15. Had to get up then because Leslie and I were going to town for his suit and then to the pictures to see "Waterloo Bridge".♣

Nina still in bed when we left. The suit had not arrived at the shop owing to enemy action around Leeds. We went up to the Abbey *(a local cinema)*, having been successful in obtaining some chocolate and nougat from Meesons – quite a luxury nowadays. The picture was quite good. Lily and Coopie were behind us. Lovely day. Incidentally we had another "do" last night. We practically repeated our programme of the night before. Went out, came back, had fire upstairs. Sat down for a few minutes and then siren went so

---

♣ *This film, starring Vivien Leigh and Robert Taylor, told the story of a WWI captain who falls in love with a ballerina. It was Vivien Leigh's first film after* Gone with the Wind.

went downstairs and sat there listening to thumps and bumps until the early hours. Am told that Wallasey and Birkenhead have had a very bad time.

Sunday 16th March 1941

Had a bit of peace last night, thank goodness. Just read and enjoyed myself by the fire, with the remains of the nougat and chocolate. Gorgeous today. Nina and I took Father down to see the ship which was sunk in the Mersey. Just funnels sticking up. Then we walked up to South John Street where the fire was. The A.F.S. were still working on it. Terrible mess. Father very tired by this time so took him home. Leslie came on way to work. Read.

Monday 17th March 1941

Everyone talking about Wallasey and Birkenhead. Seems they really have had a terrible time. Thousands homeless. Somebody said it was equally as bad as Coventry. Quite a few of the girls in Nina's office had their homes damaged and several of them were injured. Stayed in and read.

Tuesday 18th March 1941

Very busy at the office with renewals etc. Went to dentist at 5.30 p.m. Kept waiting till 6 p.m. He finished off the filling and I think that is the lot but am going again on Wednesday next week at 5.30 just to let him make sure there is nothing else to do.

Wednesday 19th March 1941

Nothing much to report. There is a "to-do" going on about Jugo-Slavia. Will they or won't they give in to Germany who are doing the usual bullying stunt. It is said the people are very much against it and are "seething with dissatisfaction" and so on but just the same I'll bet they go the way of all Balkans. There have been some very heavy raids on various parts of the country. "They" seem to have resumed their former tactics of "blitzing" places systematically.

Monday 24th March 1941

The official figures for the Merseyside raid are 500 dead and 500 injured. Clydeside, who were raided I think on the same nights have 500 dead and 800 injured. Nice work by members of the "finest and most enlightened race in the world". The Jugo-Slavian problem is still giving people to think. It is rather like a tug-o-war. First we go one way and then the other. The weather on Saturday was delightful. Pouring down in sheets all day. We went to Forum to see "Freedom Station".* Clive Brook and Diana Wynyard. Very good. Then collected Leslie's suit and then home. The cigarette question is becoming very vexed. Could only get a packet of "Park Drive".

Sunday was a day of National Prayer. Quite well supported I think, in view of the fact that Dolly out of the shop actually went

---

Freedom Radio was actually the name of the film mentioned. It was a flag-waving film set in Vienna during the War. The husband of a Nazi actress runs a secret radio transmitter for Allied propaganda.

to church. Nice day but bitterly cold. We went to church in the afternoon. Exposition. Leslie off. Stayed upstairs and actually had no raid. Bit of all right.

Raining again today. Perhaps it is just as well. Mr. L. went home early. Not feeling too good. Went to Mrs. Mather's for a couple of books and actually got some toffee and chocs. No cigarettes. Had a nice quiet evening. George on lates.

Tuesday 25th March 1941

Mr. Lawrence not in. Pay day but no pay. Couldn't get any cigarettes at all at the usual places. Miss Pitt eventually got some "Tenners" at a kiosk somewhere. They do say as how the tobacconists have large stocks which they are hanging on to until after the Budget. If so, dirty dogs say I.

Wednesday 26th March 1941

Mr. L. came in and paid us. Got our War Bonus too.

Thursday 27th March 1941

News this evening of Yugo-Slavian coup. It seems that the people have revolted and thrown out the fellows who signed the Pact with Hitler. I don't think I have said that the Pact was signed but it was and now they have been kicked out. Nice work. Young Peter is now reigning and I'll bet Hitler is mad. What a pity a few more countries didn't shew the same spirit. They are greatly to be admired because it can't be very pleasant to know that you are only twenty minutes by air from the German air-fields.

Saturday 29th March 1941

Went to church – 9 a.m. – came home and had breakfast. Went to town and bought brown shoes, brown gloves – all for the summer. Got some "Players' Weights" in town. Met Leslie in Lewis's Café. Went home and managed to get a packet of Kensitas – or rather Leslie got it. Went to Mrs. Mather's to change books and to my astonishment she slipped me a ten "Players" and a packet of chocs. Nice work!

Sunday 30th March

Bitterly cold although sunny. Leslie, Nina and I went to Birkenhead to see the damage. Not as bad as I expected, but bad enough, especially Birkenhead Park station and round about. Oxton Road had had a landmine by the look of it and round about the "Plaza" didn't look too good.

Monday 31st March

News has been trickling through of a big battle in the Mediterranean with the Italian Fleet. Several of their best ships have apparently been destroyed. Good work due to Admiral Cunningham.

Tuesday 1st April

Pouring rain. Lovely April day, I don't think. Went to "Lamb" for a short while in the evening then Leslie went to work. Revised figures given by Mr. Morrison for Clydeside two nights' raids – 1100 killed and 1000 seriously injured.

Wednesday 2nd April

Auntie Mary rang me up to find out what kind of beer Father drinks. Told her and she had six bottles sent up from Brennan's much to Father's joy. It was his birthday and he did pretty well. Went to Church by myself. Had been to dentist to have my teeth polished. I have finished with him now for a few months I hope.

Thursday 3rd April

Evening news that Benghazi[*] has been evacuated by our troops. Don't like the sound of that. No details. Belgrade has been declared an open city. War appears to be considered inevitable between Germany and Yugo-Slavia. Don't know what Germany is holding back for. They don't usually. Hungarian Premier has committed suicide – Count Telecki.

Saturday 5th April 1941

My day in at office. Pretty busy. Went home for lunch and then proceeded to town to see "Strike up the Band" [**] with Mickey Rooney. Not bad but not as good as the "Hardy" pictures. Then home and stayed in. Leslie off.

---

[*] *A port in northwest Libya which changed hands several times during the war. Captured by the British in February 1941, it was re-taken by Rommel in April. It was recaptured by the British for the last time in November 1942.*

[**] *An American musical comedy directed by Busby Berkeley, which starred the young Judy Garland.*

Sunday 6th April 1941

Got up as usual about 9 a.m. Funny how when one has been expecting a thing like the invasion of Yugo-Slavia for a few weeks, when it comes it is still a bit of a shock. Germany invaded Yugo-Slavia about 6 o'clock this morning, so the battle-front has been enlarged still further. The B.B.C. has been buzzing with the news all day. Belgrade has been bombed, in spite of having been declared an open city. Salonika has also been attacked. The Germans are also thrusting at Greece – poor Greece. Hitler addresses his troops telling them to be humane if they are met humanely but if they are treated brutally to be equally brutal. In other words he is paving the way as usual for all sorts of atrocities. He also addressed the Yugo-Slav people telling them not to interfere with the Germans. For every German killed ten Yugo-Slavs will be shot. Sweet guy.

Monday 7th April 1941

According to the papers this morning there is a large force of Empire troops in Greece – Australian, New Zealand and so on. About 350,000 according to the papers. Russia has signed a non-aggression pact with Yugo-Slavia and great importance is being attached to it by a lot of idiots here. Naturally if Russia does anything which appears decent it will be for her own ends. After the Russo-German pact which burst upon a thunderstruck world a couple of years ago I don't know how any sane person can possibly place any trust in them. Lot of rotters. See also their treatment of Poland.

We had a siren last night about 11.30. I was in bed and stayed there for some time but then I heard some gunfire so thought I had better arise. Stayed downstairs for an hour or so and then went back to bed. "All Clear" soon afterwards. We have had one siren so far today and I shouldn't be at all surprised if we have a visitation tonight, although Monday isn't really "blitz" night. We usually get ours a bit later on in the week. Haven't been able to get any cigarettes today but fortunately have enough to last till tomorrow.

Tuesday 8th April 1941

Got a letter from Walter last night. Doesn't seem very happy where he is now – Newcastle on Tyne. Washed my hair. Nina and I just thinking of having supper, being washed and going to bed when siren went. This would be about 9.40 p.m. We didn't think it would be anything much, but it developed into quite a decent length raid. Very heavy gunfire from time to time. We eventually – after a very lengthy lull – got fed up and were so tired that we decided to go to bed. We did and shortly afterwards, about 3.30 or a bit later the "All Clear" went. Haven't heard where exactly the damage was. Mr. L. says that three or four houses not far from him were destroyed, that is, in Meols.

Not much news about Yugo-Slavia and Greece. Very fierce fighting going on apparently somewhere around the Struma Valley, wherever that may be. I think the Yugo-Slavs will prove to be pretty tough people with somewhat unconventional methods of warfare. One wonders what good this is against mechanised weapons but as the district is said to be very rocky and mountainous the advantage may be with the Slavs. However, we will see.

Apparently the advantage wasn't with the Slavs as they have now gone down for the count. Greece is still going strong with

Anzacs and Aussies helping them but I suppose it is only a matter of time.

Thursday April 10th 1941

Office is closing down till Tuesday. Lovely.

Tuesday 15th April.

Back at work. Not so good. Had a lovely rest. Charlie came to see us. He was hoping there would be a "blitz" while he was here as he has heard so much about them but as he is going back today it looks as if he has missed it again.

Wednesday 16th April

Sure enough we had a "do" last night. Lot of heavy gunfire. It seems from the news today that it was Belfast who were really getting it. Some damage done in Liverpool and several casualty lists up.

Thursday 24th April 1941

Haven't done any diary since last week. Since then however, the King of Greece has left Athens and is taking up his abode in Crete, a certain proportion of the Greek Army has capitulated – for which I don't blame them. They have been absolutely marvellous but having to face the Germans now is a bit too much to ask. Our forces are retreating gradually but no doubt the delay they have caused the Germans will have, if nothing else, annoyed Hitler somewhat.

Wednesday 30th April 1941

Well the battle of Greece appears to be over. Our troops are being evacuated as quickly as possible. I daresay the casualties will be pretty heavy. I feel terribly sorry for the Greeks; they have fought so hard and for such a long time and were doing splendidly against the Italians, and now all their sacrifice and effort appears lost. I suppose Turkey is next on the list, and as far as they are concerned I think they deserve all they get. We had a rather sharp air raid last Saturday lasting from about 10.30 p.m. to 2 a.m. Quite a bit of damage and a whole list of casualties. Not a "blitz" by any means.

Thursday 1st May 1941

Quite a change in the weather today, thank goodness. It must have known that it was the first of May. Lovely sunshine and blue skies. I haven't been feeling too well during the past three or four days – bilious – but seem to have recovered now. Leslie off this evening. Went out for a walk and then had a fire upstairs. Siren went at 10.30 p.m. – I knew it would go sometime – then the guns started up and we went downstairs. Heard two or three heavy thuds which sounded bombish. Over at about 12.30 a.m. Short and sweet.

Friday 2nd May 1941

Another lovely day. It does one good to see the sunshine. Apparently Wavertree got it pretty badly last night so it wasn't so far away from us. I am told that Wellington Road was hit and that the "Grid-iron"* was damaged. To think of all the long "blitzes" we have had when Wavertree has been smashed about terribly and they have never managed to hit the railway and yet in one short raid of about two hours they got it. Not many people hurt which is something to be thankful for. We had no Head Office mail today and are pretty slack.

On Thursday night, the 1ˢᵗ May 1941, we had our first air raid for some considerable time. We were thinking that it was about time we had another one as we knew it wasn't likely that Hitler was going to leave Liverpool alone for ever more. Leslie was off that night and when the siren went at about 10.30 p.m. we trooped downstairs and Mother, Nina and I went under the stairs. George, Father and Leslie were sitting about in the kitchen.

There was a good deal of gunfire and at one time we heard a bomb coming and Leslie and George threw themselves on the floor motioning to Father to do likewise. He, however, only got as far as his knees and he told George that in future he had better tell him before the bomb started coming! The next day we heard that the "grid-iron" had been hit and one or two other places but it didn't appear to have been a heavy raid.

On Friday night the siren went at practically exactly the same time and as usual we took our places under the stairs. We heard several thumps and bumps denoting bombs but nothing very close. It was not until the next day that we realised how bad

---

* *This was the huge railway marshalling yard near Edge Lane. The Luftwaffe bombers tried time and again to put them out of action, but never really succeeded, despite the damage meted out to the surrounding houses, shops and schools.*

it had been. Leslie and I had arranged to see "This England" (I ended up seeing "This Liverpool"). At about 11 a.m. when I was having my breakfast – it being my Saturday morning off – Leslie arrived with the news that a land mine had dropped at the bottom of their road demolishing a garage, billiard hall, several houses and taking the roofs off and windows out of most of the houses round about.

Nina and I went along in the afternoon to see if we could give Mrs. Smith a hand and it was truly a terrible sight. I had to go to town for a coat which I had bought at Hughes and thinking it would be better to go down on the Wavertree side I got a 4 car. I soon discovered that it wasn't going further than Edge Hill Church as there was an unexploded bomb there. We proceeded along Durning Road, down Upper Parliament Street, along Catherine Street where there was a bomb crater right outside the Women's Hospital which had all its windows out. I heard consistent rumours on the tram that Woolworths was the only shop standing in Church Street, but needless to say this was an exaggeration.

I got off the tram at Clayton Square as it wasn't going any further and proceeded on foot up Church Street and Lord Street. Bunney's windows were smashed as were most of the windows up there. When I reached Castle Street I nearly passed out with shock. It looked as if there was nothing left of South Castle Street. There was glass all over the place and yards of hosepipe. Firemen were all over the place and the general effect was chaotic. I went down James Street which was in just as bad condition.

There was a huge piece out of the Overhead Railway and when I reached the Pier Head I found that the Dock Board building had been gutted. Brunswick Street was in a terrible state and I felt extremely miserable at seeing the terrible amount of damage that had been done. When Nina got to her office that morning she found all the partitions down and all the windows out. All the girls promptly set to clearing up the rubble and debris and managed to get the place a bit ship-shape.

Little did we know what we were in for that Saturday night. The weather, of course, was marvellous. Lovely moon and very dry. Ideal for firing the city. It was with a certain amount of trepidation we awaited the coming of darkness. On this day the change of time came into force. That is, we were instructed to alter our clocks on Sunday morning for the extra hour of daylight.

At ten-thirty prompt the siren sounded. George just managed to get in in time. We took our places under the stairs, said our prayers and waited. Then the guns opened up and we heard the approach of the first planes – buzz – buzz – buzz. From then on for at least two hours there was not a moment's break in the sound of planes. I began to imagine that the noise must be in my own head. We heard several explosions and at one time we heard three bombs whistle down fairly close. The time dragged on and about quarter to four things slackened off somewhat. The fire-watchers from next door came in for a cup of tea. We could see a terrific fire in the direction of town.

Nothing much happened after that and at about four-fifteen a.m. Nina and I decided to go along Church Road to have a look at the fire, never having seen one before. All the time we were out there were bangs going off – time bombs I suppose – Guy Fawkes' night wasn't in it. We stood and watched the fire or fires across the "Mystery" *(the Wavertree Playground, a local park)*. Someone said it was Lewis's and others said it was the docks. Whatever it was it was a terrific fire. The flames were leaping up and it looked as if they would never get it under control.

We returned home as the "All Clear" was sounding and Father and I stayed downstairs whilst the others went up to bed. We had just settled down when there was a terrible explosion which shook the house. There must have been hundreds of time bombs in Liverpool that night and morning as they continued to explode all day Sunday.

I went a little walk in the afternoon and heard that Lewis's and Blackler's had been gutted. Smithdown Road was roped off from the Grand up to the "Mystery" because of a time bomb, and I discovered that the bombs that fell near us had demolished three or four houses in Fallowfield Road, which is across the road from us. There were quite a lot of people crowding on to buses going to town – I suppose to see the sights. Can't understand why they allow that sort of thing. The trams are all standing around exactly where they were left during the raid. It seems very quiet everywhere.

Crichton called in the afternoon and told us that a shelter by the "Rocket" *(a pub)* had been hit and it was feared there would be a good many dead and injured. When it happened the wardens went around asking for volunteers for the rescue work and about a dozen women grabbed spades and waded in with the men.

On the Monday morning, 5th May, Crichton was supposed to be coming for me in the car. There had been a fairly heavy raid again on the Sunday night and, of course, I didn't know whether Crichton would be all right or not. Anyway, I waited until about 10.30 and then decided to go. I got a bus which went all round the world and eventually disgorged us in Renshaw Street. The scene that met my eyes was almost indescribable. Looking towards Lime Street one could see nothing but ruins. Lewis's was absolutely burnt out and the buildings by the Palais de Luxe were on the ground.

I turned down Newington into Bold Street and saw several shops there destroyed. I got as far as Whitechapel and found Lord Street roped off. Horne Bros. was gutted and all the other shops appeared to be badly blasted. Went up a lot of side cracks and eventually got into Union Court. Saw the Arcade in Cook Street which was also burnt out together with the Bank on the corner. Looking along Castle Street toward South Castle Street I could see nothing but smoking ruins. Brunswick Street was in a similar state.

When I arrived at the office I found Mr. Lawrence sorting what post had arrived. The office was filthy and everything seemed to be upside down. There was no water on at all. Crichton arrived soon after but no Miss Pitt. She floated in about twelve o'clock and I said "Still alive" at which she promptly burst into tears. I thought "Good Heavens, I must have put my foot in it". So I asked her what was the matter and she sobbed "Oh we have had a terrible time". I asked her if anyone was injured or anything but it appeared that all her people were all right but that all the windows were out and the roof off. We all felt very sorry for her and Mr. Lawrence said that Crichton should take us home in the car. Nina came up and we all piled into the car and tooted up to Anfield. We saw scenes of ruin on all sides on the way up.

When we turned into Miss Pitt's road I was looking for a ruined house but they all seemed to be fairly all right. She asked me to go in so Crichton and I followed her up the path. When we reached the front door she looked up and said "The fan-light is smashed as well". I too looked up and saw a small crack in the fan-light. I was by this time beginning to feel somewhat embarrassed as I had come all prepared to sympathise and condole but there didn't seem to be anything to sympathise about. We said a few words to Mrs. Pitt who appeared to be just as upset about nothing as Miss Pitt. As soon as we got back into the car Crichton said "What a little liar". I really think, though, that Miss Pitt was genuinely sure that they had had a terrible time, although had she seen our house at Christmas she might have had a better idea of what it is really like to have all the windows out and doors hanging off.

We had another fairly heavy raid on the Monday night and Crichton called for me in the car the following morning. We proceeded by devious routes till we got to the Cathedral and it was obvious that there had been a lot of trouble round about there. There were firemen all over the place and hosepipes all over the ground and the traffic was in a terrific jam. We managed, however, to get as far as Victoria Street, where we parked the car.

It was only in the afternoon that it suddenly occurred to me that Royal Exchange was near the Cathedral and I could hardly wait to get home to find out if Leslie was all right. As it happened, however, he had arrived home the previous night just before the siren went so was quite safe. I had great doubts as to whether there would be any Royal Exchange left but Leslie went down to see and it must have been there because he didn't come home.

We were now getting to the stage where it didn't occur to us that there could possibly not be a raid and I never attempted to go to bed. Nina went early with the idea of having a rest before it started. On the Tuesday night they came again at about the same time as the previous night and we were once again up till about 4.30 a.m. It didn't sound very near and I wondered where they were concentrating. I found out the next morning.

Crichton called for me again and this time we got pushed further and further across the city until we landed up somewhere around Eldon Street. It seemed practically impossible to get anywhere near the city itself as every road we turned into was closed. There were military police everywhere; also policemen from other cities. Everywhere one looked there were fires being fought, most of them nearly out but still smoking. A terrible smell of burning had been hanging over everywhere for about four days. The poor people round Vauxhall Road must have had a hellish time. Their houses for the most part are tucked away in amongst factories, warehouses and so on and even had the German pilots the best intentions, which they haven't, it would be a difficult job to hit the warehouses etc. and miss the houses. We saw at least three churches in ruins – Holy Cross, St. Mary's, Highfield Street and another which I didn't know. We left the car somewhere off Vauxhall Road and proceeded on foot in and out various little side-streets, climbing over hosepipes and glass. We saw three poor women stop an A.F.S. van and ask "Have you any food in there?" Poor things!

Into Tithebarn Street where a sugar warehouse had been gutted and a building further along was still blazing. Past buildings with notices up "Keep away. Dangerous Building" and so on. Exchange Station all smashed up. Moorfields roped off and covered in glass and so on. Past Tempest Hey where it looked as if our Insured's, Tempest Hardware Stores, had had a packet. We turned into Exchange St. East and found people brushing up glass like mad. We wondered what was the cause of this and soon found that the "L. & L. & G." building had had a direct hit. By this time we were beginning to wonder whether we would find our own place standing.

The Town Hall had no windows and the walls were pitted as if some huge hand had been hurling bricks at it. We discovered that our end of Castle Street was still standing and we found the office in a filthy state. The furniture was all over the place and it looked as if a storm had hit it. Miss Pitt didn't turn up and as this was the second day she had been absent we began to wonder if anything had happened. The telephones were all cut off because of the G.P.O. being burnt out but we thought her father might have let us know what was the matter. Mr. Lawrence and Crichton went up to her house in the afternoon and discovered that she was in bed. Mr. Lawrence was very annoyed that Mr. Pitt, who had been in town on the Tuesday and Wednesday, had not had the decency to call and tell us.

Mr. Lawrence was very windy about our staying in Castle Street. His main idea is to move the office out of Liverpool as fast as possible but as nobody else is keen he can't do much about it. Anyway he decided to stay but very reluctantly.

Nina again went to bed early and had a few hours rest before the siren sounded. It was about 12 or 12.15 a.m. when we heard it and at the sound of gunfire we all piled under the stairs. George had gone upstairs for something and we had just started to say the Litany when we heard the sound of a plane approaching. Before you could say "knife" there was a terrific crash which absolutely shook the house. My heart jumped into my mouth and we were all fairly frightened. George said he had been coming down the stairs and saw a big light and the next minute this terrific explosion occurred. About two minutes later there was another one just as bad. I was badly scared and thought we were for it, but after that all we heard was planes and they seemed to be chasing each other round and round without stopping. Some of them, of course, were our fighters. At about four a.m. we went out and everyone sprawled down somewhere to wait for the "All Clear".

We heard the next morning that a land mine had dropped in Daffodil Road and another near Booker Avenue. Apparently the plane was being chased and simply unloaded his packet to get rid of it.

Thursday and Friday nights the siren sounded but nothing much happened. Saturday we had a respite and last night, Sunday, there were two sirens in the early hours but nothing developed.

London had a terrible raid on Saturday night and damage was caused to Westminster Abbey, the House of Commons and other places.

In all the eight nights of our raids the following places were either totally or partially destroyed:

Lewis's. Blackler's. Most of South Castle Street. India Building. St. Luke's Church. James Street Station. Exchange Station. Liverpool & London & Globe Ins. Building. Central and Bank Telephone Exchanges. The General Post Office. Overhead Railway. Numerous Churches and schools. Thousands of houses. The High Court of Justice Building.

May 12th 1941

In the nine o'clock news tonight it was announced that in a statement to the German people Hitler had said that Rudolf Hess, a prominent member of the Nazi party, had disappeared. It was said that owing to a malignant disease from which he suffered Hess had been forbidden by Hitler to use an aeroplane but that, in spite of this, he had taken a plane and disappeared in it. His adjutants had been arrested for allowing him to use the plane. This all sounds very queer but rather significant, but as it was given a very lowly place in the news nobody attached much importance to it.

However, in the midnight news bulletin we were informed that in a statement issued from 10 Downing Street it was announced that Rudolf Hess had arrived in England. We were all absolutely stunned. It seems that on Saturday the 10th May it was reported that a Messerschmidt 110 was approaching in the direction of Glasgow. As it was known that a plane of this type could not carry sufficient fuel to return to Germany the report was at first discounted. Later, however, a similar plane crashed somewhere in Scotland and a German officer was found, having landed by parachute.[*]

He was suffering from a broken ankle, and at first stated his name was Horne. He afterwards said that he was Rudolf Hess and produced photographs which he had brought with him to prove his identity. Several persons who had known him personally were able to say that he was Rudolf Hess and a Foreign Office official had been dispatched to the Hospital to

---

[*]*Rudolf Hess: Deputy Leader of the Nazi Party and one of the most powerful men in Germany, he was believed to have piloted a Messerscmitt 110 fighter to Scotland on 10th May, baled out and surrendered, claiming to have come as a messenger of peace. He was arrested and imprisoned, but the British Government made very little political or propaganda use of his capture, and after the war, having been found guilty of crimes against peace, he remained in Spandau prison until his death in 1987.*

Since then, doubt has been cast on these events. A 1941 Me 110 did not have the range to fly non-stop from Germany to Scotland, and medical authorities who examined his body think it was not that of Rudolf Hess. The theory now is that he may have been shot down by the Luftwaffe, and that the man who landed in Scotland was someone else. Although books are still being written on the subject, nobody really knows the truth, and probably no-one ever will.

see him.

What all this portends is an absolute mystery, but naturally people are agog with suppositions. Is it a plot or has he sought sanctuary in this country – of all places – from something threatening him in Germany? It is all very queer.

May 16th 1941

The excitement over Hess has died down somewhat, partly I think because no one really knows anything about it and we have exhausted all our theories. Mr. Churchill has promised to tell the long-suffering public something about the matter when he judges the time suitable. Meanwhile Germany is doing a nice line in bargaining with the Vichy Government. One can only come to the conclusion that the French mean to look after themselves – in a very misguided manner – and leave everyone else in the lurch. They have betrayed us absolutely, their latest infamy being to allow the Germans to use bases and airports in Syria for their activities.

Lovely sunny day but still bitterly cold. Will it ever be warm I wonder.

August 1941

After the May raids Mr. Lawrence decided definitely to remove the office to his home at Meols and preparations were made accordingly.

We arrived here toward the end of May and the first morning we were greeted by torrents of rain. This lasted for nearly a week. Then I had a week's holiday commencing on the 9th June. The weather was fine and sunshiny most of the time but quite

Leslie and Grace on their wedding day

cold. The following week Nina went away and had heat-wave weather. This lasted with hardly a break for the whole of June and most of July. A most beautiful summer.

Leslie had his medical exam. about the 17th June and on the following day we spoke of getting married. We told Mother we were thinking of it and bound her to secrecy. We then went to see the Rector of St. Anthony's to ask his permission to be married in Our Lady's, which he duly gave. From then on we were running round like lunatics, especially Leslie, getting things fixed up. By this time, of course, it was July and we thought of making it the 26th July but when Leslie went to see the Registrar he found we were just too late by one day to give the necessary twenty one days' notice, so it was decided that we would arrange for August 2nd. Nina wrote to Uncle Theo inviting him and Auntie Bea down and they accepted. From then on Nina and I were busy getting the house ready and trying to get things for ourselves in between.

At last the great day arrived. It was a lovely day and very hot. Leslie and I went to nine o'clock Mass and then he rushed home for breakfast and I had mine – waited on by Nina. Auntie Bea and Uncle Theo were there and after they had had their breakfast they got down to the job of making sandwiches. Mother was rushing round the shops getting the messages in and she seemed to be in a bit of a daze. Charlie called during the morning with a lot of cakes and then he went round to the "Lamb" with Father to get the beer. Nina was upstairs getting the table ready for the "do".

The excitement was terrific, although I think I was the calmest of all. Nina went for the flowers at about 12 o'clock and they were very pretty except that her roses and Leslie's rosebud were a bit tatty. Mine were pink carnations and the others were pink and blue and mauve sweetpeas. These were duly sent to Leslie's house – at least three sweetpea buttonholes for his father and mother and Walter, the best man, and Leslie's little rosebud. Syd called during the morning for the attaché case which Leslie wanted to put his things in.

We had our lunch – a very scrappy affair – and then about 1.30 p.m. Edie arrived, looking very smart in bluey-grey and a cute little hat. I went upstairs then to get dressed, accompanied by Edie and Nina. I put my brown frock on and Edie tied the pink sash and pinned the carnations on me. Then my big hat and I was ready. Then we went and helped Nina to get dressed. Edie was very excited and one would have thought it was her wedding not mine.

The cars arrived about two o'clock and the first lot of people went off, leaving Father and I to follow together. We left the house about five past two and, unfortunately, arrived at the church a little early. Father and I went into the porch and looked inside to see if the priest was there but there was no sign of him. Mrs. Galgey was walking about with David in her arms. We stood there for about five minutes and there was still no sign of anything happening then Nina and Walter came to us and said that the sacristy door was locked and nobody seemed to be there. I felt very annoyed really but there was no point getting upset about it.

Walter and Nina went to the house and when they came back they said the Registrar was in there talking to the servant girl and he was in a terrific temper as he had another wedding at Garston at 3 o'clock. Father was getting very het up and it was all I could do to restrain him from kicking up a fuss. Eventually Father Mahoney appeared. He came to the back of the church and got holy water out of the font and the next thing Father Connolly appeared.

Father and I then advanced down the aisle and Leslie and Walter stepped out on our right and Nina on my left. I handed Nina my gloves and the ceremony started. I don't really know whether I felt nervous or not but I thought Leslie might be so I squeezed his hand and we hung on to each other. We managed to say the responses quite loudly and clearly – so we were told afterwards – and the ceremony seemed to be over very quickly. Then we went into the vestry. We then stood in front of the Registrar with Nina and Walter behind and went through the "legal" form of marriage. By this time I felt very used to being in the limelight and that went off all right. The Registrar was at first a little crotchety but he ended up by being very affable – I don't know whether he had caught sight of the ten bob note Walter had in his hand to pay the fee. At any rate Walter got no change out of it.

After that we turned about and formed a procession and proceeded out into the church, where Edie caught my eye and winked at me encouragingly. We started off up the aisle and

Leslie had to restrain me because I was dashing along. There was a man in the back of the church who turned out to be one of the men from Royal Exchange. Very nice of him. When we got outside we found Hilda and Mrs. Devlin and they emptied the contents of two bags of confetti over us. There was another man outside who smiled at us and he turned out to be Hayes, another man from Royal Exchange. Leslie and I got into the first car and drove off. He took us along Lance Lane and roundabout so that we wouldn't get home in front of the others.

When we eventually reached our front door we found a Crowe's handcart right outside and so we couldn't pull up right outside the door. Then I suddenly spied Hilda Close with her two babies in the pram and I jumped out and spoke to her. Leslie dragged me into the house and we went upstairs where we found Mrs. Galgey and David and Mrs. Smith.

The next lot of people arrived soon after, including Syd and Win and Bob and we all trooped upstairs and started eating. The table certainly looked very nice and Nina and all the Mothers handed round sandwiches, which were lovely, and cakes of all sorts. Then tea. When I thought everyone had had enough to eat and drink I produced the wine and filled all the glasses and gave one to everybody. Then I started to cut the cake. I made rather a mess of it and eventually Edie took over and did it very well. I thought Father should give a toast but before I could say a word Walter started off. Father was rather annoyed about this, as I found out afterwards, but it went off all right. After that it was just a case of eating and drinking and rushing downstairs to have snaps taken and singing and so on. I thoroughly enjoyed it.

Feb. 4th 1942

I have not done any diary for months now, but that is not to say that nothing has been happening. On the contrary, an awful lot has happened during the past few months. For one thing the Russians appear to be having some successes against the Nazis and to be pushing them back a considerable way.* We have, thank God, had no raids this winter, with the exception of one or two which have only lasted a short time and not much damage has been done.

Round about Christmas Mr. Churchill paid a visit to America and Canada and had a great reception in both places. We heard his speeches on the wireless.

The most important thing that has happened is the entry of Japan into the war. They suddenly attacked the Philippines and Pearl Harbour at the beginning of January and had great successes. The Americans, for all their efficiency and so on, appear to have been taken by surprise and sustained losses in their navy which will take some time to make up. The Japs are, so far, taking all before them. In Libya, too, we are not doing so well. After all our success there, Rommel has taken the offensive again and our troops are withdrawing. It seems we haven't yet got the right kind of tanks and guns out there.

American troops have been landed in Northern Ireland for some reason or other, probably in case of invasion.

In January 1942, the Russians had crossed the River Donets south of Kharkov, and Timoshenko's troops were advancing into the Ukraine to threaten the main supply base for the German Army Group South at Dnepropetrovsk. By the end of the month, however, German defences had been bolstered and the Russian advance halted.

Nov. 11th 1942

It is over a year since I wrote anything in this diary It is not because nothing has happened. Indeed, it has been a most eventful twelve months.

26/7/43

I have been terribly lazy over this so-called diary, but really must record the fact that a fortnight ago our troops landed in Sicily and most of the island is now in our hands. Today it is announced that Mussolini has handed his resignation to the King of Italy. That's the end of one Dictator – we hope – what next I wonder.

Monday 5th June 1944

News through. Rome in Allied hands – not defended by Nazis – Thank God.

6th June 1944

Allied Invasion of FRANCE commences!

(Grace Smith's diary ends here.)

Chapter Three

Call-up and Basic Training

In 1939, the British Regular Army was a small professional force backed up by the comparatively poorly trained and ill-equipped Territorial Army, made up of volunteers. It was the hard core of career soldiers who made up the British Expeditionary Force that was evacuated after the Fall of France from the beaches of Dunkirk. By 1940, limited conscription had raised its numbers to 50 divisions, and by June of that year over 1,500,000 men were in uniform. It was not until the end of 1941 that the National Service Act allowed for the conscription of all men between the ages of eighteen and fifty for military or other purposes, and of unmarried women between twenty and thirty.

It is easy for those of us who grew up after the end of the War to be distracted by the uniforms, the steel helmets and the weapons, and to make the mistake of thinking that the soldiers of the Allied armies had somehow chosen a military profession. Far from it. Of the three million who were in uniform at the end of the war, well over two-thirds had never thought of joining up until the call to arms came. For most of the half a million who were killed, wounded or taken prisoner during the hostilities, nothing had been further from their minds. For a few, including my father's brother, Charlie, who fought with Wingate's Chindits in Burma, the War was an opportunity to volunteer for what they saw as an exciting, if dangerous, adventure, but for most, especially family men, the arrival of the call-up papers was something to be dreaded. However, in the spirit of the times, they accepted it and took it in their stride. There was nothing to be done about it, and besides, they felt that everyone must "do their bit" for the war effort, even if that might one day mean leaping through the surging surf of a foreign beach into a withering hail of enemy fire.

In July 1942, it was finally my father's turn to leave his wife and family and become a cog in the slowly grinding wheels of the British Army. This is how he wryly recalled his army medical: "I walked into the room and the Medical Officer looked up at me over his glasses. 'How do you feel?' he asked. I hesitated. 'I feel fine,' I answered slowly. 'OK. A1.' He scribbled on a piece of paper. 'Next!' And that was it!"

And this is how he records his call-up in his diary (with later additions):

8ᵗʰ July: Received my calling-up papers ▯ to report to General Service Corps at Prestatyn on 16ᵗʰ. Postal Order for four shillings enclosed.

16ᵗʰ July: Left Lime Street 10.45. On train met R.E. Smith from Southport, operator at Wigan. Arrived Prestatyn one o'clock. Marched to camp ▯ former holiday camp ▯ chalets, wooden huts and Nissen huts, toilets marked "Lads" and "Lasses"! Various interviews for personal particulars, etc. Issued with kit. Filled palliasses with straw. Lights out 11, top bunk in wooden hut. Fair night, but cold.

And so started six weeks of the most energetic period of my life.

17ᵗʰ July: After breakfast dental exam, after dinner medical exam. Took kit to be marked (I am now 14234557 ▢ the number they say one never forgets). Put uniform on. After tea paraded in religions ▢ we went to church, others in ballroom. Talk by priest. Then back to ballroom for talk by M.O. Canteen.

18ᵗʰ July, Saturday: Talk by major and lieutenant. Amongst other things were told that the new system was for all recruits to be given six weeks infantry training, so that we could give a reasonable account of ourselves as soldiers if necessary. Heretofore every recruit had gone straight to the branch for which they were destined.

I think we were part of the first intake under this new system, and I could see the sense in this, particularly as I was later to meet colleagues who had never, for instance, handled a rifle (and probably wouldn't have known what to do with it if they had!)

Prestatyn.

As a seaside resort on the North Wales coast, Prestatyn has long been popular with holidaymakers from Merseyside, as has Rhyl, its brasher neighbour a short distance further west. Unprepossessing as a town, it nevertheless has sweeping sands and grassy dunes, the hills of Snowdonia in the background and fresh sea air in abundance. The Edwardian castle at Rhuddlan broods nearby, and in the graveyard of the Marble Church at Bodelwyddan lie the bodies of many soldiers from the Army

Camp at Kinmel. Most died of natural causes, but some were killed in the 1919 mutiny of Canadian soldiers dissatisfied with the speed of their repatriation after the First World War.

Kinmel camp had been in existence since 1915, and was linked to Rhyl by a narrow-gauge railway. Close to Prestatyn also was a group of wooden huts which in 1939 housed a searchlight unit, but which was later used as a prisoner-of-war camp for captured Germans, many of whom worked on local farms and became friendly with the locals, the last of them returning home in 1948.

The camp where my father did his basic training, however, was the Tower Beach Holiday Camp, part owned by the L.M.S. Railway and Thomas Cook. It was built in 1939 to luxurious specifications including a swimming pool, ballroom and gymnasium, but by 1942 was housing recruits in less glamorous wooden huts. The Holiday Camp closed in 1985, and the distinctive tower and remaining buildings were demolished in 2001 to make way for a housing development.

The Palladium Cinema mentioned in the letters, where the W.V.S canteen was, stood in the High Street until its demolition in 1979. Boots the chemist now occupies the site. The Ffrith, also mentioned, was a well known beach, but also a public house on the edge of Prestatyn.

The letters mention a trip to Rhyl which included having a cup of tea, going to the pictures and having a glass of beer. This is described as extravagant – yet a cinema seat in the 1940s cost from 6d (2½p) for the front stalls, up to 2/- (10p) for the best seats!

The Royal Corps of Signals

It was General Omar Bradley who made the comment that "Congress can make a general but only communications can make a Commander", thereby underlining the importance of the Royal Corps of Signals in passing the accurate information vital to the conduct of military operations.

Since the earliest times, various kinds of signalling have been used on the battlefield, from beacons and smoke-signals, flags and semaphore, to the "gallopers" of the Crimea. It was here, of course, that the devastatingly erroneous message was given by Captain Nolan to Lord Cardigan that led to the Charge of the Light Brigade. But times change, and it was in the same campaign that Morse Code and the electric telegraph were used for the first time.

Later in the 19th century, the Royal Engineers formed a Signal Wing, which became the Telegraph Battalion and then the Royal Engineer Signals Service, which provided communications during World War I, an era of growing prominence for the Despatch Rider and the wireless.

In 1920 the Corps of Signals was formed, and the "Royal" was added by George V a few weeks later in recognition of its importance. The Corps grew rapidly in size, and at the height of World War II had 150,000 serving officers and soldiers. Today, with over 9,000 men, it represents just under 10% of the British Army, a total well justified by the increasingly complex nature of the work it carries out in this era of so-called "information warfare".

The Royal Signals cap badge is a figure of Mercury, more commonly known as "Jimmy" to members of the Corps. As an emblem, it dates from 1884, when it was adopted by Major Beresford, Commander of 2nd Division, 1st Telegraph Battalion

The Section — L.M. Smith back row 4th from left

of the Royal Engineers. However, it was only in 1921 that it was approved as the official cap badge of the Royal Signals. My father's cap badge, as he mentions in his letters, ended up in the possession of a Belgian girl in Brussels.

The motto of the Royal Signals is "Certa Cito" *(Swift and Sure)* and they march to the tune of "Begone dull care".

79

Our Stolen Years

Leslie Smith

Letters: (Leslie Smith) 14234557 Signalman (*later Lance-Corporal*) Smith

14234557 Pte. L.M. Smith
6 Platoon, Hut E5,
1 Coy, 6 P.T.C.
Prestatyn.

Wednesday 22nd July 1942

Darling,

Our days are very full and I have to squeeze writing into the time after finishing, which is supposed to be 7 p.m. but is usually nearer 7.30, and 'lights out' at 10.30, after supper, cleaning etc. This first six weeks of intensive training is to give us the basic training all soldiers should have. At the same time we are to have tests designed to assist the selection of personnel to place men where they will do most good. If one is selected for the Signals one stays here for a further fifteen weeks for the necessary training. If not selected for Signals one goes at the end of the six weeks to the unit selected for. To-day we had to fill in a form giving all sorts of particulars about our education, jobs etc., and intelligence tests – general knowledge, fitting missing pieces into designs, dividing figures up to form squares etc., arithmetic, then an agility test – taking rings off pegs and putting them on to others (I think we saw that on the pictures?)

We have had quite a lot of drill, some rifle instruction, P.T., a gas lecture. Yesterday we had some Bren gun instruction and field work.

It is really a fine place, the food is quite good – you should see me drinking tea out of a mess tin, you've seen soldiers carrying them, haven't you?

It's pay day tomorrow thank goodness. I've got 2/8d. We are allowed to buy 35 cigarettes a week in the canteen, but when I get out perhaps I will be able to get some in Prestatyn.

Sunday 26th

On Thursday night, owing to the C.O. being very keen on short hair, I had to queue for two and a half hours for a haircut, and if some of the results I have seen are any guide, I don't want to see the back of my head. Most of them look as if a basin had been put on their heads, but being fair, perhaps mine doesn't look so bad. Friday night we were shown how to arrange our kit properly, and then had to do it, which took some time – every fold so, two socks there, so, etc.

Yesterday we had the usual drill for 45 minutes in the morning (commonly known as "square bashing"). Then we had a game of baseball, of which none of us knew very much, and I was last out, or rather, I was "not out". Then we had a few strengthening exercises and some unarmed combat. By then, by the time we had changed from our gym clothes, it was dinner time, and finish for the day. After cleaning up, Dick (that is, R.E. Smith, of whom I told you, and who is a very nice chap) and I went out intending to go to Rhyl by bus, but they were so crowded we walked to the station and caught the 3.20 train to Rhyl. We wandered about for a bit and I bought a couple of pairs of socks for my boots – they are a bit big, then we went to a forces canteen at the Town Hall and had tea and cakes. We were wearing our own shoes and our feet felt very tired – I think we'd have felt better with our boots on – so we decided to go to the pictures. The picture was not due to start for half an hour so we sat on the prom for a time and then went back and saw "Roxie

Hart",⁎ and it was quite good – we felt quite civilised again. We came out at 7.30 and the train did not leave until 8.10 so we had a couple of drinks. This was the first time we had been outside the camp on our own, and we enjoyed it. I have about 1/9d left after yesterday's outing so will not make a habit of it.

We had no drill to-day, but just before dinner there was a tailor's parade, when our uniforms were inspected, but no drastic alterations are made – only things like an inch off the collar and the pants. My blouses are rather baggy owing to the length of my arms, so it is either that, or shorter sleeves. After dinner we were finished for the day, so after washing some socks and hankies I came to the lounge to finish this epistle to you, my love.

While we are in training we have to wear denims, which are the same style as the battledress, except that they are about twice as big and made of a sort of gabardine. We all look like sacks of potatoes.

We have P.T. every day, most days we have rifle and Bren gun instruction. We have also been out on visual training – how to search the landscape for the enemy, how to take cover, etc. It is amazing how hard it is to find a man a few yards away if he knows how to take advantage of the natural cover and colour of the ground. There is certainly a great deal to be learned in this respect. One day we went through the gas chamber with and without our respirators – only tear gas, but not very pleasant all the same, my eyes were streaming and I was glad to get out. We are to have another later on. There is an assault course here, walls, ditches, barbed wire pits and entanglements etc. We

---

⁎ *This was a comedy about a 1920s showgirl confessing to a murder she didn't commit in order to gain publicity for herself. It starred Ginger Rogers and George Montgomery. Later it became the successful musical "Chicago".*

haven't reached that stage yet but are being toughened up for it. I believe next week is to be quite a hard one

The food here is quite good, once one is used to the conditions, the only trouble is that if I leave here the food will not be better, or even as good, and I am being spoiled. For breakfast we may have, say, porridge or cornflakes, bacon and mashed potatoes, bread and butter and tea; dinner – meat, potatoes and peas, beans or cabbage, and rice or something like college pudding and custard, tea, cold meat and lettuce, and jam and tea. Supper (which is optional, a lot of fellows prefer the Naafi – tea and cakes) beans on toast and tea or cocoa.

There is a swimming pool, ballroom (also used as a cinema), tennis courts, table tennis, billiards and a cricket field. Planes are roaring over and along the sandhills all the time – I've never seen so many so low before.

On the first Saturday we were put into age groups and "re-hutted", – there's another plane just flashed past – and they are quite a decent crowd in E.5. Dick, being 27, is in the same hut, although at the other end. In the next bed is a chap named Van Neste, who is a Catholic. We are four, McLellan from Bolton, and another fellow from Chester, originally Liverpool, who is only very nominal, being "R.C." just because he was baptised one.

It is 4.30 now so am going for tea, and the post collection is at 4.50, so will close for the present. I hope this finds you as it leaves me – in the pink – although I'm a mass of aches at the end of each day. If only I could combine being with you and doing all this I wouldn't mind at all – I believe it is doing me good.

Ta-ta for now,
Leslie

Tues 28th July 1942

My darling,

Yesterday was mainly devoted to Bren gun and rifle instruction, field training, and the usual P.T. To-day we had some drill, Bren gun and rifle, field training, P.T., some tests for D.S.P. (Dept for Selection of Personnel) and an interview by a D.S.P. officer. The first test was with headphones – writing down numbers spoken (on a record) by someone gradually retreating from the mike – I got most of them – then pairs of morse sounds, when we had to put down whether they were the same or not. Then a complicated, but really easy, written test which I finished – I think correctly.

The interview seemed to indicate that I was already earmarked for the Signals, in spite of what the tests may indicate. For one thing as far as I know, none of the operators have had the practical mechanics tests which I know some fellows have had. Still that doesn't matter.

Last Thursday I received my first pay – 12/6 – never have so many gone through such a to-do for so little – salute, hand over pay book, sign, receive money, soap coupons and cig coupons, receive back pay book, salute and march off. All this after waiting for ages.

All my love,
Leslie.

Wednesday 29th July 1942

Darling Gracie,

I quite agree it would be more sensible to wait for each other's letters, the snag being that they seem to take so long – for instance, I received yours this afternoon. I am writing this now, but can't post it till morning, which means you won't get it till the next day (Friday). This means roughly one each per week – still, as you say, it is the only way of preserving order, but that doesn't mean strict adherence, does it, my love?

Am I having a busy time! To-day hasn't been quite so strenuous. This morning it rained, and after the usual "square-bashing" (the rain had stopped by then) and P.T. we had some Bren gun, then another field session, during which we had to approach a barn without being seen, which necessitated crawling on our stomachs across a wet field with rifles in our hands. The afternoon we had a couple of map-reading sessions, more P.T. consisting of a game of basketball, then more drill and rifle.

As regards the tests I haven't done anything but paper work, except the agility test, when I was about average. We are not told the results of the others, but I think I did pretty well. In any case, as I said in yesterday's, it doesn't seem to matter, except to show one has some intelligence.

I don't like getting up early very much but I don't have any difficulty – I shave at night, so that saves some time in the mornings. Still it's always a rush, having to have blankets, boots, pumps, valises, knife fork and spoon exactly so on the bed. It has to be left on the bed all day, so that even if one had the time there would be no comfortable spot on which to sit. We have a ten minute break each hour, but that is usually occupied with things such as changing from and to P.T. kit etc.

I haven't come across any religious bias yet. One has to get used to "R.C." instead of "Catholic". Officially everything is made as easy as possible for us, such as being able to have breakfast after early Mass, and we can insist on going to Mass if anyone tried to give us something else to do.

I certainly was extravagant at Rhyl but thought it justified in the circs, and it certainly was a very welcome break.

Being such a lovely evening I went for a swim and enjoyed it, but didn't stay in long.

I'd better leave you now, darling, – it's near lights out. Goodnight,
Leslie

Friday 31st July 1942

My darling,

A few minutes to spare after dinner and after changing into P.E. kit. I doubt whether I'll be able to post it to-day, but if not it will be ready for additions.

Yesterday and to-day have been lovely, but too warm, especially dressed as we are, although after dinner we were told to parade in our shirt-sleeves. We have to wear small valise, belt, and bayonet almost always now. Yesterday we had two sessions of drill and I'm afraid we're about the worst platoon in that respect, but are improving. We had a gas film and a lecture on trench digging, also three Bren gun sessions – it takes some knowing.

To-day, after the usual drill, we had a demonstration of barbed wire fencing and then had to do it. Surprising how easy it is – you know when looking at it it looks a terrible job. After dinner P.T., then grenade throwing practice – not live ones yet. Then we were shown "Next of Kin",[*] just fancy that after our

---

[*] *Made in 1942 and originally intended as an instructional propaganda film, which showed how careless talk cost the lives of commandos during a raid, this film was so entertaining that it achieved success in the commercial cinema. Directed by Thorold Dickinson and with music by William Walton, its cast included Basil Rathbone, Naunton Wayne and, amongst others, Geoffrey Hibbert, whom my father encountered a few weeks later in uniform.*

queuing for it, but the apparatus isn't too good, so I didn't bother much – in fact I fell asleep once. Then tea and more Bren gun, after which we went to collect our suit which had been altered and left the other to be done. Finally we had to clean the hut ready for the C.O.'s inspection tomorrow.

We are allowed to send six articles every week to the laundry, anything over to be paid for.

To-day I sweated, I think, more than I have ever done, in spite of the comparatively easy programme. When I took my tin hat off it splashed me. Even sergeants of long service say it is unfair to us to have to cram so much into six weeks – our heads sometimes are reeling with facts about the different lessons. Still, we can take it. I hope. Actually we are the first batch here to be called up for the P.T.C. (Primary Training Centre), although the previous lot, who have just been sent to their units, were called up for the Signals, transferred to the P.T.C., and went through the same course. We have P.T. in the open when the weather is fine, and have to take our vests off, so that when I put my equipment on it isn't very pleasant round the shoulders. It is nice to have some sun, but I wouldn't like too much of it at once. At the beginning of next week we have to do some trench digging. Tomorrow comes our second lot of inoculations, also vaccination, so I suppose it will be C.B. for the weekend again.

After writing about ten lines I realised I wouldn't be able to post this to-day, as I had hoped. Sunday being our first anniversary I wanted you to get this on Saturday, but it doesn't matter really, as I can still wish us both "many happy returns of the day" and hope we will be much closer on our next.

Actually it was a fortnight last Wednesday since I last saw you, but it seems ages, it is ages – longer than we've ever been separated before, and I don't like it a bit. As you say it is just as well I'm so busy. What about you – you're busy, but doing the same old things, only more so. I know you won't think me conceited when I say I'm the luckier one in the circumstances.

Goodnight, my darling, for the moment.

<u>Saturday afternoon.</u>

This morning drill as usual, followed by inspection by the C.O. Then a short lesson on aiming at moving targets, followed by a break, giving us just time to dash to the canteen for a cup of tea before the next parade. Then we were taken to a field bordering the main road to practise aiming at targets on the road – people and traffic, first kneeling, then lying in the grass. We haven't fired a round yet. After that we went for inoculation. We were inoculated again in the right arm, and vaccinated in the left and about three fellows passed out – I think it is more the thought than anything else at the time, because the operations themselves are simple. One of the fellows who passed out surprised us because he is a tough looking specimen – he is one of our characters. Some of the chaps are sleeping in the hut, and my arm is beginning to ache, my right one. Some say this second lot affect one more than the first, others less, – it depends on the individual I think.

After the inoculations we are excused duty for 48 hours, but C.B. I am in the lounge now, and probably before I finish this I will go for tea.

After dinner I went to the Naafi for a cup of tea – we don't get any at dinner time, collected my laundry, and returned to the hut where I found your letter waiting, also the parcel. The stamps were a nice thought, my sweetheart, I had run out of them, and the cigarettes are more than welcome, although I'm not down to my last yet. The ration has been raised to 40 per week, out of which 20 have to be Woodbines, etc. By the way, we only get one soap coupon per fortnight now – has the civilian ration been cut?

Your letters cannot be too full of all your doings – the more the better, and the closer I feel. Sometimes I think about my being in the army at last, and it seems like another world, but I want to stay in yours and mine as much as possible until I can return to it properly.

Regarding my Missal – each time I've written since you first mentioned it I've intended asking you to send it and each time I forgot. Perhaps it would be better if you sent a prayer book – or would it? Has it got the Confiteor in it? I don't know it off by heart yet, and you may remember you typed it out and stuck it in my Missal? I'm quite attached to it really but it is rather bulky, isn't it?

Mother sent me a notice to report to Hood St. for firewatching last Wednesday ha-ha-ha.

There was a French or Belgian despatch rider sitting opposite me at tea to-day and his English was very good – in fact until I noticed the flag on his shoulders I just thought he was from another part of the country – one hears so many accents.

I have heard there are quite decent digs in Prestatyn. Denbigh would necessitate a late pass and even then the difficulty would be getting transport to be back by 23.59. There is also a "sleeping out pass". Denbigh could be managed I'm sure and would probably be more to our taste. In the meantime I will try to get a day pass one Sunday. One can also get a pass for bringing visitors to entertainments, dances etc. at the camp. If you were in Prestatyn that would be handy.

Being, as you know, terribly superstitious, I won't mention that my feet haven't troubled me much, but some of the chaps have had blisters and all sorts of things. My heels have skinned but without being sore, except being tired and achey.

Under this new system of P.T.C.s and D.S.P. there are what

are known as "feeder trades", such as plumbers may become coppersmiths, locksmiths – armourers etc., unless the tests show he has more aptitude for something else. If a man does not come under the "feeder trades" but shows inclination and aptitude for a job he will be set to it, subject of course to the requirements of the services. Apparently telephonist is one of these former, but even if one is put to learn a certain job and at the end of his training fails to pass the test, he will be put to something else. I believe operating in the Sigs is a terrible thing to learn. Still, whatever it is I get, I don't mind.

How do I really feel about it all? I don't think I'd like to stay in the Army, but I haven't had time to get used to it yet. I'm making the best of a bad job, realising it's got to be done. How can I explain like this, my darling? I want to sit with you and try to tell you. I feel more useful here than at Royal, certainly, and feel, at the moment, that I am training to do a real man's job. There is more in soldiering than one thinks, I think. One thing, in the evenings I don't feel as though I ought to go out to get some fresh air – I get plenty of that. Above all, I miss you.

Nina is ironing, the cat is playing – "the damn cat," or "the poor little precious", depending on what he's doing – George is sitting, smoking, listening to the wireless, shaving, getting coal, breaking wood, chasing the cat off the garden. Gracie is cutting bread, washing, peeling spuds, washing up, wringing clothes through the mangle – that's how you get pains in your stomach – ask George to turn the handle for you.

Allerton Road, bathed in sunshine (swept by wind and rain if you like) queue for the trams, my love and I walking along, to the Plaza, to the "Rose", sitting on a seat, or just walking, talking.

All my love,
Leslie

(That's July gone, and I must say that it's been very energetic. In between each spell of activity we had only ten minutes to get our breath back and to change for the next session, which meant sometimes changing from uniform or denims into P.T. kit and after that changing back again, perhaps for a lecture in a hot Nissen hut, when one had difficulty in not dozing off. But at the same time I must say that I realised, even then, that it was doing me good.)

Tuesday 4th August 1942

Darling,

I'm in a hurry again I'm afraid. It's 8.15 and I've only just been able to start. After finishing at 7 we had our usual bath parade, which we have had before as the last parade, finishing at 7. Yesterday was a fairly easy day because we didn't start until 1 o'clock. We had some rifle drill, started on the anti-tank rifle and the "75" grenade, and had the usual P.T. The "75" grenade is chiefly used for stopping armoured vehicles and as land-mines (minefields) and is quite a different shape from the "pineapple" which is the "36". To-day we had some rifle drill, Bren gun, P.T., a discussion – the lieutenant presiding – during which suggestions and complaints were heard, field exercises, and were shown how to use a pick and shovel! There has been a lot of changing around of N.C.O.s – we started off with Sgt English, a good soldier but a bad psychologist, and a decent L/Cpl & Cpl. After a few changes we now seem to have two sgts, who seem pretty decent, and a swine of a L/Cpl.

Last night, for the first time since last Monday, we went out, to Prestatyn, wandered about and finished up at the W.V.S.

canteen over the Palladium cinema.

I don't get my letters from behind the front door – they're sometimes thrown. The corporal comes in and starts shouting names, and when he comes to "Smith" its usually "Which one, Corporal?" You've no idea how heavenly "L.M." or "57" can sound!

I'd better go now love, tea is at 4.30 and I've had nothing since, so will go to the Naafi for a cup of tea and a bite of something, before going back to shave, clean rifle, buttons and boots – they should be done in the morning, but if I do them at night they just need a rub over in the morning – it's such a rush then.

Love to you, sweetheart,
Leslie.

Thursday 6th August 1942

My darling,

There is nothing much fresh to report. We have done drill, rifle drill, visual training, range-finding, A.A. rifle drill, gas drill, sandbag filling, lectures on field manoue/manouevres/manoovers, (how the h—do you spell it?) etc., etc. The weather has been lovely again. Today there was a fresh intake – poor fellows! I have seen no familiar faces yet.

So you think it is possible to get something in the nailbrush line, suitable for polishing buttons, and a big mug – I don't like drinking out of mess tins. A lot of the fellows have mugs, pint ones.

Apparently even if one goes into the Sigs, the training period isn't so easy, even if not so strenuous physically, but they don't finish much earlier. Still we can take it.

I think regular meals are upsetting my stomach a little, but nothing to worry about. Our sergeant today expressed the same views as myself as regards lack of time to do anything, especially G.P. Today we "blancoed" some of our equipment for the first time, and what a messy job it is. On Saturday we have to scrub out the hut.

We did not get any cigarette coupons to-day as they are starting a new rationing scheme, which necessitates cards, and we have not been issued with them yet, consequently I am at the moment smoking my last but one.

I can faintly hear, from the N.C.O.s' canteen, the news, so it is nearly time I returned to my chores

Love to all,

Leslie.

Tuesday 11th August 1942

Lovey,

I meant to write last night, but after "finishing" we had to erect some double bunks in place of our single ones – it was a bit like a joiner's shop, we actually had to screw them up, etc.

On Sunday I arrived at Prestatyn about 10 and had to pay my fare then – 3/2. I ate my sandwiches walking to the camp and the cake next morning. Coming through the camp I could see searchlights – I think over L'pool.

Darling, I love you terribly. It was lovely being able to see you on Sunday – only one thing wrong with it – not long enough.

Yesterday we had some bayonet practice, another map-reading lecture and the usual Bren, rifle, etc. This morning, a terrible morning – wind and driving rain, we marched about 2 miles to throw grenades, live ones this time. We threw two each.

After that P.T., dinner, rifle, Bren, anti-tank gun, and an ABCA (Army Bureau of Current Affairs) lecture by Lt. Garside. Tomorrow we are firing on the outdoor rifle range. That's about all I can manage now, my Darling –it's nearly 10 and the lights go out at 10.15. Oh, darling, I worship you.

Love to all,
Leslie.

Wednesday 12th August 1942

Darling,

Another day gone – a fortnight next Tuesday we should "pass out", maybe we will! To-day has been mostly windy and cold, and this morning from 8 until dinner time we were on the rifle range. I did quite well and I think I was top scorer, or at least within a couple of points, and if I had not slipped up on the five rounds fired while wearing respirators I would have been miles ahead. It surprises me because I didn't think I would be any good at it – I don't know why. By the way, we seem to have a bugler now! After dinner P.T. then Bren revision, rifle revision, more Bren revision. Just before tea we had rifle drill, and had just been shown how to "present", when a general, who was inspecting the camp, came on to the square with the colonel and other officers, and we had to "present arms". It seemed pretty awful to me, I don't know what he thought. After 7 o'clock we had "bath parade", which we usually have on Tuesdays.

I see in orders tonight that I am down for dental tomorrow at noon. I think I told you that we were examined when we came, and I am down for scaling only, I think. It is being done alphabetically. Quite a lot of the fellows are in hospital with vaccine fever, there are two from our hut. I think it affects those who have never been done before, more than others.

I haven't had your parcel yet. As you say we didn't have much time together – that would have been one of the advantages of having our own home, however selfish. Still there'll come a day, won't there my love?

All my love,
Leslie.

Monday 17th August 1942

Darling,

I arrived all right, but had to stand from Chester to here, owing to helping a couple of girls with a case when we changed – they were going to Rhyl for a holiday. Dick was on the train and we met at Chester – he saw us at Mossley Hill but could not get to the window. It's a pity you have to walk home alone, lovey, but it can't be helped, can it?

It is 9.30 p.m. and I have just shaved etc. Slocombe, one of the vaccine cases, now out of hospital, is playing his oboe. Some of the lads have been and are on "Fog picquet", so I suppose it will be the rest of us for guard on Thursday.

To-day has been lovely, the weather and our work. We started off with rifle drill in respirators, followed by P.T., then two periods of map-reading. Dinner, then to the armourer with our rifles for inspection. Then we went to the sand-hills, where we had a rifle test, aiming and firing from cover, during which my rifle was choked with sand, also my pockets and face. Tea, then a gas lecture, after which we went into the gas chamber – two minutes with respirator, then two minutes without, and then had to put our respirators on and march about for ten minutes. It was that gas I told you about, and although some suffered much more than I did, we were all sneezing etc., and our gums were aching. The idea is to give us confidence in our respirators.

Later we are to have an application of Mustard Gas to give us confidence in the ointment. We finished at 6.40 and at 7 I went for supper. Now if I have time before lights out I will clean my buttons, boots and rifle. I've made my bed, and am now writing to my wonderful, lovely, darling wife. I do love you, Gracie.

As far as I can see the best train for you would be the 9.40 from Lime St., which arrives here at noon. It probably stops at Mossley Hill or somewhere. I think there is one from Low Level at 10.5 which catches the same connection at Chester, but that would mean going to town and then changing at Rock Ferry or somewhere.

I don't think there's much else. They have just broken into "She'll be comin' round the mountain". Vic Beese from Newport, Mon. is a record fan and used to buy several each week, all sorts. Yesterday, as I said, there was a rifle inspection and those of the absent ones were in the Q.M. stores so I had to borrow one for first parade. It's "Old Faithful" now.

Will go now, my sweetheart, so look after yourself, and give my love to everyone.

Goodnight,
Leslie

Wednesday 19th August 1942

My darling,
The above won't be my address for much longer I hope. As you know we "pass out" next Tuesday officially, although it has been going on for a few days. Yesterday was lovely, and to-day hasn't been so bad either, although we had some rain this

morning. On the whole they have been fairly easy days for us too. Yesterday we spent the period between dinner and tea on the range, firing Brens this time. I didn't do as well as with the rifle, but it is a handier gun to fire – it is, of course, an automatic gun, although one can fire single rounds if desired, and we fired both ways. During the morning we started with P.T., then bayonet fighting. The day's "work" finished with a discussion with the C.S.M. presiding. He is a Scot, and typically, very keen on better education. He seems a very decent sort of fellow.

To-day we started with drill, then Bren revision, followed by a gas lecture.

During the morning we heard a rumour that we had landed in France, then it deteriorated into "just a raid" and at the moment we hear that tanks have been landed. Probably you will know more about it, and perhaps we shall before we go to bed.*

After dinner, until tea-time, was occupied with fieldcraft, handling of the Bren behind cover, and tactics. After tea – 5.15 – 6.00 – we were on the square, practising sentry- drill, ready for tomorrow night. At 6 o'clock we went on bath-parade, which we usually have after "finishing" at 7 o'clock. After my bath I went for supper, which was very good – the same as for dinner, with the addition of cocoa. Lately I've been unlucky with the suppers. It depends on what time one goes, and how the stuff lasts out, but there is always something, even if the menu

---

* *This ill-fated raid on Dieppe established once and for all the impossibility of a full-frontal attack on one of the German-held Channel ports. Out of 6,000 Canadian and British troops used in the raid, 4,000 were killed, wounded or captured. Partly as a result of this, the concept of the floating Mulberry Harbours was developed, and the Normandy beaches eventually chosen for the invasion of France.*

changes half-way through.

I always seem to be talking about myself, but I know you want to know everything – if I had time I could probably tell you much more, all the little details, just as we always did. Perhaps I will have a little more time if, and when, I am a signalman instead of a private – the same rank, of course, but a different name. I hope I get into a chalet instead of a hut. Of course even if I go into the Signals I may not stay here – who knows?

It's pay day again tomorrow, and that means a new ration-week starts – I got some cigs to-day – from a shop opposite the main gate, so am not waiting so impatiently as usual for Thursday.

I hope your mother is feeling full of beans now – and talking of beans, we had beans on toast (or rather fried bread) for tea. We have quite a lot of beans, sometimes at breakfast, with bacon.

I don't think there's anything else, love, and it's time I was going, so goodnight, darling and sleep well.

Leslie.

Thursday 20th August 1942

Darling,

It's now 11.45 p.m. and I am in the guardroom waiting for my next spell on guard, from 1 until 3. I was the first of our platoon to do sentry on the main gate, from 7 until 9. We do 2 on and four off. This morning during drill fifteen of us were picked for guard, and of these, three of us were chosen for main-gate duty, the other twelve patrolling the camp in pairs, keeping their eyes on things – much like bobbies on nights, trying doors, etc. They do the same hours. What a hectic time we had getting ready for it – blancoing all our webbing equipment and changing into battle dress after tea. We also had to shave etc. Of course, we still have to parade as usual in the morning.

This morning we started with drill, followed by a practice kit lay-out, then a lecture on anti-tank action. After dinner we had a couple of trial runs over the assault course. Actually it is only a miniature, but it was quite enough for us. We start by jumping a ditch full of barbed wire, then crawling under a barbed wire entanglement, followed by a network of trip-wires, then throw a couple of grenades over a wall, jump onto the wall, with barbed wire on the far side to clear, more trip wires, down and up a sandy depression, bayoneting a couple of dummies on the way, cross a ditch full of barbed wire by running along a pole, run up the sandhills, finishing by firing five rounds rapid out to sea. (It makes me wonder what it's like in Libya, where they have quite a lot of sand to get into rifles). Then the blanco period, followed by a gas lecture just before tea.

The postings were up to-day and although I didn't have time to look, I'm told I stay here, as I thought.

I'll be seeing you, lovey.
Leslie

Tuesday 25th August 1942

Darling,
Fancy having to wait five weeks or so before being able to talk for a few hours! I hope you enjoyed it as much as I did, anyway, and that you reached home without any trouble. I am writing this in the W.V.S Prestatyn, where we have dragged ourselves after the most tiring day of all, although very little happened. It has been pouring on and off – mostly on – all day and the pass-out was a wash-out. We spent most of the morning preparing for kit

inspection, which lasted about five mins. At about 10.30. After that we had another practice march-past, on the square. After dinner we prepared for the big moment but the rain won and we were merely inspected in the drill sheds, and then "marched past" the C.O. along one of the camp roads. Our corp. was quite pleased with our showing. Up till then we had done quite a lot of standing, which, as you know, is most tiring. We thought we had finished then, but no, then we were paid, which entailed about an hour's standing. Then we had to hand our rifles in; we took them to the stores, waited for about half an hour and then were told to go back after tea, which we did, and after waiting about an hour were told to go back to our huts and return by platoons. We were eventually free about seven o'clock – all this after being told that we would have a free afternoon. To make matters worse, yesterday we went out on a little scheme, and in climbing a fence I landed awkwardly on my right foot, and it was very painful for a few minutes but soon passed off. Incidentally it was very hot while we were out. This morning, when I got out of bed I could hardly bear to stand, but when I had been about a bit it wasn't so bad, although it has made things most uncomfortable. We are all feeling footsore and weary. Tomorrow we move from E.5 to ?

On Sunday after leaving my darling wife, I walked here for a snack and found Dick and several of the fellows here.

Last night we had to scrub the hut out, as well as do the blancoing, and it was all we could do to squeeze in a cup of tea at the canteen.

Wednesday night

After leaving here last night it was raining, and we had just passed the chip shop on the main road when it started tippling down, so we went into the chip shop and had three penn'orth of chips each – there were five of us – and what chips and what a huge three penn'orth! When we had finished them it was still raining so we went back into the room behind the shop and had a cup of tea each. We landed in our hut about 10 – "lights out" 10.15. After "lights out" two or three more came in, more or less under the influence

This morning was one of great activity – packing all our kit, etc., and what a complicated business it seems fixing all the straps and things. For once, though, after packing, we had time for a leisurely cup of tea during the break at 9.45. At 10.30 we had to parade with all our kit. Luckily our kitbags, with blankets around them were taken by van. At about eleven-thirty we set off for Prestatyn, carrying large valise, haversack, respirator at the "alert", and gas-capes and was it warm, phew! We marched to a house in Prestatyn, where we collected a palliasse and bolster and two tin plates. Then we were taken to our billet – a house (empty but for us) in a road off the main street, and Dick, Dick Williams, Treloar and I managed to get together in a room on the top floor, together with Wadsworth and Van Neste and another fellow. It was a treat to get our packs off. We went to dinner higher up the High Street and it was very good. The place seemed to have been a large garage or stables at some time. Then we were marched to the reception centre where we were interviewed and most of us were told that we would be going away for a little training. I will be a switchboard operator apparently.

Darling, isn't it a mess? Just when I thought I was settled here for a few months and now I may never see the place again. I asked the officer whether he knew where I would be sent but he didn't know. He said that "living in L'pool 'they' would probably send me to London and if I had lived down there they would probably send me to Aberdeen, that's the sort of thing 'they' do".

We've been told that there will be some Day Passes granted this weekend, but am not very hopeful having already been home and some haven't.

Love,
Leslie

> *14234557 Sgmn. L.M. Smith*
> *Reception Centre*
> *Clwyd House*
> *Bryneithin Avenue*
> *Prestatyn*

Thursday 27ᵗʰ August 1942

Sweetheart,

It's very warm in here tonight. The 9 p.m. news is just about to start, Big Ben is striking – what are you doing at this moment, my love? I don't suppose you'll be able to remember.

There are 39 men in our house, and we sleep on palliasses on the floor – we are seven in the front top room. To-day has been lovely. At 8.40 we had to parade, taking our gym kit, and were marched about half a mile before falling out for a smoke. After about a quarter of an hour we fell in again and our corporal said he hoped we had enjoyed our P.T.! Oh, before we went off the officer-in-charge had a little talk with us and explained that while we were there, the maximum stay usually being ten days, we were to have a comparatively easy time after our strenuous six weeks. We have already noticed the difference in the N.C.O.s. Sometimes they say "please"! We were then marched to the NAAFI where we were allowed to spend half an hour. Then, at 11, we marched about two miles towards Talacre, returning in time for dinner.

After dinner we paraded for P.T. and went to a field near the baths, where we undressed and did our P.T. – pumps and shorts only – in front of an audience in the road. We returned for tea and then were off duty. We were thinking of seeing "The Day will Dawn" but decided to leave it until tomorrow, we hope. Tomorrow we have to report at the mess-room for cookhouse fatigues, so I don't know what time we will finish. On Sunday I am firewatching at the billet – that is, of course, if I am still there. The food is even better than in the camp and we are not quite so rushed at mealtimes. The washing facilities are not too good and we also have to wash our own plates, and what a job it is.

Nothing else at the moment, love, so goodnight and every bit of my love,

Leslie.

Monday 31st August 1942

My darling,

Thank you for a wonderful day – did you enjoy it too? Of course you did, even if the weather wasn't too good – it's been warm to-day, although there hasn't been much sun. Did you have any trouble getting home?

When I left you I met Dick and Dick in High Street and was told that Dick Smith had to report in the morning for medical, which means posting. We were all rather disappointed at this news, but it can't be helped. He leaves at 8.30 a.m. tomorrow (Tuesday) for Huddersfield or Hendon – the former we think and he hopes.

By the way, when you mentioned the piano playing I forgot to mention that hardly a night passed in the Naafi without someone playing the Warsaw Concerto and what may have been either Concerto for two or its derivative – sometimes very well. This morning in our Naafi the P.T. L/Cpl. Was at the piano and played very well – such things as "Canadian Capers" and so on.

This morning we paraded as usual with our P.T. kit and stripped again in full view of the populace, had a game of all-in rugby, then some "jerks". At 10.15 we broke off and adjourned to the Naafi until 11, when we returned to the field and played football until dinner time. At dinner parade Dick Williams and I were told to be at the Company office at 1.40. The corporal said it was for an easy job so, being optimistic, I took my pen with me. When we arrived there we found several others waiting and the cpl. marched us to the camp. Two men were sent to the officers' mess and the rest of us were taken to the coal dump to shovel coal. Needless to say we didn't overwork ourselves, in fact when we finished things were as we had found them, because when we had cleared a space a fresh wagon-load came in and filled it up. At half-time we went to the Ffrith, which was only a few yards from where we were working, and after that the L/Cpl. In charge of us seemed to think we had done enough, so we all sat about and discussed the war, the army etc. And who do you think was with us? – Geoffrey Hibbert! Before we set off for the camp our cpl. took our names and I heard someone say "Hibbert" but naturally thought nothing of it. When we reached the camp we were hanging around for a few minutes and I was chatting to one of the fellows. We were sitting almost back-to-back so I couldn't see his face, except that I knew he was wearing spectacles. During the conversation he mentioned that he was down as a clerk and I asked him whether that was his usual job and he said he was an actor. A few minutes late I was able to see his face, and putting two and two together, decided he was Geoffrey Hibbert, and later when we were working I asked him and found out I was right. He seems a decent sort of fellow and has come here from Aldershot. He belongs to Hull and is twenty. He prefers the stage and wants to get into the entertainment side, in one of the companies doing straight plays. He told me that when they were shown "Next of Kin" he had to do fatigues instead, and he has been working on the new Noel Coward film – or is it a play – about the Navy, and was also due to go to the "Court".

Tuesday
Dick went this morning – to Hendon. I am billet orderly to-day and we are expecting the C.O. around some time this afternoon. My partner is Van Neste and we have to brush out all the rooms, wash the downstairs rooms, and generally keep the house clean and tidy. Because of the expected inspection a fatigue party scrubbed out all the rooms this morning. We have bunks now, but this time they were put up for us. Wadsworth also went this morning. We have had some rain to-day but at the moment the sun is shining

I can't think of anything else that's happened, only that the sooner something happens the better, so that we will know where we are for a time. I don't suppose my move will be permanent, but only for training and then to somewhere else.

Ta-ta for now my darling,
Leslie.

Thursday 3rd September 1942

Darling,
Yesterday I was billet orderly again and it rained all morning, but was fine in the afternoon. To-day is pay-day and

thank goodness. I was booked for fatigues in the camp, but by the time we had marched there and then marched back for pay it was too late to do anything before dinner, so we were told to make ourselves scarce until two o'clock. We had dinner in the camp and reported back as instructed. There were two of us on the General Trades Stores, and we started by carting a couple of rails back to the stores – I think they had been used as altar rails in the ballroom. Then I emptied the ATS L/Cpl's waste-paper basket. It was about 2.30 then. Our next job was to move a pile of chairs back to the ballroom, but we had to wait over an hour for a wagon so it was a hectic rush before tea. Did we say some sweet things! We were just in time for tea. I had intended going to Benediction at 6 o'clock and then to a Symphony Concert in the camp by the Western Command Symphony Orchestra, but was too late for Church and couldn't be bothered walking to the camp for the concert. Dick (Williams) and I went for a drink, where we were joined by Sigm. Hibbert, and then came here to the Naafi for some supper – did I mention that in this unit supper is not provided? Last night in the WVS G.H. was playing the piano and singing, but only to himself. He is working in the Coy. Office and has managed to get himself a weekend pass.

In orders tonight I am down for "medical" in the morning, so shall probably move on Saturday – all from our room are down for it. Information indicates Cheltenham or Hendon, with Cheltenham based on, I think, the more reliable sources. If only it could be here or Liverpool where I could be close to you, my darling.

Goodnight and all my love,
Leslie.

Chapter Four

Movements

Over the course of the 21 months from early September 1942, my father, like many thousands of other servicemen, was posted to a variety of places in England and Wales, including Cheltenham, Kidderminster, Wimbledon, Narberth and Tenby. After the initial shock of call-up and separation from home, life settled down into a fairly mundane routine, but with its own persistent preoccupations. The big frustrations of army life included having absolutely no control of where you were sent or what you did. Soldiers were posted at short notice, and often for no apparent reason, to new units and new billets. Once posted, they had to learn to live with the subtly different attitudes of their new N.C.O.s and officers, and had to adapt to their new comrades, and to make friends within their unit.

Constant themes emerge: pay was one, with soldiers (British, not American) chronically short of money, waiting for postal orders from home and worrying about debts and the cost of a cinema seat or a bar of chocolate. Another was the food. No matter how good the catering may be, it is always frustrating living within an institution where you have no control over the content of your meals, and the army was no exception to this. My father sometimes describes in loving detail a completely unexceptional meal eaten at a services canteen, but memorable because it was his own choice.

Another big frustration was being ordered around by other men, whether they be corporals or colonels. In the Regular

Army, rank depends largely on qualifications, seniority and the desire and ability to gain promotion. In a conscripted army, however, it is far more random, and intelligent, educated men would often find themselves being bossed around by N.C.O.s who, in the world outside, would not be their professional or intellectual equals. Mindless or menial tasks, petty rules about the laying out of equipment or the wearing of uniform (which varied from unit to unit), restrictions on movement, punishments for minor infringements, uncomfortable billets – these were all things with which the conscripted soldier had to learn to cope.

Letters from home were eagerly awaited, and vitally important for the morale of the troops. Fortunately, the post was seen as a priority by the Army, and letters arrived with a speed and efficiency that is not always matched sixty years on, although soldiers still moaned frequently about the post. My father and mother wrote frequent, lengthy letters, but it must have been so much worse for the less literate and articulate soldiers, unable to convey their experiences to those left behind, or to have their spirits lifted by news from home. Many a relationship must have foundered in these strained circumstances.

Finally there was the question of leave. When a man like my father left home to join the Army, he had no clear idea of when he would see his home or family again. There were constant rumours of when leave would be granted, but there was no certainty about it. Passes were given for 24 or 48 hours, but these were of little consolation to soldiers stationed far away. Men were moved at short notice, and there was no leave in between Basic Training and posting. There was certainly no guarantee of leave at normal holiday times, as my father found out when it came to his first Christmas in the Army. So life became a constant dream of the next leave, and in the meantime you got your head down and tried to make the best of it.

"Never be first, never volunteer for anything, if it moves, salute it, if it stands still, paint it." There is a grain of truth in all these typical sayings of enlisted men, which have a certain ring of resignation and resentment. Life went on day by day, month by month, as the war ground forward, with battles raging in North Africa, the Far East and on the grim Russian Front. But for the average soldier still in Britain it was a seemingly never-ending existence of tedium and separation, where normal life had been suspended for an indefinite period, and the possibility of action began to sound like a merciful relief.

However, with the thought of action and postings came the worry about their destination, and soldiers were continually resigning themselves to the thought of months or years overseas, with little or no contact with their families. Rumours were rife, and men had to accept the fact that they would be sent abroad at short notice. Where, they knew not. The Second Front was being talked about in early 1943, but its exact location was a well guarded secret until 1944.

14234557 Sigmn. Smith. L.M.
No. 2 Coy. W/O/ Signals,
Lauriston House,
Queen's Parade,
Cheltenham, Glos

Saturday 5th September, 1942

Darling,

It is Cheltenham after all, worse luck, but it seems all right here, so far, although it's rather early to know We had our F.F.I. (Free From Infection) inspection yesterday and did very little else except have a bath. At tea-time we read in orders that we (thirteen of us) were to hand in our palliasses etc. and parade at the Coy. Office at 9 this morning, when we learned that we were going to Cheltenham.

This morning we caught the 9.46 train, changed at Crewe, the train was late getting into B'ham, so we missed the connection. Luckily, we had only an hour to wait for the next train, and were here by 4 o'clock. We are billeted in the Queen's Hotel – a very posh place, the biggest hotel in Cheltenham – and there are also ATs and Americans in it. It's about half the size of the Adelphi. There is hot and cold water in every room but we sleep on the floor – on palliasses. After a big meal we were told that breakfast is at 8 a.m. and we have to parade at 9.50 for interview by the C.O. This is War Office Signals and apparently we are to take over from the non-P.O. men and ATs who have hitherto done the job. We are supposed to be fully-trained signalmen now, but we will soon find out, I expect, where we stand. We are in the YMCA at the moment, after a short stroll around the town, and I will finish this tomorrow in case there are any new developments.

The place is simply swarming with American troops and in the town one sees at least fifty of them for every one of our own. We were told that this is quite a decent place if one is not interested in girls – you can guess why, I suppose, but why it should be I fail to see, as the majority of the Americans are a scruffy looking lot and that without prejudice.

Of course, Van Neste is overjoyed – he is only about a mile from home, but even so we were out before him tonight. If this were Liverpool, they wouldn't see me for smoke.

I'll say goodnight for now my darling – how I wish I could wrap my arms around you while saying it, but still, time marches on. I'm in my eighth week now. I believe wireless operators don't get any leave during their course, which lasts about five months!

Goodnight, love,
Leslie.

Tuesday 8ᵗʰ September 1942

My darling,

On Sunday morning we had to parade for interview by the O.C. – a captain who, although he looks rather a weedy and cissy-ish sort of fellow, seems quite decent and human. He interviewed us one by one, taking particulars which we are tired of giving, and then spoke to us altogether, telling us what sort of work we were to do, and impressing on us the need for secrecy about our work, so please, darling, if you value your husband, keep what little I can tell you strictly to yourself. Then he told us where we were to go – five here, four there, and four of us somewhere else. Four have gone from here, but the rest of us stay in Cheltenham and are taken into the middle of nowhere each day to our station. We are all part of the Defence Telecommunications Network. Myself and three others are at a place where we are the first of the operators who will take the place of A.T.S and non-G.P.O. men. We are welcomed, as we don't need any training really – the board is different from what I have been used to, but the mere fact of being familiar with a switchboard at all is a great help. I can't say I'm keen on the job, but maybe it won't be so bad.

On Sunday I worked from 1.30 – 8.30 and the same yesterday, but to-day was 8.30 – 1.30. In between is the night shift. I believe the method is the two former on alternate days for a week, and then a week of nights. One couldn't call it hard work – we have frequent breaks and on nights, I hear, we get about four hours sleep.

We were told that there will be no leave for us until after the completion of four months in the army, so we have quite a time to wait, my darling.

The food is pretty awful after what we have been used to, but perhaps that will improve. At least we have mugs for drinking, which is something.

All my love, sweetheart,
Leslie.

Thursday 10th September 1942

Sweetheart,

It was lovely getting a letter from you at last – that's the worst of moving, and having to wait until you have my new address. I felt such along way from you – even further than I am, but everything's lovely again.

Cheltenham is much bigger than Prestatyn – I was surprised to find how big it is, but it seems to be a very posh sort of place – rather snobbish I think, but it is certainly very pleasant. The main thoroughfare, with the Queen's facing the top, is wide and tree-lined with pavements almost as wide as the roadway. It's called the Promenade although we are about sixty miles inland. Bristol is about forty miles away, and Gloucester ten, I think.

I haven't come into contact with the Americans yet, except one sergeant who was very pleasant although I could hardly understand a word he said, and one chap we were chatting to last night while he was waiting for a girl from Liverpool. He came from New York, and said he thought it very pretty here, misses his family, and would like to be in London. He told us that he had no embarkation leave, but was simply taken from where they were and put on the boat without even time to let his people know he was going. He also was very pleasant and chatty – yes, indeedy.

I think the best thing to do with Income Tax demands is to mark them "Serving with H.M. Forces" and return them. We did that with Charlie's and heard no more. After all they can't deduct it from a non-existent income, and as you say, we have no other money to pay with! I say let them sort it out – they don't ask for it, but say they will deduct it, and if they don't – well...

If you could send me a pair of round, brown laces for my shoes it would be appreciated. We are not allowed to wear boots in the switchroom, so either have to wear shoes, or take our pumps. I wear my shoes to save changing when we get there.

Our sergeant made his first appearance this morning – he has been on leave. He seems to be regarded as a pig and a cissy, but was quite decent to us. I think these fellows could do with a dose of some of the P.T.C. N.C.O.s. They're terribly slack here.

We are grateful for our training now as we know more about real soldiering than most here – the other night one of our chaps on guard was showing them what to do with a rifle.

Next week we will be on mornings every day, with lectures in the afternoon. We have to do map-reading and later on will have a trade test, when, if we pass, we will get a few more coppers I hope. I think they expect a lot from us as regards our job – quite naturally perhaps.

I don't know why they didn't call us up sooner, as they are terribly short of men used to switchboards.

Now I'll say "Goodnight", switch off the light and draw the blackout back.

Goodnight, my love, and God bless you.
Leslie.

Saturday 12th September 1942

Darling,

I'm in the Y.M. at the moment, and it is 10 o'clock. This particular canteen is a British Restaurant during the day and at 6 o'clock becomes what it is at the moment. A few minutes ago an American officer – a major I think – came in; can you imagine one of ours doing that. Democratic perhaps, but I think they could do with less, and ours with more.

There was a procession this afternoon – Army, RAF, H.G., A.T.S., WAAF etc., for Tank Week and Major-General Lee of USA took the salute and made a speech. I caught a glimpse of the procession – the Yanks slope their arms on the right shoulders – it looks funny. They seem to do everything the opposite way – just to be awkward. Our A.T.S were very smart. They're quite a different sort from the Prestatyn crowd.

<u>Sunday afternoon.</u>

I went to 9 o'clock Mass this morning after a breakfast of sausage and cold potato, one piece of bread and no tea. When I came out of Church I went to the YM (we are well catered for here by them) for a cup of tea. I met one of our fellows and we were chatting to an American sergeant. He mentioned that he had spent £20 already this month! He expressed disgust at our rate of pay and said that the shopkeepers were putting up prices because of their presence, thereby making things very difficult for us. He and his friend told us about the attitude of the South towards them – apparently the Civil War is still on. After that I was speaking to a young sergeant who seemed more refined than most of them. He was from New York and was keen on going back, but not because he disliked being here – he liked the country and found everyone very friendly. He was expecting to go to an officers' training school. A lot of them wear those round hats and overalls – just like a farm worker on the pics. Their salutes amuse me – just like "hi-ya buddy"!

The Gloucester Regt. wear a small badge on the back of their caps and I wondered why. I was told yesterday that it is because they fought with the enemy behind them, that is, on both sides – I don't know when.

Ta-ta for now,
Leslie.

Monday 14th September 1942

Darling Grace,

The C.S.M. (Company Sgt.Major) interrupted me last night. It was 10.45 p.m. and the black-out curtain was blowing –

'lights-out' is at 10.15, but no-one bothers about that. He's a sour looking blighter, but his bark seems worse than his bite. He just said "What's the bloody light doing on, and the black-out blowing", glared at me, and walked out. I was lying on the bed in my undies – not a very comfortable position for writing, I know, but we are not provided with chairs and tables in our boudoirs.

My rate of pay is 2/6 per day (17/6 per week) of which 6d per day (3/6 per week) goes to you, leaving me with 14/- (on paper). Actually, while at Prestatyn I only received 12/6 per week. In October I should get about 19/6, which sounds quite princely after 12/6. At the moment I have 4½ d

I didn't know the "Daily Worker"* had been "unbanned" until I saw one the other day.

Love,
Leslie

Friday 18th September 1942

Darling,

...On Wednesday evening there was a free concert for the forces in the hall of the girls' college, just round the corner from the Queen's. The artistes were Merle Oberon, Patricia Morison, Frank McHugh, Allan Jenkins and Al Jolson. Merle Oberon was commere and did some back-chat with McHugh. The latter and

---

* *The Communist Party newspaper, had been suppressed by Churchill on 21st January 1941 (a fate also suffered by its French counterpart* L'Humanité) *because of its criticism of the war effort and its links, perceived or real, with Moscow. This, of course, was before the U.S.S.R became one of our allies.* The Daily Mirror *also attracted the wrath of the Government and narrowly avoided closure.*

119

Jenkins wise-cracked. Pat Morison sang "Begin the Beguine", "Night and Day" and a couple of others. Al Jolson sang "Swanee", "Buddy can you spare a dime" and "Sonny Boy" and others. He is a good showman. He said that he had been to Alaska, Iceland, the Dutch East Indies and lots of other places doing shows for the troops. General Lee spoke at the end. Merle Oberon seems nicer in the flesh than on the screen. At the end the audience sang "The Star-spangled Banner" and our National Anthem.

We have been having lectures each afternoon – Signal Office procedure, switchboard procedure, map reading, military abbreviations, and more to come …

I believe that War Office Signals are the highest grade of Signals. I don't know what difference it makes, except that our despatch riders escort the P.M. and carry the BBC news during blitzes, and that sort of thing.

All my love to you, my darling.

Leslie.

Monday 28th September 1942

Dear darling Gracie,

I've been learning a bit about Magnetism. I am getting ready for the D II trade test, for which a knowledge of electricity and magnetism is necessary, and the passing of which, I believe, means another shilling a day. I'm becoming a real money-grabber, ain't I?

Often when I've been writing to you I've thought the same thing – that often we've spent a whole evening talking about practically nothing, and I sometimes wonder how long it would take to exhaust the discussion of our doings and feelings now. It's not the same writing, is it, lovey? How I'm longing for the time when you'll say again "Start at the very beginning", but I suppose too much has happened to do that now. As you suppose, I haven't seen a fire for ages, although I believe the Yanks have one. While actually in the switchroom it isn't so bad, but during our breaks, which last about as long as our time on the board, we have to leave the main building and go to a stone hut where we have a cup of tea, and which is like an ice-box. Yesterday I wore my pullover. We go either in a truck or a bus with no windows – you've seen them.

The American soldier we were talking to the other night was an exception to most of them here, the majority being clerks and so on, who have only been in the army two or three months. Some of them, though, have what I thought were medals. Worn over the left breast pocket, shaped like a Victoria Cross, some of them having bars hanging from them – I've seen as many as five or six bars – with "Machine Gun", "Rifle" etc. on them. They were explained to me one day by a wearer, who said they denoted proficiency in the weapon named.

I don't know all the American marks of rank; as you know, there are so many of them, some fellows look like zebras. One stripe is a private first class, two and three stripes corporal and sergeant – the same as us. Three stripes with three semi-circular stripes underneath is a master-sergeant – roughly the equivalent of our sergeant-major. The sloping stripes near the cuff are service stripes.

I know just a little about the officers. One gold bar is a 2nd Lieutenant, an oak leaf is a major, and I think an eagle is a colonel. There are silver bars, oak leaves and eagles, but in each class silver is higher than gold…

Au revoir, darling. I'm dying to be with you again.
Leslie.

19th October 1942

Hello Darling,

I don't think there's anything I want for Christmas, love, – what do you want? Silly really, isn't it?

As you say, my love, – "roll on time". I suppose my leave will be the quickest week I've known – wouldn't it be lovely if I were coming home to you in our own home and you not having to be out all day? I wish we could decide what to do about being "properly married" *(starting a family)* – are we sensible, are we too sensible, or what? Pray hard, my darling, that we may know what to do. How do you really feel about it? After waiting so long it seems a pity to start now, when we're separated most of the time. I, too, would infinitely prefer it to be in our own home. I used to think and hope that we wouldn't have long to wait for the war to end, but now it seems a terribly long way off. Did you see in one of the papers the pictures of utility furniture for "bombedouts" and "newlyweds" – are we "newlyweds", darling?...

Cheerio, darling, for now.

Leslie.

26th October 1942

My darling,

CNW is where I work, and I don't know what it means, except that I believe the CN is a sort of abbreviation for Cheltenham. I don't think that the officer-in-charge really knows. We are a trunk switching centre with lines to places all over the British Isles. We don't use the P.O. lines, the Army have a network of their own. I was surprised to find how many private lines they have. Some of the switchboards have lines to

P.O. exchanges (such as Derby House) but although we have lines to Cheltenham and Gloucester they are very rarely used.

Are you still keeping your diary? I haven't heard of it for a long time and was thinking about it only the other day...

I'll have to go now love, so ta-ta for now,

Leslie.

(Around this time my mother gave up her job to stay at home and look after the family home, where my grandmother and grandfather were both in poor health. Of course, in those days shopping, cooking, washing, ironing, and general housework were much more time-consuming chores than nowadays.)

29th October 1942

How's my darling housewife? Feeling happier now, I hope?

Did I tell you I got my badge and a jack-knife? I don't know what the knife is for, but it's a bit of all right. It has one blade, a tin-opener and a "thing for getting stones out of horses' hooves". When I got the badge Clarence sewed my shoulder flashes on and they have been much admired.

I just missed a mouse with my boot last night.

The central heating has been put on and the radiator in my room is just at the head of my palliasse, under the window. They thought I'd picked the worst spot, but of course we never expected the central heating to be put into commission. The rest hut at CNW is still unheated though, and the place is like an ice-box....

Cheerio for now,

Leslie.

28th November 1942

Darling,

There has been an issue of rifles and these have to be carried when going on duty or leave – I was lucky this time. There is a route march in the morning which I miss, being on nights. There has been an appeal for volunteers for the Signal Brigade attached to the Commandos and there was a very good response. If I'd no ties of any sort I would have volunteered with the others. Then they found that Switchboard and Keyboard Operators were not accepted. Postings are still in the air, though, three men are attached to H.Q. "pending posting".

I don't like being here very much, darling, I'd much rather be with you – that, in my opinion, is the acme of understatement. I enjoyed my leave though, and I'd like some more very much. I love you an awful lot.

There is an announcement in orders that women are wanted as telephone and teleprinter operators. The telephonists need no experience, but will be taught, but the teleprinters are required to be able to type, preferably touch-type, and the commencing wage is £2/10/-. Soldiers' wives and lady-friends are invited to apply. Wouldn't it be nice if it could be managed, love?

God bless you,
Leslie.

14234557 Sigmn. Smith, L.M.
"N" Section, 3 Coy. W.O. Signals,
Park Attwood House,
Bewdley,
Worcs.

11th December 1942

Well, my darling,

I bet that was a surprise! This morning being "on pass" I went to 9 o'clock breakfast, and at about 9.20 I was told that I had to go for a medical at 9.45 and pack my kit ready to catch the 12.12 train to Kidderminster. There are four of us – two were on duty at CNW and had to be fetched from there. We were told we were going on a hush-hush job to Kidderminster. I wasn't shaved and hadn't cleaned my boots, buttons or anything. I dashed back to my room and shaved and then reported at the Coy. office at 9.50

It was raining then, so I had to put my coat on. We ran most of the way to the medical centre and then had to wait quite a time before being examined. It was about 11 when we returned to the Queen's, and then had to pack everything – what a rush! Luckily a Yankee press man offered to take our kit to the station, so we hadn't that to carry, only what we were wearing – that is, large pack, small pack and respirator. By the way, we were told that we would only be here a fortnight. It is supposed to be some job which cannot be done by anyone but Signals, for security reasons, but has nothing to do with switchboards. As far as I can make out we are a sort of labour gang!

We were met at Kidderminster by a truck, the driver of

which dashed our spirits by telling us that we were going about six miles out – no buses, no pubs, no nuffink. The country is lovely – up hill and down dale. The house must have been lovely too. We are billeted in rooms where the grooms probably slept, over what were the stables. This is a most important wireless station – I know there's no need to tell you to keep things strictly to yourself. We are rather mystified as to why we, trade-rated men, are chosen, when there are others who could move more easily, but ours not to reason why.

The only transport into Kidderminster is a truck which leaves at 6 p.m., and if one wants to go in it one has to notify them in the morning! The alternative, of course, is to walk.

There is a canteen here, open 6 – 9 and the only drinks are beer and lemonade – no tea. Apparently the favourite diversion – if one can call it that – is going to bed early. There's nothing else to do except read and write, when one is not on duty. Reveille is at 7, which is a change, breakfast 7.30, parade 8.30, and then I suppose we shall find out what we are to do. Tomorrow we may walk into K. I wonder whether I'll be here for Christmas – I think so, somehow.

We were all rather elated at our change, but the location of the place put us off. Personally, I don't mind very much. I think we'll get plenty of fresh air and it ought to do us good. The washing and sanitary arrangements cannot, naturally, compare with the Queen's – not even hot water. I'm on a top bunk. We have a stove which fills the place with smoke. The place is guarded by Military Police and one can't get in and out very easily. They have a huge Alsatian.

<u>Saturday 7.40 p.m.</u>
I'm at the Y.M. in Kidderminster and have just had

sausage and scallops, b & b and tea – 10d! We intended to walk, but were told that if we walked some distance from the main gate the truck would stop for us. We left about 5.45 and had walked about a mile when the truck came – officially it holds twelve, but I'm told it has carried as many as twenty-three.

I slept well last night in spite of the smoke. At about 7.45 we had breakfast – porridge and sausages. At 8.30 we paraded with the rest. We were detailed off with an N.C.O. in charge and a couple of other men. We were given rubber boots and collected all sorts of tackle. It was a lovely morning, but we certainly needed our boots as the grass was very wet. We took down a 96ft. aerial mast and re-erected it in another field, which brought us to dinner-time. Actually we were at a critical stage then (12.30) so we had dinner at 1 o'clock, and were we ready for it! We all had that "glad to be alive" feeling. At 2.15 we repeated the process on another mast – it's a very ticklish job. We "knocked off" at tea-time – 4.30. There are several more to be done. What we were told we were coming for was to dig a trench for a cable, but that may come later. I don't mind how long it lasts. At tea-time I was told I was very red – I hope the job lasts until near my next leave – just so you can say I'm not looking pale!

It's just the opposite of Cheltenham – there we have good billets and a job I don't like, and here I'm enjoying the job and can put up with the rest. They say "a change is as good as a rest". Perhaps this change will seem to make the time go more quickly for me, until I'm with you again.

God bless you,
Leslie.

13th December 1942

My darling,

This morning none of us wakened until 7.50, and only just managed to get breakfast. I left at 9.50 with Dvr. Barnett to get to Mass at an R.A. camp two miles away. It was a lovely morning. I had my coat on, only because it might have rained, but it was very warm walking. Mass had just started when we arrived. It is held in one of the sleeping huts, with a trestle table for an altar. There were eight of us – two A.T.S., four R.A.s and us. We sat on forms and knelt on folded blankets. The Chaplain comes from town to say Mass. There was a stove between altar and "congregation" and it was very warm. The priest said afterwards that he was roasted, and no wonder, with his vestments over his uniform. The priest recognised me as a newcomer, and complained of the fact that although there are about eight Catholics at Park Attwood, my companion is the only one who goes there.

On the way back we looked down into Habberly Valley, and went down a few yards, but it is too steep and deep to go further. It was very windy but not unpleasant. We walked a little further and then decided to try a short-cut across the fields, as the road winds so much. It was all up and down, with several fences and ditches to cross. I saw a lot of holly with plenty of berries on it – does this mean we shall have a hard winter? When we were near the house we went through an orchard and there was one tree with apples still on it and plenty on the ground. We knocked some down and filled our pockets – they are rather small apples, but quite nice. The orchard – one of several – belongs to the estate, and I'm told that tons of apples and pears rotted for want of labourers to gather them.

We arrived back about a quarter of an hour before dinner. While I had been away the others had taken two more masts down, but it was too windy to put them up again.

After dinner nearly everyone in our room was having a siesta, but I decided to go for a walk. I walked along a muddy lane running from beside the house, and after about twenty-five minutes I came out on a main road – Bridgnorth – Birmingham I believe. I had heard this is a short-cut to Kidderminster, so now I know part of it. It was cold and windy when I started out but I was soon warm and enjoying my walk. It was rather tiring walking back, as it was a gradual climb and the lane was muddy. I landed back just before tea, when we had canned herring and slab-cake.

Monday evening.

I am quite happy here – as happy as I can be without you. This morning was dull but not very windy, and we started putting another mast up. We had to knock part of a tree down as it was getting in the way of the stay-wires. At about 10.15 we had a break and went to the canteen, where I collected your letter – re-directed from Cheltenham – bought my ration of ten cigs, and two penn'orth of biscuits. When we had the mast up we started putting poles in for a cable. Then the O.C. Lt. Peter Hadland came along and had a discussion with the man in charge of our party. Then we three went off to another field – a ploughed one – to fix the site for another aerial. Peter was quite pally, asking me how I liked being there and so on, and said we would probably be going back on the 23rd or 24th. I had to walk about the field with a pole, while he directed me, taking bearings with a compass, to fix the positions of the four masts. Each aerial has to be just so, so as more easily to pick up messages from the part of the world it is meant to receive from. This particular one is for a place very much in the news – shh. We finished just in time for tea – bread and cheese and a piece of swiss roll.

From the little I've seen of Worcestershire, I think it's lovely – it certainly is around here. We are six hundred feet up and one can see for miles, although the visibility hasn't been too good since we came. It's certainly a big change from Cheltenham – the air seems fresher round here. As I said we are out in the wilds – Bewdley is just an address. This afternoon we started digging 4'6" deep holes for the supports – in the ploughed field, and it's brown clay-ey soil. It was caked thickly on our wellingtons. Personally, I rather enjoyed it!

In the next field is the Malay Peninsula mast, which of course isn't used now.

All my love, my darling.

Leslie.

16th December 1942

Grace, my darling,

To-day we finally got the first of the new masts up. It was cold and foggy, and just before we finished it started raining. We finished at 1 o'clock, after working without a break since 8.45. I spent about two hours hanging on to a cold, wet rope. I hear we shall be here for another fortnight. We still have seven masts to put up, as well as a cable on posts – seven miles we heard.

I'm not getting enough food for my appetite on this job and am having my leg pulled for my constant hunger – I'm ready for my next meal all the time. I've managed to buy a few bars of chocolate, and have eaten a couple. The wind is howling now and the moon is shining. Somewhere below I can hear Morse coming in – maybe the latest communique from N. Africa. All the press reports come here too, from the battle-fronts. I feel here as if I'm really doing something useful, even if it is only a glorified labourer's job...

Once more –"goodnight". I wonder how many more times before I'm with you for always.

All my love, darling.
Leslie.

14234557 Sigmn. Smith. L.M.
No. 2 Coy. W/O/ Signals,
Lauriston House,
Queen's Parade,
Cheltenham, Glos

22nd December 1942

My darling,

I've some unpleasant news for us, I'm afraid. Tomorrow I go to Hendon, which means, eventually, overseas.

This morning we were just about to start work, when the clerk came out and told me to take my denims off as I was to go back to Cheltenham. Of course, I was very disappointed at this, especially as I was the only one going back. That was just after nine. At ten I was ready to go. The truck was going to Bewdley, so we went there first and then on to Kidderminster. I was at the station at 10.30 and the train wasn't till 11.26, so I wandered round the town and had a snack. By the way, I gave the driver a small parcel of chocolate to post – I hope you get it all right. I changed at Worcester and Honeybourne and arrived in Cheltenham at 2.45 – nearly an hour late. When I reported at the Coy. Office I was told to lay out all my kit for inspection. The clerk showed me the Unit Orders, which stated that 6 of us are posted to 7th. Air Formation Signals. I was told we were going to Hendon, although Dick Smith is in the 7th. A.F.S. and he is at Whetstone. I had the kit inspection and was told to report for medical at 9 in the morning. While I was in the office the O.C. – Capt. Jenkins – came in and asked me how I liked the idea of going and I said I didn't know yet. Then he said "It means overseas, you know" and I told him I wasn't pleased with the idea, but of course that doesn't make any difference.

All my love darling,
Leslie.

> *14234557 Sigmn. Smith, L.M.*
> *2 Coy.,*
> *7th Air Formation Signals,*
> *Whetstone,*
> *London N20*

24th December 1942

Darling Gracie,

By the time you get this Christmas will be over and I hope you and the family have had a happy one. I hope I didn't alarm you too much in my last letter – I don't think there's much chance of my leaving here for the present.

I've had a hectic time since my flight from Bewdley. We caught the 11.26 train which went straight through to Paddington, stopping at all sorts of little places as well as Gloucester, Swindon, Didcot and Reading. I was feeling quite excited looking forward to seeing London for the first time. I caught my first glimpse of the Thames – at least I supposed it was the Thames – somewhere between Swindon and Didcot, and saw quite a lot of it after that. We arrived at Paddington at 2.45. We had a cup of tea there and then took the Tube to Sloane Square, from where we walked to 94 Eaton Square, the H.Q of W.O. Signals, to report for further instructions. It was about half a mile from the station, and halfway there a taxi driver took pity on us and took us and our kit the rest of the way. We had tea there and left again at about 5.30. We walked quite a long way to Victoria and went from there to Charing Cross, where we changed. We arrived at Totteridge Station at about 6.45, and had to walk from there to Unit H.Q., where we arrived at about 7.15, feeling very hot, dirty, tired, hungry and generally fed-up. No-one seemed to know much about us. They took the inevitable particulars, and tried to find some-one who knew where we could sleep. We were given blankets and then advised to go to the Naafi which, thank goodness, was quite handy, until "someone" could be found to take us to the billet. We went to the Naafi and had something to eat, but no-one came for us, so we returned and did some more hanging around. Eventually we were shown to "Westgate", which is about ¾ of a mile away. We had to make two journeys as we couldn't carry all our kit and the blankets. We finally landed at the billet at about 9.45, and found there were no beds or palliasses for us, so had to sleep on the floor, but we didn't mind where we slept by then.

We were up at 6.30 this morning and walked to breakfast,

then on to the Coy. Office, and after waiting about half an hour we set off for the M.O.'s. When we arrived he had gone so we returned to the office. On the way back I suggested to one of the other men that this evening we should go to Midnight Mass at Westminster Cathedral, but some time after we got back to the office, the C.S.M came along and said "You, you, you and you, on guard tonight." I was the first "you".

I'm in the guard-room now – 11.50. I was on guard from 9 – 11 and will be again from 3 – 5.

5.15 a.m. Christmas morning.

Just finished my second two hours. Outside it reminded me of what you say about coming home from Midnight Mass – a lovely moonlit night – or morning.

What I feel most at the moment is the lack of a letter from you, my darling – I hope any you've written will find me. I don't suppose I'll get any mail to-day – Christmas Day too. I believe we're having a very good Christmas dinner – I hope so, as I seem to have had very little food the last three days. I won't forget in a hurry either my first Christmas in the army, or my first visit to London. We will probably go into town this afternoon.

I don't know what I'd do without you to think about – yesterday I was more fed-up than I've been during all (!) my service, but thinking about you cheered me up. You've no idea what you mean to me and how you bring me through my depressed periods, my lovely wonderful darling.

Boxing Day.

Yesterday we went to 10 o'clock Mass, at St. Mary Magdalene's, about ten minutes' walk away, after which we had a cup of tea in a low dive – the King George Café! At 1 o'clock we had dinner. The dining-room was decorated with holly and there were flowers and bowls of apples on the tables, and strips of green paper down the centre of them. The tables were arranged in long rows. We had been told to take our mugs. First we had soup – it had tomato in it, so I suppose it was tomato soup. The officers and sergeants waited on us and brought the beer round in buckets – tea buckets. Then we had turkey, beef, potatoes boiled and roasted, sprouts, carrots and stuffing followed by Christmas pudding and custard. I left the table feeling satisfied and comfortable, having enjoyed my dinner. There was a "whip-round" for the cooks, who certainly deserved it.

At 3 yesterday we left Totteridge Station and arrived in Leicester Square at 3.30. It was 1/10d return. Apparently, one isn't allowed to go into London without a pass, but we chanced it. We just wanted to see a bit of the city we'd heard so much about. We walked from Leicester Square along to Piccadilly Circus, crossed Pall Mall and Buckingham Palace Road. We passed through a little park – St. James' Park? And soon saw Big Ben, the Houses of Parliament and Westminster Abbey. We didn't go in, but walked to Westminster Cathedral, where we found Benediction in progress, with, we are almost certain, Cardinal Hinsley at the altar. Just after we arrived the choir sang "Adeste Fideles" starting with a boy soloist, and at the end they sang "God rest you, merry gentlemen". It was lovely. I was wishing you were with me, as I did all the time I was in the city. I wanted you to be the first one to show me London for the first time. We'll see it together one day, won't we, love?

We continued our tour, but it was getting dark. We passed Buckingham Palace and walked down Pall Mall, and at the other end passed through Admiralty Arch to Trafalgar Square. There we went in a canteen in the crypt of St. Martin-in-the-Fields, where we had pie and mash, apple trifle, a cake and a cup of tea for 10d. While there we heard the 6 o'clock news, when they told us that Darlan* had been shot – seems one way out of that difficulty…

All my love,
Leslie.

16ᵗʰ January 1943

My darling Gracie,

Sorry I couldn't write properly before now, but it just couldn't be helped. On Wednesday we had another inspection, and, in spite of the fact that all agreed my webbing looked fine, the O.C. didn't think the colour quite right. I admit it wasn't as light as it should be, which was only to be expected after six months' application of the darker blanco we've always used before. The O.C. has a supercilious air which annoys me – he picked up one of my boots, but couldn't find any fault with it and dropped it on

---

* *Commander-in-Chief of the French Navy, it was Darlan who ordered the French Fleet to sail to bases in North Africa, instead of delivering it to British ports. This brought about the disaster of Mers-el-Kebir, where the Royal Navy sank many of the French ships to stop them falling into German hands, but with the loss of more than 1,200 sailors.*

Darlan became Vice-Premier of the Vichy Government, collaborating with the Germans while encouraging Allied intervention, which earned the mistrust of both sides. In late 1942, after Hitler had ordered the occupation of Vichy France, Darlan committed himself to the Allies, but his endorsement as head of French North Africa provoked outrage. De Gaulle, in particular, protested against his appointment, citing his apparent recent pro-Nazi sentiments. This embarrassing and potentially explosive situation was solved when he was assassinated by a young French monarchist on Christmas Eve 1942.

to my towel. Then he held my large pack between finger and thumb, as though it smelled, and said "When did you last <u>think</u> of blancoing this?" I can well understand how some less intelligent, or more impetuous fellows go for their superior (!) officers.

The result was that about half the personnel of the billet were released from the partial C.B., whilst the rest of us were still "as you were" until Sat., when there was to be another inspection. I had to scrub all my webbing nearly white the same night. This was because we are now ordered to use "Goddard's blanco" obtainable from the Q.M.'s stores – we think someone must be making a bit out of it, although we do get it cheaper than in the shops.

The other day the C.S.M. called a meeting of all the N.C.O.s. He wants discipline, and, in effect, the men are to be treated like dirt. There must be no familiarity with the men. He is a regular soldier and means to go further and ensure a good pension, and is not going to let a scruffy company spoil his career, and so on, etc.

Our colonel is not fat or balding, in fact he's rather young. He wasn't responsible for the C.B., which was a company matter. The Colonel, actually a Lieut-Colonel, commands the whole unit (7th A.F.S.). He is the C.O. – Commanding Officer. Each company in the unit has an O.C. – Officer Commanding, usually a major or captain. It was the C.O. who inspected us in full regalia last week.

All my love, darling,
Leslie.

23rd January 1943

Darling Gracie,
The dinner-time raid – the one where the school children were killed – we were marching from lecture to billet, ready for dinner, at 12.30, and heard three or four dull thuds in the

distance. Then the siren went and the guns opened up. We were ordered to "double march" (run) for part of the way. We went to dinner wearing our tin hats and while we were having dinner could see the puffs of smoke in the sky. When we were queuing to wash our plates we saw four planes go over, with shells bursting behind them. A short while later we heard, but couldn't see, what we thought would be our fighters after them. The same night we had a siren at about 11.00 and another a few hours later, but nothing else...

God bless you darling,
Leslie

26th January 1943

Darling,
Last night I was told that the whole squad had to report for F.F.I. at 7.45 this morning, as we are being posted to-day. It is 11 o'clock now and we're all packed and ready to move as soon as instructed. It seems fairly definite that we are going to Wimbledon.

7.50 p.m.
Well, my love, we've arrived. We left Whetstone at 3.30 and changed to the Southern Rly. at Waterloo. Our station was Raynes Park – the one after Wimbledon. We marched about half a mile from the station, and were apparently expected here. In next to no time we were allotted a billet, issued with brand new blankets and plates and mugs, and taken to tea. Of course, it's too early to know much about the unit, but there's certainly more organisation than at Whetstone – admittedly that doesn't mean much. The Signals seem to have taken several roads over – all the houses in Laurel Road, where our billet is, are taken

over, except one. Our billet is nothing to write home about, but it's no worse than Whetstone. We brought stores with us – field kitchens, dixies, shovels, storm lanterns etc. They were brought by road, as were our kitbags. The name of the unit is L. of C. (Lines of Communications) Signals. All the places – offices, billets, mess-rooms etc. are fairly close together, which is a change from Whetstone, where every part of the unit was a day's march from every other. The "inmates" don't think much of the place, but they haven't been to 7th A.F.S., so we'll find out for ourselves.

The latest information is that we are to be telephone operators in the Swiss Navy, so you can gather how much we know. I hope I'm wrong, but I have a feeling my next leave may be embarkation leave. Not one of us knows anything definite, but they took our sizes again the other day, and they wouldn't do that for nothing. Don't get the wind up, my darling, but be prepared.

Your loving husband,
Leslie.

14234557 Sigmn. Smith, L.M.
2 Coy.,
96 Cambridge Road,
Wimbledon SW 20

30th January 1943

Darling,

Don't worry about my being "put upon" by the other fellows. I can hold my own without losing my sense of decency and without becoming "tougher" than is necessary. I don't think

I'm any different now.

It looks as if they're collecting the necessary sections for a complete Sigs. Unit – switchboard operators, teleprinter operators, despatch riders and linesmen. There's one good thing about being posted as a section, as we were – we're more sure of getting embarkation leave. I feel it so much being away from you at all, and yet I have to think of resigning myself to being away from you for months maybe And yet, if I do go, I'll be seeing new places, while you will have to carry on in the same old way. As you say, curse this - - war! To think we could have been together all this time. I never did fancy myself in a brown suit, and now I have to wear one all the time. Again, I wouldn't like to be back in "civvy street" while the war's on, yet I want to be with you all the time. The only way seems to be for the war to finish soon, and then I can tell you and our children how I won it! One of these days, I suppose, we'll look back on this episode and think how short it really was, but it seems ages now.

The news is on – first daylight raid on Berlin. I think we're winning, don't you, love?

God bless you,
Leslie

2nd February 1943

Darling Gracie,

Don't worry about my being mixed up in any fighting, love. My work will be at bases well behind the front line. I should think the only enemy I'll see will be prisoners. I'll be safe all right, sweetheart. I only hope I see a part of the world worth telling you about. I wonder where I'll go, if I do go? The only places I can think of are France and India (to push the Japs out of Burma). I shouldn't think they'll be needing us in N. Africa, unless, maybe, for communications in occupied territory…

All my love, and love to all,
Leslie.

5ᵗʰ February 1943

Here I am again, lovey,

I'm glad I've taken a load off your mind. I'm a switchboard operator, and obviously we couldn't be up with the fighting with a switchboard, although we may connect to a telephone that is. Even so, other corps, infantry and so on, have their own signal sections. As a rule, Royal Signals work further back, except perhaps for wireless and linesmen. It all depends, I suppose, on how conditions are – whether fighting is fairly static or not.

I suppose, if we do go through Italy, I could always run to the Vatican if we were chased, couldn't I? I wonder where I will land up.

From what little I've seen of the news, the Russians don't need us, anyway, thank goodness. I don't fancy the Steppes, or anywhere around there…

All my love,
Leslie.

23ʳᵈ February 1943

My darling,

Some of the sections have been given "pamphlets" on "Health in the Tropics", though, of course, that in itself doesn't necessarily mean anything..

No, love, I don't like the sound of the "medical" either. It was an F.F.I. (Free From Infection) which happens whenever one leaves or joins a unit. The latest about the "scheme" is that it is scheduled to start on the 2nd, but may start any time after Saturday, which is the 27th. We are to have a lecture about it by the C.O. tomorrow.

Yes, some do think that the "scheme" will be the second front, but no-one knows, and I think it is just a "scheme" even if the actual thing isn't far off. A "scheme" is the name for an exercise or manoeuvres. I suppose they could send me away without giving me leave first, but I don't think that will happen.

I don't know whether I'll have a settled address or not, but I doubt it, so I suppose I won't get any letters for a week...

Leslie.

"Somewhere",
England.

1st March 1943

Darling,

Soon after 11 yesterday we squeezed ourselves into the lorry and made ourselves as comfortable as we could, which wasn't very, there being fifteen of us, wearing small pack and respirators on our backs, and we were sitting on our kitbags and packs. It was after midnight before we started out. We tried to sleep after a time, but it was cold and we were cramped, but we did manage to doze a little. The convoy – about fifty trucks – made slow progress, stopping often and not going fast even when moving. At about 2 we were allowed to get out for a smoke, not being allowed to smoke in the truck. Then we started off again. I hadn't the faintest idea where we were or in what direction we were going. When we had stopped we seemed to be miles from anywhere. I must have slept quite a bit after that, for the next I knew it was 6.45 and we'd stopped again for a smoke. It was bitterly cold. We moved off again and went a short way before we left the road and drove into a wood. This, apparently, was our rendezvous. We were all feeling very cold, tired, stiff and generally miserable.

We took off our packs and started gathering wood for a fire. (We should have brought our camp kitchen with us, but had been told that being attached to A.F.S., they would cook for us.) All the wood was damp and we had great difficulty in keeping a fire going while we tried to boil water in our mess tins. Before we had succeeded bacon was cooked for us on a stove, and we had some, but nothing to drink. A few of us collected breadcrumbs in our mess tins and put milk and sugar on them and quite enjoyed the result. It was still cold and our feet were frozen, but the sun was beginning to show itself. Then, as expected, the section was split up and I was one of four who were told to go with one party, who were to be attached to forward positions. We had to move our kit to another truck and collect our party's rations from the section rations. By this time the sun was quite warm and we were not moving off till after dinner, so we lay down in the sun and slept a little. I was wakened to be told that I was staying with the main body of the section, who would be manning the Signal Office at Rear H.Q. My face was quite red – it's the first time I've been sunburnt in February! It was really lovely

I learned that we were near Billingshurst in Sussex. At one o'clock we moved off again and passed through some beautiful country and lovely villages. After about two hours we arrived at Witley Camp, occupied mainly by Canadians. It is about five miles from Godalming and we are on or near the border of Sussex and Surrey. Billingshurst is about fifteen miles from the Channel. We are working with the Canadians, who are supposed to have landed at Portsmouth and arrived here, which is Rear H.Q.

We were put into a barrack-room, some having to sleep on the floor. We soon had tea and then were free, as the scheme was scheduled to start at 6 p.m. Sunday. We washed and shaved – in hot water, a luxury we hadn't contemplated. I'd thought that our experience in the wood was a foretaste of what we were to expect. Three of us went to the Naafi, where we bought a little choc and could have got cigs, both without coupons. We had a couple of doughnuts – with holes in them. I heard someone ordering "chop and chips"! The Canadian troops certainly get better food in the Naafi.

When we got back to the barrack-room we only had one blanket each, so two of us decided to sleep together, so we could share our blankets and overcoats. We didn't have much room, but were warmer. Several others followed our example. We paraded at 8.30, after a good breakfast of porridge and bacon. We did nothing before dinner, except that I went for a little walk. It is lovely around here – plenty of trees and I think we are on or near the Downs. After dinner I took my groundsheet and overcoat and slept on the grass. We eat our meals outside and it is quite pleasant in the sun, so long as one doesn't stay too long, because there is a breeze.

Tuesday afternoon.

To-day the weather is still lovely. Planes are flying over by the minute and occasionally one can hear distant gunfire. We don't know how the "battle" is going. While I was lying in the sun three "brass-hats" passed – probably umpires – there are about fifty over the rank of Lieut-Colonel knocking about ...

All my love, my darling.

Love to all,

Leslie.

7th March 1943

Darling Gracie,

One of these days, my love, we will be looking back on our separation as a bad dream. I often think how I used to wonder whether I'd ever be away from Royal, and here I am feeling quite at ease in my uniform, as if I'd always worn it, and at the same time wanting to take it off for the last time. I suppose I could use the pants for gardening, unless I'm so fed up with them that I couldn't bear to see them again. I hope it won't be long before we're sitting in the "Lamb" again...

God bless you, darling,
Leslie.

A moment of relaxation – May 1944

L.M. Smith second from left

12th March 1943

My darling,

The show is over – more or less. It finished at 9 this morning, but we still have to keep up communications until the units have dispersed. Our objective was the enemy's "capital", Huntingdon, and we won, I believe, although I don't think we actually reached Huntingdon – and don't care. It will probably be two or three days before we leave, but we're all very pleased the "scheme" is over. It was the biggest ever – I suppose you'll hear about it eventually…

Goodnight, darling, from your hot water bottle's would-be substitute.

Leslie.

(After the return to Wimbledon at the end of this exercise, another year and more was to elapse before the next phase of the war began, which was to see my father's unit moving abroad as a vital part of the Allied invasion forces. In the meantime they were posted to various places throughout the country. In the spring of 1944 my father was in hospital in Newmarket with a recurrence of his skin infection, but was sufficiently recovered to rejoin his unit by the beginning of June.)

Chapter Five

Normandy: June 1944

On 6th June 1944, the day came at last that the free world and the occupied countries had long been anticipating with hope and with prayers – the opening of the Second Front. Hitler had rashly torn up the Molotov–Ribbentrop pact of non-aggression in June 1941 and turned his armies against the Soviet Union in the ill-fated Operation Barbarossa. Since then, his former ally had borne the brunt of the fighting and the casualties in the struggle for Europe. Numberless Russian soldiers had died in savage battles, including Stalingrad and Kursk, and women and children had starved and frozen in the sieges of many towns. The German Army had finally foundered, like Napoleon's Grande Armée before it, in the snows of the East, where after every hollow victory, more millions of men came implacably out of the heart of the Motherland to replace their dead and captured comrades. But Russia alone could not summon the reserves to defeat Hitler. And they cried out for help from their British and American Allies.

It seemed at times to many that this help was slow in coming, but the long months before D-Day were spent in carefully gathering information about landing beaches, gun emplacements, German troop deployments and all the details upon which the assault would depend. Commando reconnaissance operations, aerial photography and information from the French Resistance were all vital. Postcards and holiday snaps of the French coast were also gathered and carefully analysed by experts, so that when the day came the troops would have a clear picture of the situation facing them, down to the details of individual houses and sand dunes.

At the same time, troops were massing in hidden locations throughout the southern half of England, preparing for their part in this immensely complex operation. In Devon, soldiers practised beach landings, and millions of troops slowly assembled in the southern counties, their lorries and tanks lining the roads and causing traffic jams on the routes to Portsmouth and Southampton. Meanwhile in Kent, artificial tanks, planes and ships were deployed to convince the Germans that any attempted landing would be directed towards the Pas de Calais.

Looking back on it, it seems inevitable that events happened on the dates that they did. However, for a long time arguments had raged about how soon it would be practicable to attempt to establish a foothold on the coast of Northen France. The first plans for a cross-Channel invasion were drawn up by British Chief Planning staff in September 1941, but it was not until the entry of the USA into the war at the end of that year that the idea became at all feasible. Roosevelt had been persuaded of the need to defeat Germany as quickly as possible in order to free troops for the war against Japan, and he and Stalin were pushing for the opening of a Second Front in Europe. Churchill, on the other hand, was cautious, and it was not until the Quebec Conference in August 1943 that a date was set for the Normandy Landings.

The invasion was to be spearheaded by five divisions, making a total of 150,000 men, mainly British, American and Canadian, but including some Polish and Free French troops. They faced great odds, although many of the German troops were not of the highest quality. The main landings were spread over five beaches. The British and Canadian beaches of Gold,

Juno and Sword stretched between Ouistreham and Arromanches, and the American beaches of Omaha (which saw the greatest casualties) and Utah were further west, towards the Cotentin peninsula.

The German High Command knew perfectly well that without a port through which to unload men and supplies, it would be impossible for the Allies to sustain an invasion of the Channel coast. The Allies also knew, after the abortive assault on Dieppe in 1942, that capturing a well-defended port would be virtually impossible. The solution, when it came, was both blindingly obvious and yet breathtakingly bold in its conception and execution. The answer was to build a floating harbour and tow it across the Channel, anchor it offshore from the shallow Normandy beaches and trundle tanks, lorries and all the other paraphernalia of war onto dry land using long floating roadways.

In the great shipyards and construction sites of Britain, skilled workmen toiled to create these strange contraptions, unsure what they were building, but using their long experience to manufacture them to the exact dimensions required. In the event, these Mulberry Harbours were an amazing success, despite the storms of 19th June which damaged the harbours and wrecked the American Mulberry off Omaha beach. By the end of the year, hundreds of thousands of men had passed dryshod onto land, accompanied by thousands of vehicles and untold tons of supplies. The first sections of the harbour were in place by the 9th June, but for many days afterwards troops were still coming ashore in landing craft, so that men of the Royal Signals, such as my father, who did not arrive on D-Day itself, could still proudly claim that they waded through the surf to reach French soil.

It came as a surprise to many of the Allies that the people of Normandy did not always welcome them with the gratitude they expected. It is easy, however, to see why. In this part of France, far from Paris and Vichy, the inhabitants had seen nothing of the German Blitzkrieg, of aerial bombardments or of people fleeing the invader with their belongings on handcarts. Food shortages largely passed by this rich agricultural region, and the German troops stationed here were often either withdrawn from the Russian Front and glad of a quiet life, or, by 1944, composed of older men and teenagers drafted in to make up for the terrible losses already suffered by the Wehrmacht. An uneasy working relationship had been established between the Normans and their occupiers, to the extent that overt Resistance activity was generally frowned upon for disturbing the status quo.

In June 1944 all this changed. A terrible seaborne bombardment heralded the landings, and the days and weeks following saw the reduction of towns such as Caen and Falaise to little more than rubble, with many deaths and other personal tragedies to set against the joy of liberation. Nevertheless, the majority of people were pleased to see the backs of the Germans, and welcomed the arrival of the Allied troops and the prospect of getting back to normal. Unfortunately, there was still a lot of fighting to take place across the peaceful cow-grazed pastures and through the apple-laden orchards before the occupying forces were finally pushed back and began their now inevitable retreat to their own borders.

Nowadays, when working-class people routinely travel to the Mediterranean, or even the Caribbean, it is strange to recall that for my parents' generation, foreign holidays were the preserve of the rich and famous. Young people have become quite blasé about going to France or Spain, yet their journeys on school trips or package holidays are swathed in comfort and cocooned in safety regulations. What a contrast to the young men landing in Normandy in June 1944, for whom danger and discomfort awaited, combined, for many, with great excitement. My father's description of his first day in France – the landing craft, the dusty roads, the search for his unit, the bivouac in a field under starry foreign skies – is far removed from most present-day ideas of a first trip abroad.

My father had been learning French, and this was his chance to use it for real. It enabled him to make friends with the locals, and he was sought after as an interpreter by other men of his section. He was hampered a little by his desire to get it right – grammar was important to him, and he was not content just to make himself roughly understood; but in the end he became a more than competent conversationalist in the language. He was obviously fascinated by the challenge, and appreciative of the opportunity his posting to France had given him.

However, as was the case with all British troops, thoughts were predominantly of home, and when no post arrived for a while, soldiers felt alone and cut off. My father frequently bemoans the intermittent arrival of letters, and yet the Army, very conscious of the effect on troops' morale of messages from loved ones, made their delivery a high priority. As a result, despite the difficulty of cross-Channel communications and the problems of finding a particular unit or section in the changing patterns of the Front, letters frequently arrived within three or four days. Sixty years on, the postal service often struggles to match this record.

My mother worried that my father might become coarsened by his experience of life in the Army, or be put upon by others;

but he appears to have chosen his friends carefully, and in any case could stand up for himself perfectly well. He was seemingly cherished by his section, especially the younger men, for his maturity and calming influence. Nevertheless, gentle person though he was, my father came to show little pity for dead Germans, and freely used the term "Jerry" to show his distaste for the nation which had dragged men like himself into Hitler's War, splitting up families and disrupting lives, even before the greater tragedies of the time are taken into account.

My father was away at the war when his son was born, and for several months had only his wife's descriptions, and later on, some photos, to convince him that he was really a father, and that his firstborn was flesh and blood. He worried constantly that his son might see him as a stranger when he finally returned home, and that he was missing so many happy moments in his baby's early life. The end of the war could not come soon enough.

Poignantly, many of the conscripted men believed that once the invasion had taken place, the end of the war would follow swiftly. They dreamed of returning home, and rumours spread that they might be back by Christmas 1944. How wrong they were. At the time of the Normandy landings, it was less than two years since my father received his call-up papers; he did not realise it then, but even at this apparently late stage in the hostilities, he was still less than half-way through his army service.

4234557 Sigmn. Smith, L.M.
2 Coy., 2 L of C. Signals,
A.P.O England

Wednesday 7th June 1944 – No. 1

Gracie, my darling,

I think that, this being my first letter after the long-awaited "D" Day, it is as good a time as any to start numbering my letters, even if it's not really necessary.

I suppose we won't forget the 6th of June. We're all pleased it's started at last, as, I suppose, everyone else is, and we are now awaiting our turn. The invasion seems to have started well, anyway, thank God, and I hope it will continue so. Yesterday we had a "Service of Dedication" in the camp theatre and it was well attended. There was no Padre, but it was led by our present O.C. The service started with "O God our help", then the 91st psalm was read, followed by "Abide with me", two minutes of "silent prayer" and finished with the National Anthem. Later that evening I heard the King's speech.

Yesterday we were given copies of the messages to the troops of Eisenhower and Montgomery which were published in the papers…

God bless you,
Leslie.

SUPREME HEADQUARTERS
ALLIED EXPEDITIONARY FORCE

Soldiers, Sailors and Airmen of the Allied Expeditionary Force!

You are about to embark upon the Great Crusade, toward which we have striven these many months. The eyes of the world are upon you. The hopes and prayers of liberty-loving people everywhere march with you. In company with our brave Allies and brothers-in-arms on other Fronts, you will bring about the destruction of the German war machine, the elimination of Nazi tyranny over the oppressed peoples of Europe, and security for ourselves in a free world.

Your task will not be an easy one. Your enemy is well trained, well equipped and battle-hardened. He will fight savagely.

But this is the year 1944 ! Much has happened since the Nazi triumphs of 1940-41. The United Nations have inflicted upon the Germans great defeats, in open battle, man-to-man. Our air offensive has seriously reduced their strength in the air and their capacity to wage war on the ground. Our Home Fronts have given us an overwhelming superiority in weapons and munitions of war, and placed at our disposal great reserves of trained fighting men. The tide has turned ! The free men of the world are marching together to Victory !

I have full confidence in your courage, devotion to duty and skill in battle. We will accept nothing less than full Victory !

Good Luck ! And let us all beseech the blessing of Almighty God upon this great and noble undertaking.

Dwight Eisenhower

21 ARMY GROUP

PERSONAL MESSAGE
FROM THE C-in-C

To be read out to all Troops

1. The time has come to deal the enemy a terrific blow in Western Europe.

The blow will be struck by the combined sea, land, and air forces of the Allies—together constituting one great Allied team, under the supreme command of General Eisenhower.

2. On the eve of this great adventure I send my best wishes, to every soldier in the Allied team.

To us is given the honour of striking a blow for freedom which will live in history; and in the better days that lie ahead men will speak with pride of our doings. We have a great and a righteous cause.

Let us pray that " The Lord Mighty in Battle " will go forth with our armies, and that His special providence will aid us in the struggle.

3. I want every soldier to know that I have complete confidence in the successful outcome of the operations that we are now about to begin.

With stout hearts, and with enthusiasm for the contest, let us go forward to victory.

4. And, as we enter the battle, let us recall the words of a famous soldier spoken many years ago :—

> " *He either fears his fate too much,*
> *Or his deserts are small,*
> *Who dare not put it to the touch,*
> *To win or lose it all.*"

5. Good luck to each one of you. And good hunting on the mainland of Europe.

B. L. Montgomery
General
C.-in-C 21 Army Group.

1944.

155

Sunday 11th June 1944 – No. 3

Gracie darling,

Enclosed are some letters and a "D" Day paper. I've had no letters since last Wednesday, but as we're moving tomorrow, perhaps I'll get some soon.

This morning I hiked to Mass and back in time for dinner. The rest of the day I seem to have spent in packing innumerable things into comparatively small compass – we haven't any kitbags now. We are the last section to move...

All my love darling,

Leslie

(They finally left England on the night of 13th June, and landed in Normandy on the morning of the 14th – D-Day plus 8. This was my father's first experience of foreign travel.)

Friday 16th June 1944 – No. 5

My darling Gracie,

This won't arrive in time for your birthday, but, however late it is, you'll know that I'm wishing you a very happy day.

I hope you received the note I wrote on the boat – it seemed just a matter of chance whether they were posted or not. We don't really know how much we're allowed to say yet, so I mustn't say too much. We don't get a great deal of news, but things seem to be going all right I think.

I'm managing to make myself understood by the inhabitants and can understand them most of the time. The children ask for "bon-bons" and the men are short of cigs. The people generally seem pleased to see us. Apart from occasional distant gunfire, aircraft (ours) and troops, we know very little of the war.

We're all well and happy, only anxious to be home.

God bless you, love,

Leslie.

14234557 Sigmn. Smith, L.M.
2 Coy., 2 L. of C. Signals
A.P.O 698

Saturday 17th June 1944 – No. 6

Gracie darling,

We find to-day that we're allowed to say we're in France, and can relate certain incidents – when they're a fortnight old!

It's 9.30 now and I'm just going to visit some friends – a young couple who live nearby. I only met them last night and they're very kind. They have a little girl of two, whom I haven't yet seen as she was in bed when I visited them, with Peter and Norman, last night...

God bless you, darling,

Leslie.

Sunday 18th June 1944 – No.7

Darling Gracie,

Last evening Norman and I went to our friends' house to write and before leaving had some strawberries and coffee. I don't know their names yet, but they are very kind. Monsieur is very grateful when we give him cigarettes, and we also take chocolate and "bon-bons". The cig ration for them is forty a month and they're horrible things, so you'll realise how much he appreciates ours. Earlier in the day I met Françoise, who is two and has lovely fair hair and blue eyes.

They told us a lot about "le Boche" – how, when they wanted something, they just walked into the house and took it

Leslie and Norman

– radio, sewing machine, bed linen, furniture, electric light bulbs etc. The house is very clean and tidy, but with hardly any furniture except table and chairs – no easy chairs. Monsieur used to work in a bank and hopes to return to it when it re-opens. They know no English whatever, and are very patient and helpful with our French, and we get on very well. Fortunately they don't speak a "patois", but just straightforward French that we can understand. They were telling us last night that Jerry had bombed the cathedral and houses in Rouen immediately after we or the Yanks had bombed the railways and factories, and had done the same at other places. Jerry propaganda linked these supposedly Allied actions with our burning of Joan of Arc! A lot of other things they told us, too.

The water situation isn't too good, although we're not short.

All our water is drawn from a pump a few yards up the road – it's not so easy as turning a tap!

Yesterday there was a fire at a farm down the road. I didn't see it, but apparently it had its humorous side – it sounded typical of the sort of thing one reads about. The natives either stood idly watching the fire or arguing as to who was to blame, while some of our lads tried to do something about it whilst awaiting the arrival of the fire brigade. The latter turned up and then argued with themselves as to the best way to put the fire out. It was caused by children playing with something or other left behind by us or Jerry

We're making ourselves as comfortable as we can and haven't much to complain of as regards living conditions. About other things I could say more, but won't – at the moment...

Look after yourself,
God bless you,
Leslie

14234557 Sigmn. Smith, L.M.
2 Coy., 2 L. of C. Signals.
B.W.E.F.

Saturday 24th June 1944 – No. 10

My darling Gracie,

Have you heard about Hitler having given us 72 hours in which to get out of France before he destroys us? We heard the story a few days ago.

The young boys here wear smocks or aprons over their other clothes, and most of the people – adults and children – wear sabots, except on Sundays, when they turn out in their "Sunday best". The people seem quite friendly and usually greet one with a "Bonjour" or "Bonsoir", or sometimes just "M'sieur". I'm gaining confidence with my French. Those of us who know some French are continually being pestered by those of the section who don't, for information as to "how to say so and so" or "what does so and so mean?"

The town is out of bounds at the moment, and I don't know how long that will last, but it doesn't worry me.

I wonder how long it will be before we take Cherbourg? It would be a great help if we had a port.

I would like three of my books when it's convenient for you to send them. They are "First Year French for Adults", "Elementary French Composition" (I hope the marked papers are still in the cover of this one, as I'd like them too) and "La Petite Chose a l'Ecole"…

God bless you, darling,
Leslie.

Monday 26th June 1944 – No. 11

Gracie, my darling,

Yesterday I was invited out for lunch, together with Norman and Peter. We arrived at 1.30 and started the meal soon after. I don't know whether lunch usually lasts so long in France, but this meal didn't finish until 4.20! It started with a small omelette, together with a little dry brown bread. Then rabbit (roasted) and veg. – potatoes, peas and carrots. We were drinking cider as well. Another helping of veg. and then bread and cheese, followed by strawberries and coffee.

I've at least had a glimpse of a German, when I saw a few prisoners passing through in cars.

I wonder whether you'd had the note I wrote from the boat when you wrote your last letter, as you suppose I'd be in France when I receive it, although, of course, you couldn't be certain that was my destination. I was certain – but couldn't tell you – because that morning we'd been paid two hundred francs. I was very relieved when we were sure it was France, because they could easily have changed their minds and sent us to Burma or some equally unpleasant and far-away place.

Here, at least, there is a chance of leave, we hope, but not, of course, for some time. Maybe our baby won't be very old when I see him or her, but of course, it all depends how things go. I would prefer that we should push on and on and wait a little longer for a leave without end. Maybe I'm optimistic, but things seem to be going quite well so far. We've taken Cherbourg at last, which should be a great help. I say "at last", but think our forces have done very well in capturing a port like that, and it will facilitate the disembarkment of troops and material.

As you say, it is a thrill for me to be in France – yes, I am there! – and I hope I'll see more of it. It would be annoying if I stayed in the one place, even though I've already made such good friends. I wonder if I will see Paris – I certainly hope so. If I don't see it I'll be disappointed, but maybe we'll see it *après la guerre.*

As regards the language, it will, of course, take sometime to become accustomed to the "rhythm", but I get on quite well so far. I can understand our friends most of the time, except when they speak quickly. They know no English – no one around here seems to know any – which is a good thing in a way, but sometimes it's difficult when we come across a word or phrase which is unfamiliar. Still, however unconsciously or slowly, we must be learning, and lose no opportunity of learning from them. They are most understanding – if they see we don't understand something they repeat it, more slowly, or perhaps using different words, and we very rarely fail to understand. It's a different matter from writing the language, naturally. We find the ordinary everyday expressions, which, in English, come so naturally to our lips, a little confusing, as it would be so easy to put one's foot in it, but there again we thank Madame and Monsieur for their help – they fully realise our difficulties. Our Army instructor once told us it took him nine months before he felt at all confident in conversation.

So the Yanks are doing everything over here, are they? I suppose they'll say they won another war for us. We know better. Anyway, their switchboard operators are "lousy"!...

All my love,
Leslie.

Thursday 29ᵗʰ June 1944 – No. 13

My darling,
So far as my limited experience takes me, the French do seem pleased to see us and glad that the Germans have gone, although I suppose there are exceptions, as apparently Jerry wasn't too bad in his behaviour here – apart from things like shooting ten for one etc!

God bless you,
Leslie.

Tuesday 4ᵗʰ July 1944 – No. 14

Gracie, my darling,
On Sunday morning I went to Mass at the Cathedral with our Canadian interpreter. The Cathedral was packed, but apparently

most of the treasures have been hidden. It does look rather bare, but is a magnificent building, even though probably smaller than cathedrals I've seen in England. It dates from the 11th to 14th centuries.

Afterwards, Norman and I paid a visit to *nos amis*. Five refugees were having a meal with them. There are three women and two girls, aged about six and twelve. The younger girl has the biggest, brightest eyes I've ever seen and she looks like a little gypsy. The other girl is fair and quite sweet. They were both abandoned by their mothers about a year ago. They and our hostess made it very plain that they would like to have every German, man, woman and child, exterminated. They certainly seem to have justification for that attitude. I've heard things that, read in an English newspaper, would sound like propaganda. They may not be true, of course, but it's the people who ought to know who tell us.

The people here are much less casual in their outward courtesy than we are. Everyone shakes hands on meeting and leaving one another – even the children. When we visit our friends, and their "guests" are there, it means eight "shakes" then, and the same when leaving. If one member leaves, he or she shakes hands all round. Sometimes we may meet Monsieur S. in the street and chat for a minute or two – same procedure. I wonder whether or not we appear to be unmannerly with each other. If we're just going for a meal it's "Bon appétit". Meeting in the morning it's "vous avez bien dormi?" ("Did you sleep well?") etc.

My DII rating pay is now in my paybook. It is sixpence a day and I get threepence of it and I suppose you will get the other threepence. My full pay is now 4/3d a day of which I get 3/3d. On 16th of this month I complete two years and so should have another threepence added, but whether you get it, or I, remains to be seen.

God bless you darling,
Leslie.

Letter (Grace Smith)

7ᵗʰ July 1944

Darling Les,

I hope by the time you get this you'll have heard that you are the proud (?) father of a son.

I came in here on Wed. night about 10 o'clock as I had been having tummy ache. I was put to bed in a ward with three girls all of whom had had their babes. I started with very bad pains shortly after and was taken to the labour ward at quarter to twelve. Dr. Cantrell was sent for and the baby was born at 2.30 a.m. Thursday morn. It was awful while it lasted but I was lucky that it only took about five hours in all — it was making up for its tardy appearance! I had to be cut and had two stitches & I had chloroform right at the end.

The baby — or Paul rather — is very good but can cry lustily when he feels like it. I feel fine altho' terribly uncomfortable all the time. It hurts to move and the bed seems as hard as hell! It's very nice here & we are well treated.

Paul has dark blue eyes, medium brown hair and a very decisive looking nose. In spite of all our fears he has a sweet little chin — not a long one! You know the way you stick your lip out when you're playing "little boy"? Well he does exactly that & looks terribly cute and pathetic.

I think it was a miracle that on the day I needed one — that is yesterday after my "ordeal" — two letters should arrive from you after a silence of a fortnight — nos. 7 & 9. Today no. 5 has arrived, so they're coming along - even tho' they're going backwards!

Harold is home but I don't know why. He sent a telegram saying "What! Another guy named Smith! Congrats." I've had one from Edie as well!

I'm glad to know you are doing all right love & getting on with the "natives". I wish you were here, of course, but let's hope it won't be many months now!

Mother came last night & said the Palmers next door are having a christening cake made! Could you get here for it do you think?

I'll write again soon. Meantime love from me and Paul.

All my love,
Gracie

Sat 8th July 1944 – No. 15

My darling,

Your letter of 28th (8) came yesterday, and I was very pleased to see it, even if the news isn't exactly up-to-date I seem to be receiving all your letters sometime, anyway. I hear they're now coming by air – Peter had one which took only two days – so probably I'll get some letters out of sequence. You say you've had mine of 17th – I wrote on 16th, too, so there's one at least missing, though perhaps you've had it by now. You can tell if you miss one, anyway. Please do send the papers, love, as I'll get them all right, barring accidents.

It does seem strange to me that I should be in France at last, but I'm getting used to the idea, although I haven't seen much of the country yet. Don't expect me to speak French fluently yet, love – it takes time to get used to it. One has to get into the "rhythm" of it. As you say, it is a great opportunity and I'll do my best to take advantage of it, having made a good start.

So far the section is more or less together, except that, as I've mentioned in a previous letter, three of us have been detached and are working in the town. I don't know whether I'll be able to see other places or not. We seem to be fairly static at the moment, but maybe we'll move later – I hope so, anyway.

I like most of the people I've actually met – they're most friendly on the whole. They seem pleased to see us, but not terribly so. Still, I don't expect them to be cheering, throwing flowers etc. all the time, although I've heard it's happening in other places. To me, the feeling seems to be that of great relief and thankfulness. There's no doubt about the fact that we're welcome. Some shopkeepers are profiteering, of course, although price restrictions have now come into force. They certainly won't grow rich at my expense. This part of France, I'm told, is a great producing area, which accounts for the fact that they're not short of food. There is plenty of meat and there is more in the shops generally than I'd expected to see.

Cherbourg certainly should be a great relief to us and should ease the strain on the beaches – and on our ears. All day long trucks, tanks etc. are roaring past – not to mention aircraft. At night we can sometimes just see the gunflashes in the distance.

Occasionally we have a Jerry plane over, but it's rather hot for him, although one day a ME shot down a Spitfire near here. I just missed seeing the action, but heard it.

Later

I wrote the above this morning, before going on duty.

Since then I've heard the news I've waited for for so long. So we have a son, my darling! All my love to you both. I just got the bare message that you are both well. I hope you are very well, my love, and that you are very happy. I'm not sure yet, but assume that Thursday this week was "the" day? I can hardly wait to hear from you. I'd better address this to Elmswood, where I hope you're being well looked-after. My darling, darling, my lovely wonderful darling – tell me you're happy! I want you to be. I suppose it's silly to ask what his Lordship looks like!

I'm just about to go to the camp, where, apparently, I'm expected to buy drinks for all, but I want to finish this to-night.

Later still!

I'm sitting in Norman's room now, having received the congratulations and leg-pulling of my friends, and had my supper with them.

Of course, as you know, I'll write as often as I can, and at the moment can't see any reason why that state of affairs shouldn't continue, but don't worry in any case, love, because I'm a long way from the fighting.

I wish I could be with you – sitting amongst familiar things. Actually, it's not so strange here really, except for little things one notices occasionally. Of course, all the signs and speech, except for ours, are in French. I'll try to tell you more about what I see, etc., but at the moment must finish this letter, so you'll get it as early as possible.

Perhaps you'll be able to get into some "decent clothes", now, love, before the summer's over. Our weather is generally good. I'm told that there'd been no rain here for months until we came – we even brought our weather with us!

The latest "secret weapon" seems to be giving quite a good account of itself. I hope Bea and Theo aren't troubled with it.

Once more wishing I could be with you, as always. I'll say "goodnight" to you and our son. I love you both – you don't mind sharing it do you? It doesn't make any less my love for you, including him as well.

My love to all,
I love you very much, my darling,
God bless you,
Leslie

P.S. Does "he" know his father's in France?

Sun 9th July 1944 – No. 16

Gracie, my darling,

Last evening, after I'd written to you, Norman and I went around to our friends. N. had told them my news earlier and Mme. S met me with her "félicitations", but was disappointed at "it" being a boy. She gave me the enclosed flower(s) – "pour Maman, Papa, et le petit bébé". They had three guests – two girls, relatives of M. who had been evacuated from the Caen area, and a Parisian with whom M. used to work for the Germans – digging on the coast and forced of course – and whom he'd met again. The latter actually hails from Marseilles, but was a Parisian by adoption and his wife is still there, he having been taken away for the aforesaid labour. He knows a little English and talked about football a lot. We promised to go there again this afternoon when M. hoped to have some wine to drink to the health of "Paul et sa mère" (that's you!).

This morning I was on duty and couldn't go to Mass. During the day we heard that Caen had been taken, which is a relief.

After lunch I walked to the billet and found that Norman and Don were already at our friends' house. Soon, M. brought out a bottle of vin blanc and they toasted "Le petit Paul, sa mère et son père" and wishing you good health. Even little Françoise had a drop of wine. Then we had a tiny glass of "Calvados", which is like whisky but more so, and then another. I couldn't drink much of that without feeling the effects. It was the real stuff – not the sort of "Calvados" one could get in the cafés. We three left for our tea and returned for a couple of hours, after having listened to the news.

I came back here with the rations, and with a small bottle of what I thought was vin blanc, which I'd asked M. to get for me. We soon found out it was Calvados.

Love to all, and all my love to you.

God bless you,

Leslie.

Tues. 11th July 1944 No. 17

Gracie, my love,

I was surprised and delighted when I got your letter of 7th (11) this evening, particularly as I'd thought you wouldn't be able to write for some days. I'm glad it wasn't too bad, although I suppose it was most painful. Was everything normal – I don't know from what you say, not being conversant with such matters. Was it as bad as you expected it to be? You didn't have too long to wait after you arrived there anyway, did you? I wonder why babies are so often born in the small hours? I hope you're feeling more comfortable now, lovey – it was sweet of you to write when you probably didn't feel like doing so – it was a lovely surprise. I'd expected to get my first idea of what Paul was like from Nina – that's no disparagement of Nina, of course, but I'd much sooner hear it from you, my darling. I'm glad he's good and hope he doesn't feel like crying as often as his father did. I'm glad you like the place and are being well-treated – you're not surrounded by "thousands" of women anyway. Are the other occupants nice? I wonder what you mean by a "decisive-looking nose"! I'm glad his chin doesn't take after his father's anyway! I'd love to see him. I'm hungry to hear all I can about you both. Does he look as cute as I do?! How I wish I were with you! Tell him his father's thinking about him and sends his love, won't you? Explain that I'm away at the war (!) and will come home as soon as I can!

I'm glad my letters have started to arrive, even though not in order & especially that the first after a "silence of a fortnight" should have arrived on your "D" day. I hope you're getting mine regularly now. Your letters are arriving in good time now, as you can see. I wish I knew whether or not mine are taking as little time as yours, as I've sent two to "Elmswood" and will do the same with this, but perhaps I'd better send the next home, if I don't hear.

It was nice of Edie and of Harold to send telegrams and of the Palmers to be providing the Christening cake – I wish I could help you eat it. Maybe you'd let me hold Paul for a minute or two, too!

God bless you both,
Leslie.

Wed 12th July 1944 – No. 18

My darling Gracie,

It's a month to-day – or rather four weeks – since I arrived in France. We were on the boat for hours before sailing. We started off at 11 o'clock on the Tuesday night – 13th – and before we were out of the harbour were ordered below. We wouldn't have been able to see much, anyway, at that time of night, although it was a lovely night. We already had on our Mae Wests, under our blouses, and we had to keep them on for sleeping. Although we were crowded together, we had a bunk each and were provided with one blanket, which was ample. Our craft was a U.S. Coastguard boat, and wasn't very big. I suppose the sea was calm really to a sailor, but our craft rolled quite a lot, and the engine kicked up a terrific din. I lay on my bunk and became accustomed to the rolling, but then it would start to toss, or the engines would change their tempo, and I thought I'd never sleep. We were provided with three bags, vomit, but I didn't need mine, nor did anyone else need theirs, which surprised quite a few. Eventually I fell asleep and slept fairly steadily until six o'clock. We were still moving, and I fell asleep again. I woke again at 9.20 and went on deck.

I always imagined the Channel to be grey and gloomy, but when I went on deck I found that it was a lovely sunlit morning and the sea was practically blue. It was very exhilarating and I felt very hungry. I was surprised to find that we were still out of sight of land, having thought that the journey was of about six or seven hours. We must have gone a long way round. We passed a few ships going in the opposite direction and saw an occasional aeroplane. I was dying for a cup of tea, but there was none to be had, although we had some soup, which, in my opinion, is a poor substitute. We began to see more and more ships, until eventually we saw the coast of France, and as we came closer could see hundreds and hundreds of ships of all sizes.

The land sloped very gradually upward from the sea and as we wormed our way closer inshore I could see traffic along the beach and on a road leading up from the beach. A landing barge came alongside and we jumped down into it. It wasn't easy for us, loaded as we were, because the edge of the smaller craft was one minute close enough to step onto and the next far below – one had to step onto it as it came up. Eventually we were all in two of them and headed for the shore. The craft drew alongside an improvised pier, along which we walked to the beach. It was about 2.30 p.m. then. Alongside the pier I saw a naval man busy painting the scene on the beach!

(Despite the "improvised pier" they still got their feet wet. It was my father's proud boast that he waded ashore on the D-Day beaches.)

We walked straight up the beach and onto the road leading inland. We had to keep moving until we were well clear of the beach. I'd heard about the dusty roads of France, but this one was particularly so. It was very warm, but we knew we had several miles to walk so we put our best feet forward and staggered along. We passed a huge anti-tank ditch and saw several "Achtung Minen" notices and I saw a few German gas masks. The ground was pretty well blasted and churned up, although the road itself, apart from its very-dustiness and lack of repair, didn't seem to have been damaged. Most of the houses we saw at first were very badly knocked about. Gangs were working clearing the debris, while a few civilians wandered about – apparently looking for their possessions. We passed through a village, where I heard some children use German words – as well as "O.K. Buddy"! At one place, at the side of the road, I saw two British graves together.

I think we walked about three miles – although it seemed longer – before we first contacted our unit. They were in a field and were living in self-made bivouacs. We weren't to stay there, however, but were taken by truck to where the rest of the unit were, in a former German barracks. I don't know whether we should have walked all the way, but we'd never have done it that day. There was no room indoors for us so we settled down in a field behind the camp. Soon after we arrived we had supper and our first drink of the day, except water, of course. When we'd sorted ourselves out and made our beds, Norman and I walked into the town and had a look round. The place was full of khaki, of course, and it was difficult to get about. Fortunately, it was a fine night and none of us wasted any time in getting to bed. Soon a bit of a raid started and I could look straight up at the "fireworks". I don't think there were any bombs, but there was plenty of A.A. That was the end of my first day in France.

I'll never forget the view of the Channel when we halted on our climb from the shore and looked back – I've never seen so many ships all at once and I don't suppose I ever will again. I've been told that the people used to wonder why we were taking so long to come, but when they saw the immense amount of shipping and supplies of all sorts they wondered at our having come so soon.

Next morning we paraded, and soon after were told we'd have to do our own cooking. We found an old German stove and cooked on that, but the only utensils we had were our mess-tins, until we managed to scrounge a couple of biscuit tins. After dinner we were told we had to move to a house about half a mile away – no, not as far as that – so we had tea in the field and then moved our kit to the house. (A day or two later I heard that our field was being swept for mines! They didn't find any.) Our new billet is on the main road and all day long traffic is roaring past. I'm not there now, of course, but visit them quite often. We'd only been there a day or so when we met our French friends. The first night we were in the billet there was a short sharp raid, and after we'd heard a couple of bombs we went out to a trench at the back of the house but didn't need to stay there long. Since then we've heard quite a lot of A.A. but no bombs. For a time we had a field gun or guns not far from us and they made a row and shook the house, but we don't have it now, and, in fact, very rarely hear artillery, although at night we can see the flashes of the guns. We see plenty of aircraft, of course, but I haven't seen a German one yet, neither have I seen a German soldier except prisoners. So you can see, I'm not exactly in the front line. You may have heard of the recent five hundred bomber raid on troop concentrations near Caen. I was on duty and didn't see them, but some of the boys saw them going, wheeling around and returning after dropping their bombs.

When we'd been here a couple of days we went to the public baths where there are communal showers. Since then the baths have been reserved for front-line troops, which is as it should be. There is another bath place which some of the lads have used, but the usual way to bathe is in a biscuit tin. Where I am working now – we live in the room next to the s/room – there is a wash-basin, which is a luxury, although there's no hot water. In the village, where the section is billetted, all water has to be drawn from a pump at the road-side. There are no grates in the billet, only big open fireplaces. At the billet, too, the "other convs" are most primitive, although one has the benefit of fresh air and sunshine! Here we have a civilised arrangement.

The town is very old, with narrow streets in need of repair and it's quite a business just walking about. There is a "labour exchange" open. Some of the shops have notices in English or would-be English, such as "Butter unrationé" and "We have not of biscuits". The people are very poorly shod, most of the footwear being of wood. It's not unusual to see a woman "dressed to kill" and wearing short socks and knee length stockings. Wool is scarce and very poor stuff. Furniture is terribly dear and shoddy. Food is plentiful, although, of course, a lot of it is rationed. We are not allowed to buy bread. The making of confectionery is forbidden.

When I'd written my last letter to you, Norman and I visited our friends and found they had still more refugees – from near Caen. They had been living underground for four weeks and their house had been razed. Monsieur had been to the coast on his bike to where he used to work for the Germans, to collect a suitcase which one of his friends had rescued from the now destroyed German barracks.

Yesterday morning I was on duty 8 – 1. In the evening I went to the billet for the rations and was also relieved to receive twenty cigs for seven francs. Soon after we arrived here we were issued with 240 cigs, soap and letter-forms. I also bought half someone else's share of cigs, so had plenty. Of course I gave a lot away, and soon was down to the seven a day we get in Compo rations. Then we got another fifty, & yesterday was just about down to existing on the seven when I got the twenty. I was on duty at eleven and started this about midnight. It's a lovely day to-day but I haven't seen much of it. I'm on duty again at five, and it's four now. So far to-day there have been no

letters, but it's not too late for me to give up hope.
All my love to you and Paul,
God bless you both,
Leslie.

Friday 14th July 1944 – No. 19

My darling,
To-day is "le quatorze juillet" – France's national day (14th July) being the anniversary of the taking of the Bastille. I haven't been out to-day so far. There was a procession and meeting with Allied officers, a Solemn Mass at the Cathedral, and this evening there's to be open-air music. This afternoon there was a football match between a French local team and British soldiers. I would have liked to have been at the Mass, but it was at 11.45 and I was on duty at one, before which, of course, I had to have my lunch. It's 7.15 now and I'm going to meet Norman shortly. He's playing in a Unit match at 6.30 – the first we've had in France.

Saturday 15th
I was lucky enough to get a lift out of town last evening. The place was a mass of khaki, and flags were hanging everywhere. There was a bit of action up above and I saw a few shell-bursts, and found out later that if I'd been walking I would have seen a couple of Jerries brought down by Spitfires – missed it again! The football match was drawing to a close, so I waited till it finished and walked back to the billet with Norman. There, I found your letter of 10th, and a little later received Mother's of 11th. Whilst I was there, there was some activity – a lone

German plane wandered about, being fired at from the ground, and the last we saw of it it was being chased to the front.

I love you very much darling, and want more than everything to be with you. Give our son a kiss from me.

God bless you both,

Leslie.

Monday 17th July 1944 – No. 20

My darling Gracie,

On Saturday I wrote to Bea and Theo – I'm starting to write to all the people I've neglected while I've been waiting for the news which has made me so happy.

I went to the billet to see Norman, and on the way saw truck-load after truck-load of evacuees in the town. I wonder what they'll do with them all. The nuns and priests are doing fine work and the injured are being well looked after.

Yesterday was the second anniversary of my enlistment, and I hope I don't manage another one in the Army. In the evening, whilst on duty, I was very pleasantly surprised when my books and the papers arrived. I hadn't expected them so soon in the circumstances.

All my love to you both.

God bless you,

Leslie.

Tues. 18th July 1944 – No. 21

Darling Gracie,

'Tis past the witching hour, in fact it's 12.35, so I suppose I should have dated this 19th.

After I'd finished my last letter, Norman and I went across to where some R.E.s have a radio, and listened to the news. We heard Gen. Montgomery say that Germany should be out of the war this year. Then we visited our friends. In addition to their five refugees they also now have two sisters-in-law of our host – one is fourteen and the other is sixteen. They come from a village near Caen and are obviously terrified when they hear a few rounds of A.A., and no wonder. They share our hostess's hatred of the "Boche" and have plenty of reason for it. One of their brothers is a prisoner-of-war, another was killed in an air-raid while working for the Germans, another was "requisitioned" and sent to Germany, and a sister was abducted and they don't know where she is. Madame told us that they used to think that the stories from Poland were just propaganda and intended to scare them, but now they've seen some of the same things happening here and know it's true. I wish some of the people I've met in England who said "propaganda" could hear the stories – probably some of them have – and I've only heard a little, as I don't like pressing them. And remember, as you say, that this part of France seems to have escaped lightly compared with others

Wednesday

After tea I went to see Norman, and on the way called to see if there was a letter for me, but there wasn't and I was very disappointed, not having had one since Friday. Don had gone up before me and collected our Naafi rations. I got 75 cigs, bar choc, soap, razor blade, matches, shaving soap and chewing gum for 55frs. (5/6). We had a chat with the lads and then called on our friends.

Monsieur S. started work yesterday, but not at his own job – he was in a bank. He is working as a carpenter and seems very pleased to be doing something. He is working for us, about three kilometres away, and was given a pair of army boots, as were all those who were poorly shod – probably all of them. We had been wondering whether it would be possible to get a pair of boots for him, particularly when we knew he was to start work, as he had only one pair of thin shoes with the soles hanging off and a pair of battered slippers. We met him when he returned from work and he was wearing the boots. He had also had a good meal. We only called for a few minutes, but it was after nine when we left. On the way back to town Don remembered he had a couple of letters in his pocket, and one of them was yours of 15th – I could have slaughtered him! I was on duty at 11 o'clock and during my vigil started this present epistle, which I hope to finish before tea and duty at 5. It's now 4.15.

On 14th July there were plenty of flags and some houses also had "Vive les anglais" and "Vive nos liberateurs", etc. outside, although as you've read, the people don't seem mad with joy, but glad we're here.

Peter has received a doll from home which he asked for for Françoise. The toys here are even more "rubbishy" than in England. F. has a little teddy-bear which she thinks the world of, but I haven't seen her since she received the doll.

Give my love to all.

God bless you, sweetheart.

Leslie

Friday 21st July 1944 – No. 22

Darling Gracie,

This morning I was on duty. It has rained all day. At tea-time I received a letter from Walter – it would come just after I've written to him!

He sends his congratulations on my becoming father of a "bonny boy" and assumes he is now the "centre of an adulating, cooing congregation"! Walter wished he could have gone to France in my place so that I could have stayed at home. He says that one of his pals has returned from where I am – I don't know whether he just means France, but assume so, as how could he know? Unless you told him, and you don't know – or do you! Obviously I can't tell you.

I suppose you've heard all about Hitler being injured and the rumoured trouble in Germany? I've only heard a little about it, not having heard the radio or a paper, although I did read yesterday's "Herald" before returning here.

We're still on "compo" rations, although we do get a little bread now – one slice per day.

I was talking to a Frenchman to-night on the subject of clothes. They get – or got – thirty coupons per year and sixty were needed for a pair of trousers!

All my love to you, my darling. Give Paul a kiss for me.

God bless you,

Leslie.

Monday 24th July 1944 – No. 23

My darling Gracie,

I hope our son hasn't a "Smith" nose – you say he has a "biggish" one. I'd love to see him. I try to imagine what he's like, but it's hard – Mother said something about him sucking his fist and I try to "see" that. When will he start noticing things? As you say, babies change so quickly, and, having missed his first days, my present ambition is to see him before that happens – taking for granted, of course, that my ever-present wish is to be with you now – "now" always.

I suppose you are sticking to "Paul" – does he look like a "Paul" (whatever that is) and does he like his name?!

Yesterday morning I went to 9.30 Mass at the Cathedral – I have to listen to sermons and notices in French now, but of course I don't understand it all. Sometimes I despair of ever being able to understand and converse in French unless they speak slowly, but I suppose it'll come eventually. It's so different – writing, and speaking the language – there's a sort of rhythm one has to become accustomed to, as well as new words and idioms. Many a time I don't understand something until it's repeated more slowly, or put in a different way, whereas if the same thing were written I'd understand it immediately. It's not that the pronunciation is any different from what I've been taught, but just the way they say it. There are minor differences in the pronunciation, of course, but they don't worry me.

In the evening I went up to see Norman and had my supper with the section, after which we visited our friends. They had no coffee – it is rationed, of course – but we had chocolate, made from chocolate we had given them. They never drink tea, but in any case, they can't get any. You know, of course, that the French much prefer coffee. They tell us that even in peacetime tea is regarded as something of a luxury, but as the majority don't like it (fancy anyone not liking tea!) it doesn't bother them.

They still have their five refugees and the two girls – relatives of Monsieur – were there. Apparently the two latter are not exactly refugees, but had come on a visit after their spell in the "front line" and they returned to their home to-day, expecting to come back again soon. Monsieur's family live in Caen, and he's had no news of them. The two girls (Renée, 16 and Lucienne, 14) speak to us very quickly, and they pull our legs when we make mistakes, but, on the other hand, are surprised and sometimes confused when we do catch something they think we can't follow. They speak more slowly when we ask them, but soon forget. They rush out whenever they know there are trucks of prisoners going past, and clap their hands.

As the B.B.C. have mentioned Mr. Churchill's visit, I suppose I can say that some of our section saw him – I didn't, of course, but I've taken calls from several people we know well by name, including our favourite radio "voice".

All my love to you both,
Leslie.

Wednesday 26th July 1944 – No. 24

My darling Gracie,

...I meant to mention the fact that, as you may remember, the 2nd of August will be our third anniversary. I hope and pray that our fourth will be the first we've spent together – the first of many. May we never be separated again.

I see that in future the Nazi salute will be the only one used in the German Army. There seems to be quite a bit of trouble brewing, but I wonder how much difference it will make.

I've had my tea now, and later on I'll go for my usual walk. It isn't a long way, but I find it rather fatiguing on a hot day. One can't walk in the road because of the traffic and the grass verge isn't very convenient for walking – every so often there are gulleys running from the road to the ditch for drainage. I've mentioned the dust before. One also has to get used to traffic on the "wrong" side of the road. Lots of children say "Bonbons" (or "sweets"), "Chocolat" and "Cigarettes pour papa" and one has to become rather hard-hearted at times – the supply doesn't equal the demand and when we finally go off "compo" rations there'll be still less in that line. There was a notice in the local paper telling parents not to let their children regard Allied troops as automatic sources of supply.

Monsieur S. has told us that when leaflets were dropped they were forbidden to pick them up, but the Germans used to read them. They (the French) used to listen to the news from London. I think that those whose sets were confiscated are now allowed to apply for their return.

I hear that the Germans are mobilising for the army all the men of the occupied countries, including the French prisoners of war. We've lost "our" radio, as the unit who have it have moved. The French used to gather in the field to listen to our French news, so they'll miss it too.

God bless you,
Leslie

Tuesday 1ˢᵗ August 1944 – No. 26

Gracie, my love,
On Sunday I heard that Rommel was dead, then only wounded, then dead – I still don't know what really happened.✦

One of the Frenchmen with whom I come in close contact was

✦ *Field-Marshal Erwin Rommel earned fame during the invasion of France, and later in North Africa. He later lost faith in Hitler, and was implicated in the abortive July Bomb Plot to kill the Führer, led by Stauffenberg. On 17ᵗʰ July he suffered a fractured skull in an RAF fighter attack on his car, from which he recovered. Later he was ordered by Hitler to kill himself, which he did by taking poison on 14ᵗʰ October.*

telling me the other night that he was wounded in 1940, six days before the armistice. He was in hospital for months and months and has some huge scars on his leg. He got the Croix de Guerre. His father and sister were killed in the Dieppe raid. He said that, as far as he knew, the French were friendly towards us and understand our bombing of places where there were factories, etc., with the consequent unavoidable destruction of non-military objectives and loss of life, but couldn't understand the bombing of a place like Rouen. He gave me the impression that they blamed the Americans more than us when a place like that was bombed.

The Americans seem to be doing well in their sector at the moment, and I hope they keep it up. We don't seem to be doing so much except in the centre, but perhaps the idea is to swing round, using the Caen area as a hinge.

I'm being very optimistic and hoping it won't be long now before I'm able to be with you.

God bless you both,
Leslie.

Wednesday 2nd August 1944 – No. 27

My darling Gracie,

...We have heard that Monsieur Sophie has to report for military service on Thursday. We went to see them, and as it was his last evening at home, we drank his health – in chocolate! I suppose there is a possibility that he may go to England, so we gave him our addresses.

I suppose my son and heir is now baptised and wonder what he thought of the proceedings – did he yell? Is Paul's hair going to be nice and wavy like his father's? I suppose he's got as much as I have, anyway! *(My father's hair was very fine and blond, and he was balding by his late twenties.*) I'm looking forward eagerly to the day when we are together, in our own home, and praying that I'll always be a good husband and father.

There's a map on the wall in our room and we keep the front up to date with a piece of string, but as it's only West Normandy and North Brittany, we're hoping we'll soon have to buy a new one. People are very optimistic here regarding the nearness of the end of the war. Things certainly seem bright at the moment. The Americans are well into Brittany, the latest we heard being that they are at Rennes and Dinan, having by-passed St. Malo. The Russians are fighting at the outskirts of Warsaw, helped by the Poles who have come into the open. We rely mainly on the French bulletins which are posted up round the town. There is one outside the shop next door to us.

Each time the local paper comes out (Tues. & Fri.) there is a list of people who have been arrested.

Our weather is still glorious.

All my love to you and our son – I hope he's looking forward to seeing that lucky man, his father, although I suppose he's more interested in his tummy.

God bless you,
Leslie.

Monday 7ᵗʰ August 1944 – No. 28

Darling Gracie,

The weather is keeping up and each day is lovely in that respect. There was a little rain on Saturday afternoon but it didn't last long.

The war seems to be going well – the Americans are moving rapidly against practically no resistance, and I suppose they're getting all the credit while our lads are slugging away at the other end, and in the centre.

The other evening I walked part of the way along a new road which has been cut across the fields, and stopped for a few minutes by a small cemetery containing both British and German graves – all denominations together, all exactly alike – in death – except that the wooden crosses differed – according to the material to hand at the time, I suppose.

I'm spending more money now that the "compo" packs have finished, but can still save quite a bit. We have just been given our weekly issue of fifty free cigs and have just bought our Naafi ration of 75 (8d. for 20!) When the war ends, it will be a blow to come home and have to pay 2/4d. for 20 …

All my love to you and Paul.

God bless you,

Leslie.

Tuesday 8th August 1944

Gracie, my darling,

I am further away from you – geographically speaking – than I've ever been. Still, so long as I can't be with you, a few more miles don't matter, and if my being so far away will help at all in hastening our reunion, then it matters still less. Each day brings home nearer – as you say, the way things are going, we stand a good chance of being together for our next anniversary – or should I say for Christmas!?

I hear tonight that we are as far as Le Mans – only 160 kms. (100 miles) from Paris. It seems as though Jerry is trying to fall back on a line in front of Paris, saving (or rather, trying to save!) his strength for a big show-down there. I wonder whether I'll see Paris? – I'm more interested in seeing Liverpool, though.

I suppose the dusty roads of France are so dusty because they don't seem to be as well cared for as ours, or maybe it's because the weather is drier – the former, I think. Of course, there's an enormous amount of traffic on them these days.

It's not fair that I should have a son five weeks old and not have seen him. I suppose it is true that we have a son?!! I can't really imagine it, but then I couldn't imagine being married, being away from you for more than a day, or being in France. It seems queer that I'm here – I who never before went further from home than my legs or my bike could take me, once upon a time. I often stop and think – "I'm in France". I'm lucky in that – I might have gone somewhere where I didn't know a word of the language, or, worse still, to India or somewhere equally far away. It'll be strange to hear nothing but English and see all the advertisements, shop signs, etc., in English. One gets quite used to them being in French.

On Monday I went along to see Mme. Sophie and found an English officer there. He is an R.E. major and when I'd said "good evening" to Madame and the refugees and him, he asked me whether I spoke French. He didn't know a word, so I was quite pleased. The major told me he was from Wigan, was a policeman there, and was in the regular army before that. His major's crown seemed to be disregarded, and he seems quite a decent sort of bloke. He had a cup of coffee and said it was the first he'd had in a French house. He left before me and Mme. told me that while she was out with Françoise, the latter was playing near where some officers were eating and they had taken a great fancy to her and given her something to eat. The major had walked back with Mme. and Françoise. He seemed to have a great liking for Françoise – she's certainly a lovely child.

At about three o'clock yesterday Norman called for me, having left Mme. Sophie and Alf Taylor outside the house. Alf is a keen gardener and had volunteered to help. We walked out of town about half a mile to the allotment. It had been neglected for a long time and Mme. wanted to save what was left. Most of the cabbages had gone to seed and there were weeds everywhere. We found some antiquated tools and started work. Norman and Alf dug up potatoes while I scraped about amongst the weeds bringing up shallots. Mme. gathered peas. At five o'clock we ate the sandwiches which N. and Alf had brought and Mme. borrowed a bottle and went for water. There are tobacco plants and coffee plants in the garden, but they weren't ready. The Sophies' strawberries came from the garden attached to the house. At about six I left them still working, and returned to tell Peter and Don how to find their way there. At about nine they returned with a bag of potatoes and one of onions and shallots, having found a truck to give them a lift...

God bless you,

Leslie.

Thursday 10th August 1944 – No. 30

My darling Gracie,

...I haven't seen, heard of, any violence against collaborators in this district – they have just been rounded up when their turn came and sent away – to work, I believe. One I knew personally went recently and from what I've heard he deserved it.

Perhaps we'd have been here sooner if the Yanks hadn't sent so much stuff to Russia so she could "liberate" Poland!

I hope I'll be home soon after leave starts. I certainly hope

I'll be home before I can be a stranger to our son. I don't think it can be long before leave starts. Let's hope not, anyway.

<u>Saturday afternoon.</u>
Another glorious day. I went for a haircut and there was an American major in there and while he was waiting he was studying what looked like a phrase book. When his turn came he started talking a few words of French. He told the barber that he spoke very little French, and that with an American accent, which was true, but the barber assured him that his French was quite good. They all say that, which makes it more difficult to judge how one is progressing...
God bless you and Paul,
Leslie.

Friday 18ᵗʰ August 1944 – No. 32

My darling Gracie,
It seems the invasion in the South* is going well, and there doesn't seem to be much opposition. On our front the Americans are in Orléans.

Talking about the Royal Corps of Signals, I can tell you now that some of the unit who came over early sometimes went ahead of the Infantry and started putting up lines and so on before the area had been cleared of the enemy and de-mined. I heard of a couple of cases where the enemy put in an appearance

---

Landings in Provence: On 15ᵗʰ August, Allied troops began landing on the Riviera, meeting little initial resistance. However, the Germans fought fiercely for the towns of Marseilles and Toulon, which were not liberated until the 28ᵗʰ.

while they were working and it was a case of down tools and pull out. The organisation on the whole, seems to have been marvellous. Units knew where their H.Q. would be before they left England. Sounds very confident, but it was justified. I dare say it'll be the same all over the country. I wonder whether I'll see any more of it. If I have to stay in France I'd like to travel about a bit. I've seen very little so far.

Time seems to be sliding past very quickly and the summer will soon be over. It's five months since I saw you, my darling, and I don't like it a bit. I wonder what Paul looks like.

Does the place still seem as full of khaki as before, or has this business made a noticeable difference?...

God bless you,
Leslie.

Saturday 19th August 1944 – No. 33

My darling Gracie,

The news last night and this morning was excellent, wasn't it – the Battle of Normandy is over and the Americans are near, or at, the Seine. Jerry has no chance of fighting other than rear-guard actions in France. We seem to be making "mincemeat" of his tanks and transport as he tries to get away. There's been fighting for transport between the S.S. and regular army men. There's certainly been plenty of aircraft over here. Tell my son his father will be home soon! I wonder? I certainly feel more hopeful now...

All my love to you and Paul
God bless you,
Leslie.

Monday 21ˢᵗ August 1944 – No 34

My darling,

The news continues good, and I see that the recent rain has hampered Jerry in retreat more than it's affected our operations.

I'm pleased to read that, at last, the Poles fighting in Warsaw have had material dropped to them, but flown from Italy and not from the Russians. It looked as if they were to be let down again. We were under the impression, about a fortnight ago, that the Russians had reached Warsaw and were surprised when we found out that the Poles were fighting on their own.The other day four truck-loads of prisoners were stationary near our billet and one of the chaps asked one of them if he spoke French. He said "Me Russki" and indicated that three of the trucks were full of Russians and the other of Germans…

It's still raining – it's the worst day we've had so far. I wonder what it's like in Liverpool now…

God bless you,
Leslie.

Wednesday 23ʳᵈ August 1944 – No. 35

My darling,

I went to the camp earlier this evening, confident that there would be a letter or letters for me, but, once again, there weren't any. It's five days since there was any mail beyond a few odd letters and newspapers. Everyone I know is extremely dissatisfied with the mail situation and it seems to me the powers that be still don't realise how much difference a letter from home makes. Even if I get a letter to-morrow it'll be six days since the previous one, which is a long time to wait.

Apart from the fact that I look forward eagerly to receiving your letters, it also makes a difference in the length of mine, you know. I haven't much news and rely to a great extent on your letters for inspiration.

Norman told me yesterday that he had been talking to a blind Frenchman who was walking across the field with his three children. He lost his sight in 1939 or 1940 and had never seen his youngest child. He is a refugee at the moment.

This morning there was a special bulletin alongside the 9.30 communiqué announcing the fact that Paris has been taken by the F.F.I. and others of the population. This is excellent news, of course, and even the French seem excited by it! This evening we heard that the Maquis had taken Strasbourg and Nancy and that the forces on the Riviera have taken Marseilles and fighting is going on in Toulon. I wonder if there's any truth in the reports of a landing near Bordeaux? There's fighting in Lisieux and I hope they don't knock it about too much...

Thursday

When I went to breakfast after coming off duty, I found that practically every shop and house had a flag hanging out – in honour of the taking of Paris, I suppose. There was more good news this morning, that, of course, being the surrender of Rumania, which is a step in the right direction ...

God bless you both,

Leslie

Friday 25th August 1944 – No. 36

A photo from home –

Paul and his mother

My darling Gracie,

I have the snaps in front of me. So that's my son! He certainly looks big for his age. I hardly know what to say, except that I like what I've seen of him so far, and as you say, he's really much nicer than that. It seems as though we've done quite well, darling. As you say, I feel more as though I actually have a son now. I'd like to hold him. He looks intelligent! ...

I suppose it is a pity I didn't go to Rome, but my Italian isn't nearly as good as my French! Even if I'd gone to Italy I might never have seen Rome, just as now I mightn't see Paris or any of the big cities. I'd like to go to Rouen and Chartres. I suppose if I do move I'll go to some poky little place or somewhere which has been knocked to pieces, such as Falaise or Caen or Argentan. By the way, didn't Constance Bennett once marry the Duc de Falaise? The name's very familiar anyway.

I've seen the explanation – or rather, the suggested explanation, for the Germans' "foolishness" – or "heroic resistance". It is that they have been told we would kill them anyway, even if they surrendered. True or false!

Mother has had a letter from Charlie. He says he's just had a hot bath, had his bobbed hair cut and his beard removed. He went for six days without food, and two of them without water. His letter was very cheerful…

God bless you both,

Leslie.

Sunday 27th August 1944 – No. 37

My darling,

This morning I went to 11.30 Mass. I'd spent a busy night. When I returned from church I was told to pack. We returned to the section at teatime. Madame Sophie is very sad because we are going, and very lonely. It will be difficult for her to make friends with our successors, now her husband is away.

It's almost dark now, so I'll say "goodnight" my love.

God bless you,

Leslie

Tuesday 29th August 1944 – No. 38

My darling Gracie,

Last night we visited Madame. Also present were her sister-in-law and the latter's husband, who is an escaped prisoner of war. We heard a few more stories about the Germans – they emphasised what we'd heard before – that the S.S. troops were the chief offenders, being the young fanatics, and the ordinary soldier wasn't quite so bad. This couple had had to move before the retreating Germans, but had managed to slip through somehow. They were given two hours in which to leave their home, but at the end of an hour they were ordered out and their furniture was smashed up, also crockery and their little girl's toys, and they even tore up photographs of the child. Among other incidents they told us of the woman who had a cow which supplied enough milk for her family and her refugees. Whilst she was milking the cow a couple of S.S. men came along and asked for some milk. She told them she had none to spare, whereupon one of them pulled out his revolver and shot the cow. Even if one discounts a lot of what one hears, it can't all be lies and these people don't hate Jerry for nothing.

Yesterday I saw a couple of towns which have been in the news. In one of them I doubt whether there are more than a dozen houses fit to live in. We've seen plenty of air raid damage in England, but this town is utterly destroyed. It makes one realise what is meant when a town is "wiped out". There were also several badly battered villages and lots of churches with most of the tower missing. In the open country there was evidence of fighting – in the fields and at the roadsides were a few destroyed tanks and cars, lots of holes and churned-up earth. One wood looked as if it had been subjected to intensive bombing or shelling and the trees – where they still stood – were blasted and bare. There were also occasional graves.

I spent quite a comfortable night. This morning a party of us went to the nearby chateau to do a little cleaning up. In the orchard were about fifteen German graves, and in the house there were a lot of blood splashes.

It's quite peaceful here. I've heard of women banging the clothes with stones to wash them, and last evening I saw two women using a sort of wooden bat for the purpose. There is a wooden shelter at the edge of the stream. They kneel on wooden "kneelers" and swill the garments in the water, squeeze, scrub a little, and bang the clothes on a ledge in front of them. I didn't see any soap. They got through quite a lot in a short time...

God bless you,

Leslie.

Friday 1st September 1944 – No. 39

My darling Gracie,

Yesterday we travelled quite a distance in trucks and saw more evidence of the fighting having passed through these parts. It wasn't very comfortable travelling as the roads are not in very good condition after bombing and shelling, and we spent most of the time being bumped about, especially when were in the dark and the driver couldn't see the holes. The moon was nearly full and as we passed through towns and villages the wrecked buildings were silhouetted and it reminded me of pictures of towns destroyed during the last war. There was a cathedral which I saw in the moonlight – just a shell, and if there had been a tower it isn't there now. It looks as though it was a very beautiful cathedral, though not a huge one.

It seems that the people are friendliest in the places where the devastation is worst. In one small town where we stopped – held up, as we were often by a convoy, we spoke to a couple of women who told us we were the first English they'd seen, having seen only Canadian and Polish so far. I don't think that would be true – maybe we were the first English they'd spoken to. The roadsides are littered with destroyed and burnt-out vehicles, tanks and guns. The other evening we went for a walk and came across a crashed German plane and then the wreckage of a burnt-out car of some sort. The surrounding area was covered with all sorts of things – letters, official books, charred clothing and boots etc.

Children run to hold one's hand sometimes accompanied by the expression with which we're heartily fed-up – "Cigarette pour Papa?"

There are lots of flags about – mostly tricolours, of course, and the people are at their doors or windows or in the street, waving and obviously glad to see us.

Most of us have had, or are having, attacks of diarrhoea. I'm all right at the moment. We don't know what it is. Some put it down to the water or tinned or dehydrated food, others to apples. I've only had a few apples – I don't know whether it's because they're not mature or because they're cider apples and not fit for eating, but I don't like them. There are orchards everywhere.

In the damaged towns and villages there are notices to the effect that death is the penalty for looting. One sees people amongst the wreckage trying to salvage things, but there's very little of use. There are also a few families on the roads with carts and bicycles loaded with their possessions, but the majority have been officially evacuated in Army or other available transport. I saw one truck loaded up with furniture and bedding, a nun sitting beside the driver and another perched on top of the load, looking very pleased with herself – like a little girl stealing a ride!

The weather is fine and warm today. I hope you are having some decent weather. The mail situation is awful...

God bless you and Paul,
Leslie.

Sunday 3rd September 1944 – No. 40

Darling Gracie,

After I'd written my letter on Friday, and had tea, Norman and I went for a walk and did some "ghouling" – we found five disabled tanks, one German, two "Polish", an American and a British. A couple of them had been burnt out inside and in one someone had obviously been unable to get out. We returned for supper, after which we went out again. It is only a tiny village, and we were surprised to find a café. We went in and had some Calvados and cider. They told us that sometimes the S.S. would knock them up at 2 a.m. and demand to be served with drinks. They had also broken most of their glasses and cider decanters.

The snatches of news we get are very encouraging – maybe we're in Germany by now. I wonder whether or not we'll get leave if Germany gives in, or whether we'll have to wait for demobilisation. We've all got the wind up in case we're wanted for Burma. There was an article on that subject which gave me some hope – something about married men with families, a job waiting, and over two years' service.

We are fed up – literally and metaphorically – with "M & V" (tinned meat and vegetables). Perhaps the fact that we get so little fresh food is the reason for the prevalence of our physical inconveniences.

We'd promised to write to Madame S., but now hear that we're not allowed to write to civilians, so she'll think we've forgotten her. I couldn't forget them; they were so kind to us. I think Françoise is the loveliest girl of her age I've seen. I wonder how Monsieur S. is getting on in the Army.

I've seen lots of men wearing the "F.F.I." armband. (Once upon a time those initials meant something different to us.)

Our advance is so rapid that I suppose it's only natural that we shall move a lot – I don't know, of course – but if so it may interfere with my writing.

Today is, of course, the fifth anniversary of the start of this business – same day, Sunday, too, and it seems fairly certain there won't be a sixth during the war.

All my love darling.

God bless you,

Leslie.

Tuesday 5th September 1944 – No. 41

My darling Gracie,

On Sunday we were told to be ready to move first thing in the morning. We had a good journey and of course, saw evidence of our attacks on the retreating Germans – tanks, cars, dead cows etc. We passed through some lovely country – the only decent scenery I've seen so far – with the river and numerous islands in it. People waved and gave the "V" for Victory sign and we felt like royalty. It was only about three days since Jerry had been moving along those roads. We crossed the river on a pontoon bridge, all the others having been destroyed. I saw a lot of barges which I suppose the Germans had used to get across – probably they were intended for the invasion of England.

This town has been badly battered, but there is still quite a lot of it untouched. The beautiful cathedral has been badly damaged and I doubt whether it's more than a shell, although there are flags fluttering from the top of the very tall, delicate-looking spire. We pulled up in the square in front of the "Hotel de Ville", alongside which there is a very big church with the loveliest façade I've ever seen. In front of the Town Hall there is a statue of Napoleon. (By the way, in case you don't know, the "H. de V." is the Town Hall.) We had a few biscuits to eat and had to give some of them, and cigarettes, away. I pulled my tin out and put a cigarette in my mouth and an old man sprang from nowhere and asked for one. Foolishly held out my tin and he took two! Whilst he was taking the two, a couple more hands came out, so I hastily shut my tin and put it away. One could dispose of one's supply in a few minutes.

We moved off again and a few minutes later stopped again. While we were standing there, a girl of seventeen who was passing suddenly threw her arms around one of the chap's necks and kissed him. It turned out that part of his section were here in 39/40, when she was thirteen. They've met several people they knew then and hope to meet more.

We heard the beginning of the news, which told us that Brussels had been taken, and then we moved on again. This time it was just around the corner, into the courtyard of a large building. There were numerous tin hats, uniforms and some ammunition lying about and the place was generally filthy. One jacket had a bloody hole through the left breast pocket. I think it was the usual thing last time to bring back a German helmet, but I don't think I'll bother unless you think Paul would like to have one!

Eventually we were allowed to enter the building. I thought the Germans were a clean people! You should have seen the inside of this place! It was absolutely filthy – empty wine bottles, jack-boots, respirators and all sorts of stuff. Cupboards and drawers ransacked and contents strewn about. The condition of the place wasn't just that of a hasty exodus, but of months of accumulated rubbish and dirt and general neglect. I think it was a seminary. There is a priest in one of the rooms. I went into the chapel and found straw all over the floor, and coke in a corner of the gallery alongside the organ! Books strewn all over the place, crucifixes lying about, altars damaged and disorder all over. There is a large decorated casket containing the bones of St. Hippolyte, broken, and the wrapping on some of the bones removed and the bones broken. There were empty wine bottles lying about there, too.

We found a room at the top of the building and have cleaned it up, used disinfectant, and made it fit to live in – in fact, quite comfortable. We had to clean other rooms out also – the Jerries certainly made themselves comfortable in their filth. This morning, when continuing the cleaning, some of the lads found a room which had obviously been used by a woman. They found that she was 17 and had a permit from the commander to enter the building. They also found other things and you can draw your own conclusions.

It's dull today and we've had a little rain. We have a good view of the city from this room, as, apart from the fact that we're on the top floor, we're on a steep hill leading out of the town. Tonight, if it's fine, I hope to have a closer look at the place.

Yesterday we heard unconfirmed reports that Southern Holland has been reached, and today that forward columns are in Germany.

This time last year I was at Fareham, and wonder where I'll be next year – with you, I hope.

Cheerio for now, darling – once again – I love you, love you, love you, very much.

Leslie xxxxxxxxxx (give some to our darling son).

Sunday 10th September 1944 – No. 43

Gracie, my darling,

'Tis indeed a glorious day. I'm sitting on a bench in the sun, in a park in a lovely city (*Brussels*). Yesterday evening we finished two days of travelling.

After tea on Thursday Norman and I went out to look around the city. We saw papers being sold, and whilst I was buying one (it turned out to be the Communist *l'Humanité*) two youths started talking to Norman and when I joined them we conversed for some time. They knew some English, but we got on much better in French. They told us a few things about the Germans, but the main point was that while they were leaving a crowd jeered at them, so they turned a machine-gun on the crowd and several were killed. As they were leaving the town the Canadians were entering at the other end.

We said we were about to do some sight-seeing and they asked whether they could accompany us. They showed us a round tower in which St. Joan was imprisoned and in which British prisoners had been kept. Further on we saw a statue of St. Joan and nearby was a square of about 3 sq. ft. marking the exact spot where the burning took place. We couldn't go into the cathedral as it is very badly damaged. Services are held at another big church which is now regarded as the cathedral. There are a lot of old and timbered buildings and it's a wonder the whole town didn't go up in flames.

I bought some postcards – one of which is rather a souvenir as it has cuts in it by broken glass caused by our bombing. Eventually we said we must return for supper and to do some packing. We walked towards our billets and soon one of them left us. They were both eighteen and students; the one who stayed with us was studying for the diplomatic service and soon was to go to Paris for his final exams and then would visit England to polish up his English. Before we left him he asked us whether we would see him later, so we said we would be outside at 8.30. We guessed that he wanted to ask his parents whether he could invite us home! We were right, and at 8.45 we were walking with him to his home, We found it to be a fairly large house and well furnished. M. and Mme. Antoine met us at the door and welcomed us very cordially. They were both very charming to us and we chatted and drank some vin blanc. They had a radio and said they'd had to keep it upstairs but never missed the news from London. They told us they knew which were British and which were American bombers, and the latter did more damage to places around the target, while the former always hit only what they intended.

Monday

The city where we are now is a capital place and everyone is mad with genuine joy and gratitude – I wish everyone who has worked to help this liberation could be here. It would make them think it worth while. The people speak French, fortunately for me, and are delighted when we speak it, although most of them know a little English. I'll never be able to tell you all in a letter, but will do my best and fill in the gaps when I see you – soon, I hope.

God bless you,
Leslie.

Chapter Six

Brussels: September 1944

As the British troops advanced through Northern France and into Belgium, the welcome grew ever more ecstatic. Sometimes convoys had difficulty threading their way through the streets of towns, as the locals came out to greet their "liberators". The travelling was not very comfortable for troops squeezed into the back of lorries with hard springs and flapping canvas tops, especially when many suffered from stomach upsets and travel sickness. Opportunities to wash were limited, and food was taken at irregular intervals. However, the welcome extended to them was something that few will ever experience, and the next few months were perhaps the best, or most memorable part of my father's life.

To be young and abroad, seeing new places and making new friends, using a different language; and above all, knowing the comradeship of a victorious army riding hard on the heels of a retreating foe – how many of our generation will know that feeling? To be cheered and welcomed by grateful people, kissed and fussed over by pretty girls, while flowers are thrown and the flags of the free countries flutter all around – what can equal that? My father's unit, who suffered few if any casualties, could enjoy it all without the terrible sadness of lost comrades gnawing at them. And combined with all these feelings of excitement was the intoxicating euphoria of believing that they would soon be home. This belief was soon to be shattered, to be replaced with the great fear of being transferred to Burma at the end of the war in Europe.

For the time being, however, my father was to enjoy his time in Brussels, with opportunities to improve his French through conversation and formal classes and make friends with a number of local people. Twenty years later, I was to spend some time with the Remis, as a sixteen-year-old studying French. Unfortunately, by then, they were old and I was young and shy, and sadly the stay was not a great success.

My father seems to have been more at home in Belgium than in France, and fell in love with the great city of Brussels. On arrival here, his unit was closer behind the retreating Germans than at any other stage. He then went on detachment with six others, advancing to within a few miles of the front, and spending some days in a position where they suffered heavy shelling and dive-bombing raids. So even his so-called "safe" job in the Signals turned out to have its rather unwelcome moments of excitement. He was, however, quite pleased to have come under fire and survived, as this made him feel like a genuine soldier who had suffered some of the dangers of front-line troops.

Back in the city, he was aware of the Resistance (whose ranks were swollen by those who joined only once the Germans were clearly in retreat) and their attitude to collaborators. Collaboration is never black and white, and while some were clearly traitors who had tried to profit from the Occupation, others might be ordinary people whose work in government offices, for example, had become work for the Nazis. They might have continued because they had families to support, and had to put practicalities before principles. Other cases involved young women who had clearly had relationships with German officers, but turned out later to have sacrificed themselves in this way in order to gain important information. The Resistance, which had fought courageously in many places, and had aided the Liberation so much by gathering essential data on German defences, was tarnished by its association with the Communists, who appeared to be working towards their own ends in an attempt to gain power within the governments of France and Belgium.

For the British troops in Brussels, after the overwhelming excitement of the first weeks, life settled into a pleasant routine as the Germans retreated ever further, through Holland and back into the Fatherland, with the winter-time Battle of the Bulge in the hills and woods of the Ardennes as their last throw before defeat became inevitable. The end of the war was in sight by early 1945, with hopes of quick demobilisation and a return home, balanced by fears of a transfer to the Far East. Would their fate be one of these, or would they continue to follow the front-line troops all the way into Germany?

Tuesday 12th September 1944 – No. 44

Gracie darling,

There's a statue here of a little boy in a certain attitude, *(The Manneken-Pis, a well-known tourist attraction not far from the Grande Place)* and the result is a fountain; I said to Norman that some people in England would think it shocking. As you well know, they're more open about such things here and the natural functions are taken for granted. They just don't bother about such things, but there doesn't seem anything vulgar about it. There isn't quite so much hand-shaking here, but still plenty of cheek-kissing.

In my last letter I left you *chez* les Antoines, so I'll see how far we get from there. The son, Roger, asked for our address – we'll have a houseful if all the people who have my address turn up at once!

Next morning we left at 7.30 – the beginning of nearly two days of travelling. We hadn't much room, but we made ourselves as comfortable as we could, and were in good spirits, although some of us were sorry to leave the town, people having been hospitable. We thought we knew what hospitality was then, but we were to find that exceeded. It was a lovely day and we made good progress. We saw the usual evidence of war having passed along, although except for the remains of German convoys and holes in the fields here wasn't as much as heretofore – I suppose he was in too much of a hurry.

Every town and village we passed through we were waved at and everyone was most friendly. We saw what had been the scenes of much fighting in 14–18, several last war cemeteries and one big monument. We passed through towns well-known because of the fighting during the last war. On top of the tower of a church in one of them (I don't remember for certain which one it was, but I couldn't mention it if I did) there is a huge statue of Christ. There was one there before and it was loosened by shelling and gradually leaned further forward. The legend grew that on the day it fell the war would end. Of course it fell on 11th November 1918.

I saw several carts being drawn by horses and oxen together – usually one of each – one with a dog fastened underneath to help a man who was pushing it.

Everywhere we were greeted with great enthusiasm and flags were everywhere.

At four o'clock we arrived at our stopping-place for the night. We parked on a grassy square opposite the school and were soon surrounded by lots of people old and young. We were soon installed in the school, after moving the desks to one side of our rooms. The cooks did their stuff and we soon had tea. Before we went in we saw some F.F.I. or Maquis (I'm not sure whether or not there's a difference) and they had three very young and fed-up looking Germans in a cart. The F.F.I. were armed with German rifles and a couple of them had grenades of some sort stuck in their belts.

We'd seen a lot of these men en route and on one occasion we saw some in charge of German prisoners working on the road – the latter could count themselves well guarded! From one party we heard that they didn't bother themselves with S.S. prisoners – and they certainly didn't let them go! These people have certainly done some good work and things have been well organised between us.

At 6.30 we were allowed out, so Norman and I went for a walk and met much hand-shaking, children following us, and everyone smiling and wishing us "good evening". We hadn't gone far before we met a man and his two sons who immediately begged us to accompany them home. It turned out that they had been waiting all day for some English soldiers they could take home. They had seen very few, if any, British troops, and we were the first who hadn't passed through without stopping. They gleefully led us to their home and on the way they took pride in announcing to neighbours at their doors that we were "Anglais". It was rather embarrassing for us, being stared at and waved at by everyone we passed.

The two boys were well-behaved and the father was obviously pleased – for himself, and because his sons were so delighted. One of the boys was about fifteen and the other about twelve. We arrived at the house and before we went in were shown the Union Jack which they'd made from a picture in an encyclopaedia. Another son of about 18 opened the door and welcomed us, and then we met the mother, she was told we had come to have supper and to sleep! We sat down and a bottle of vin rouge was produced – saved for this occasion since 1940, they said. They told us how pleased – that's putting it mildly – they were to see us – the English – and how they'd been confident we would come. The elder boy's fiancée was there and they were both very young. We had a couple of glasses of wine and chatted for about half an hour. The things they told us and the way they repeatedly told us they were happy now "les Anglais" had come, was most touching and made us feel very proud – in a humble way, if you see what I mean. I wish you could have been there to get a little of the feeling of relief and happiness which was there.

They told us of how they'd never missed the news from London. They had welcomed our bombing. They'd seen the Germans running away as we approached, on all sorts of conveyances, including bikes with no tyres. That was only four days previously. Some of the Germans had been quite decent, but only if alone, as none of them trusted another. The boys feasted their eyes on us and said "Tommy" and were most anxious to have their say. We were shown into another room, comfortably furnished, where the table was laid. They had already asked us how we liked our eggs! The first dish was four fried eggs and as much fried tomato as we wanted, and brown bread. Then meat, potatoes and beans, plums and then a sort of pie with sliced apple on top . I was wishing I hadn't had any tea! They thought we hadn't any appetite!

We had to refuse a second helping of the last course and felt very rude, but we just couldn't manage it. The French certainly "make a meal of it" when they eat. During all this we were drinking beer, and then another glass of wine, and finished off with coffee. Towards the end of the meal, more visitors arrived – to see the English soldiers. Of course, we feel rather guilty about it as we don't fight for these places, although it isn't our fault. Still, it should be the fighting men who get all this fuss instead of us enjoying the fruits of their labours. I suppose we are necessary, though..

A woman came in to meet us having been unsuccessful in getting some soldiers to her house. Another two boys came and an English-speaking (almost) man, followed by his father and mother. The father is an active member of the Resistance movement and was proud of the fact that he had captured three Germans – one an S.S. man – the day we arrived. There's certainly been some marvellous organisation between the Allies and the underground people. They told us of how, earlier in the war, he had gone to a workers' camp in Germany to speak to Frenchmen and under the noses of the Gestapo had exhorted them to "go slow" and had recited it to them in patois so that the interpreters couldn't understand how rude he was being. He gave us a rendering and it was certainly most uncomplimentary to Hitler. We didn't "get" all of it, but understood the general idea. He told us several stories, too.

One of the boys played the "Marseillaise" and "God save the King" on the piano. The "glorieuse armée anglaise" was toasted and received three "British" cheers and we got the same personally. It was most touching and Norman and I were almost in tears several times during the evening. It made things feel most worth-while and I'm proud to have met such people. We had to write the words of "Tipperary" out for them. They all know it in English. At the finish we were escorted to our billet by the boys. It had been a memorable evening and I'll never forget it. It's hard to convey my feelings. They thanked us over and over again for coming and had never doubted that we would. The F.F.I. man said that in the last war they had wonderful generals, such as Foch, but in this war we had Montgomery (what a man – Alamein, Tunis, Italy and now here!), Alexander and Wavell. And Churchill is the greatest statesman there ever was! They've followed every one of our moves since '40.

This evening made up for our lukewarm reception in Normandy a thousandfold. Of course we don't include such people as the Sophies in our condemnation of the people there. Our eyes have been opened as to how people can feel on being liberated. There's nothing they wouldn't do for us. Tell everybody that we're welcome here and no mistake. Over and over again we've heard the sentiment expressed that every German – man, woman and child – should be exterminated. These people told us of tortures – it hasn't all been propaganda, tell those sceptical people. I know I'm sentimental and all that but it isn't only I who hears these stories and of the genuine gratitude of the people. I heard a man in the street here, on meeting some friends, say "now we can breathe again!"

God bless you,

Leslie.

Thursday 14th September 1944 – No. 45

My darling,

Today I received your letters of 5th, 7th and 9th.

I told you in my last letter of our memorable evening in ----. We moved off next morning about eight, cheered on our way by a small crowd, and the waving met us everywhere through the town and wherever we went. Soon we came to a barrier and were passed from one lot of cheering people to another. We passed through a very famous town of the last war, and eventually came to the outskirts of this city where we stopped for dinner. There were lots of hangers-on and we improved our knowledge. We were told that more beer than wine is drunk here. Eventually we moved into the city and I won't bore you again by attempting to describe our reception. Incidentally, the trams are running and all the normal services are in working order except telephones. The previous place – where we had supper – was the first place where we'd seen trams running, although in the one before that we saw trams which hadn't run since '40 I think.

We pulled up at our billets and were all anxious to get out and see the city. Norman and I went out, walked round and then went to a café where we had some beer. Our French money wasn't worth quite so much, but they took it all right. There was a good dance band and a small place for dancing. Everyone was happy. The band played "Tipperary" more than anything else, I think. The place was brilliantly lit and drink was in unlimited supply – if one had enough money, which we hadn't. The city is full of such places and I've never seen a place like it. We spent most of the evening in this place. Everyone is wearing emblems of some sort and there are thousands of flags everywhere. The people have great desire to use their English and say "Allo Tommy" and "Good evening", etc. One cinema has been renamed the "Churchill". We were told that the previous week there were no British flags in the city and they'd all been made since the previous Sunday, when the city was taken – appropriately 3rd September.

We were shown one building which had hung out a flag prematurely and could see the broken stonework where the Germans had machine-gunned it. One shop is smashed up because it belonged to collaborators and a couple of people from there were fighting for Jerry on the Russian front.

It is a very clean city – the cleanest I've seen and there is very little bomb damage. The place is rather a contradiction, as the shops are full of luxuries, although necessities are scarce and "ersatz". The black market flourished and was encouraged by the Germans. Those who had money were all right, but it was very hard on the others. People are well-dressed – the women certainly know how to dress and do it well. One sees a well-dressed girl with Army signs sewn onto the sleeves of her coat – practically every woman and girl, and some men, have some "souvenirs" fastened to their clothes.

They certainly love their "liberators", especially the British, and are not half-hearted about expressing it. One well-dressed elderly lady, after some hesitation, asked Norman and me to have our photos taken with her, walking along, by one of those photographers one sees in the street. All the children want autographs and souvenirs – we can give the former, but souvenirs are not unlimited. I've given coins and stamps away. One almost gets writer's cramp signing autographs. One thing is that they don't show any class distinction – they don't care whether one is an officer or not. The fact that one is an Allied soldier is quite sufficient. One man and his daughter stopped us for a chat and he told us that he had married an Englishwoman in Leeds and the ceremony was performed by the priest who became Bishop of Liverpool.

You've no idea how the city must feel – we're absolutely "it". They've waited so long and haven't got over the joy of our being here. I wish you were here with me, love – you'd enjoy it. The shops are lovely. One can buy lovely ice-cream, grapes are from 10 to 20 francs a pound, tomatoes 5 francs a kilo (a kilo is 2lbs. 3 oz. That's about 3d. per lb!), plums, pears, apples and plenty of them. Paris couldn't be any better than this and London isn't in the same street.

The second night we were here, Norman and I went to a café – a huge place, with a good dance band (even the smallest place has a band, however small). The place was very crowded but we pushed our way in and were looking for a seat when a man called us over and invited us to have a drink. He had with him his wife and sister. He told us he was with the 55th Div. in the last war and spoke English quite well. He was literally trembling with emotion and told us that the expressions of gratitude we saw and heard were straight from the heart. He gave us his card and asked us to visit him and would be delighted and proud if we would. He said that before the war he'd had a flourishing business, but due to his refusal to buy ersatz goods, or to trade in the black market except when absolutely necessary, things weren't quite so good, but he still had some pre-war rum and cigars. The café was full of people going round – imagine Christmas Eve or New Year's Eve at a dance and magnify it a thousand times and you'll have some idea of what it was like. This was going on in all the cafes in the town. He said "you should have been here last Sunday (the first day)!" What it was like then I can't imagine!

As we were talking to him, the band struck up the National Anthem and everyone stood up, then the Marseillaise and everyone sang it, then God Save the King and those who could sang, then the U.S. National Anthem, finishing with one I couldn't recognise. Then the band played "Tipperary". Before we knew what was happening we were torn from our friend (we had been standing by his table) and were dragged around and round the place – in and out the tables, round and round, in and out, until we were hot and weary, every soldier the girls could lay hands on, until there must have been hundreds going round. The band wasn't allowed to stop for a long time. It wasn't a case of dancing, but running, hopping, skipping, etc. – just an outlet, and it goes on every night. The city was en fête for a week, but apparently the "week" is still going on. The band played "Tipperary", "Run, Rabbit, Run", "Siegfried Line" and others. It was a very good band and it's a pity there isn't a proper dance floor. They also played "In the Mood" and "Tiger Rag".

When the band did stop we were besieged for souvenirs and I couldn't get away without parting with my badge. The recipient, one of the two girls who had dragged Norman and me on to the floor, kissed me on both cheeks when she finally got it.

We returned to our friend's table, but hadn't been there long before we were rushed off again, but it didn't last so long this time. However, we couldn't get away, although we parted with no more souvenirs. We couldn't move either way and found ourselves wedged against a rail with a small crowd around us. They seemed delighted when we spoke French. They wanted to know all about what we'd seen in France, about England and so on. We felt like celebrities being questioned by reporters. In the middle of all this Norman discovered he'd lost his cap, so I asked the band-leader to announce it, without much hope of its return and we didn't get it. (Norman "loses" his cap at least once a day, but this time it had gone for good.) Eventually two girls asked us to their parents' table and we joined them for a drink. We had to be in by 10.30, so had to leave them after about half an hour. Norman had to return without his cap, but managed to get one next day.

I don't know how long we'll be here and I want to see as much of it as I can in case we leave.

You're my darling and I love you very much. Love to all. Give my love to our son.

God bless you,
Leslie

Sunday 17th September 1944 – No. 46

My darling Gracie,

Seven of us are on detachment and at the moment are in a field waiting for something to happen. We left the section on Friday evening and spent all day Saturday (yesterday) on the road, although for a great part of the time we were stationary – there's so much traffic on the roads these days

We haven't seen a newspaper for about a couple of weeks and get very little news – you know much more about the war than I do, even if I do know where I am and you don't! At least I did know where I was, but am not so sure now, except that I'm still in Belgium.

Apart from being away from you I'm quite happy – not that I wouldn't sooner be at home, but apart from odd moments I'm all right here. I'm seeing places for nothing I didn't think I'd see, but I'd swap it all to be with you now. It must be fine for most of the fellows, but I wouldn't change places with them for the world. I've experienced some proud moments over here, but they're nothing to what I'll feel when I'm back with you and our baby. So much has happened since we saw each other, and it seems ages since then. It's just six months since I was home. It can't last much longer, I don't think, love.

After we left the cheese factory at Morteaux-Couliboeuf, near Falaise, we moved on to Bernay, where we were housed in a very comfortable billet, with sprung beds, hot showers etc. It had been used as a hospital by Jerry, but was probably a Friary as the church attached was served by Franciscans. We were there a couple of days and then moved on. We crossed the Seine at Elbeuf and again at Rouen – it winds a lot, you know. Maybe you guessed I was there, as you guessed I was at Bayeux? It's a fortnight since we left there so I can't take you any further yet. It was there that we visited the Antoines. The place had been bombed a lot.

On Thursday after tea Norman and I went out intending to visit our friend of Sunday, Mr Honinckz. We boarded a 49 tram. By the way, we didn't have to pay on the trams – I believe some of the cinemas were free also. The trams are single-deckers but run in pairs. There's no smoking and we were told that was an order of the Germans because so many uniforms were burnt by Belgian cigarettes. Unfortunately, we went in the wrong direction and had to go all the way back to the other terminus. We saw quite a lot of bomb damage away from the centre of the city. On the way back through the city I saw them carrying wounded from an hotel where a delayed-action bomb had just exploded.

Eventually we reached the other terminus and after about five minutes' walk arrived at our friends' house. We were warmly welcomed by him and his wife and went inside. After that, he did most of the talking and was most interesting. He speaks quite good English and preferred to use it. I wish I could remember all he said. He never lost faith in our return and kept on telling his friends that so long as England was free "we" would win the war. He regards England as his "second Fatherland". He gained the confidence of a few Germans and even had them listening to London. He only now realises how lucky he was to have kept out of the clutches of the Gestapo. Once an informer was on his way to the Gestapo when he was talked out of it by a German woman who had married a Belgian of the Army of Occupation. This man was sincere, love – there's no doubt about that.

We ate a peach and lots of grapes and drank a couple of glasses of wine. We left at ten and caught the last tram. On it we met a man who spoke good English. With him was his son who had returned after three days with the Americans. He had seen 200 Belgians hanging and had shot three Germans in a wood. He was only a young lad in shorts. Before we went in we went to a café for a drink, after the usual "solicitations" – one can hardly move for prostitutes.

Next morning Norman and I went for a stroll around town and round the shops. You'd have a fine time in the shops, love – the place is a woman's paradise in that respect. Of course a lot of the things are dearer than England, but the counters are much better stocked. On our way out we heard bells playing – "Tipperary"! We returned for dinner and learnt that seven men were wanted for a detachment, so our relief volunteered. We were to leave at 4 so decided to see as much as we could of this lovely place before leaving. We took a tram and saw the King's Palace, which I think is being used by the Red Cross. We walked back and into the cathedral, had a drink in one of the numerous, clean, cafés, and returned at 4. We had to go in two parties, and Norman and I were in the second. We thought we were only going just outside the city but the jeep was away a long time before returning for us.

About 6.30 we left, amidst the usual waving a vehicle gets, and went well away from the city. We went about 30 miles until we arrived at our destination only to find the first three still sitting amongst their kit, waiting for something to happen. An officer was trying to fix us up, but it was taking a long time. There were a few houses and a café. We went to the café and had a couple of beers and a cognac. Eventually we were provided with a couple of small tents, but three of us had fixed up to sleep in a house. It was a small back-kitchen with just room for the three of us on the floor. The people were very nice and anxious to do what they could. They lent us an alarm clock and provided water for us to wash in the morning. (While Norman and I were guarding the kits while the others had their drink, a man on a bike pulled up, gave us each a large peach and rode off before we could even give him a cigarette.)

Next morning we had breakfast and were ready to move off at 8. We didn't leave till about 10.30 and while we waiting we opened a bottle of champagne, and drank it from our mugs! We were held up a lot in convoys, but it was a glorious day and we were quite happy. We were given apples, plums, tomatoes and pears, sometimes for nothing, sometimes for info., once for money, biscuits and sardines. We lived on fruit all day (are tomatoes fruit?) until tea-time when we arrived at the place where we had to pick up some stuff. We had tea there and moved on. (Since we left Rouen I've noticed a great number of new houses, evidently the result of the destruction of the last war. During yesterday we didn't see so much destruction, except the destroyed and burnt-out tanks and transport.)

It was almost dark when we arrived here. We were given supper and provided with a tarpaulin which we fastened to the side of the truck to form a tent. We slept well. We put our watches back an hour last night – I hope that's right. It is 3.30 now and we are supposed to go somewhere else, but are just waiting at the moment. Round the edges of the fields there are tents and transport. My companions are sleeping amongst our kit. Until dinner time the sun was shining but it's quite dull now. There is a radio at the nearby "cookhouse" and we heard that the Yanks have breached the Siegfried Line in four places and are 12 miles inside Germany. Also that the Americans who are fighting in Europe will not have to go to the Far East – I wish they'd tell us the same!

All my love to you and Paul. I love you very much.

God bless you,

Leslie

Friday 22nd September 1944 – No.47

Darling Gracie,

Things are going well, aren't they? There's some heavy fighting going on, but we're still advancing. This morning I saw nearly three thousand prisoners herded together – and what a miserable-looking lot they were! Young lads and middle-aged men, dirty, unshaven and dejected-looking, although some look pleased, and I've no doubt that not one of them would escape if he could.

I've heard the one o'clock news, which said that the corridor in Holland has been widened and strengthened and that heavy fighting is going on. I was told that on this morning's news there was something about demobilisation, but they didn't mention it this time.

I certainly didn't stay long enough in France or French-speaking Belgium to finish off my French. I'm wondering whether I should ask you to send my German book, as I suppose I'll land in Germany eventually. We're certainly seeing more than the soldiers of 1914–18 did. We passed right across the area of most of last-time's fighting in about a day.

We spent Sunday 17th just hanging about awaiting further instructions. Fortunately it was fine and quite warm as we had no shelter. Just before dark we were told we were to stay the night, so we rigged up the tarpaulin in the form of a tent. It started to rain as we were doing this, and it continued all night. We heard that an air-borne landing had been made in Holland – the biggest ever – and that the operation was going favourably. We went to bed at 8.30 (!) and slept well.

On Tuesday morning we moved off after breakfast and travelled a few miles to join the party to whom we were to be attached. We stayed with them all day, expecting to move at any moment. The seven of us were each allotted a vehicle in which to travel and sleep. There wasn't much room, but it was quite cosy. In the evening we went into the village and visited several cafes. The beer wasn't much good, so we didn't linger. Don't think I'm becoming a toper, love, by the frequent mention of cafés (which, of course, are the equivalent of our "pubs") as we only had about four glasses altogether. The Naafi beer ration is a thing of the past – not that I drank any of the only two lots we did get.

In the evening Norman's truck was taken away, leaving him without a "bedroom", so we fixed up a bivouac in a field for him, from a large groundsheet we have between us. I slept well, though rather cramped, and it rained all night. Next morning we were called at five and moved off at about seven. Progress was slow, as we were held up a lot by other convoys, and at 11.45 we pulled into the side of the road for half-an-hour's rest. We stayed there all day and watched other material going past – and there was lots of it. In the evening Norman and I were on guard and our tour of duty was from 10.50 until 1.40. Traffic was still moving up and we spoke to several people, including Dutch soldiers, who were looking forward to their trip.

Yesterday (Thursday) we were up at five and moved about seven – a few hundred yards. We stayed there all day. I heard that Brest had surrendered. We moved as it went dark and travelled all night. I slept most of the time, and woke just before we pulled up, just after crossing a canal. We're now hanging about and waiting for the next move.

I suppose you're right that the results of war might upset me, although one gets used to them – without becoming hard or callous. It is certainly pleasing to see the wreckage of the retreating Germans' transport and tanks, although it is a pity about the wrecked houses and so on. The civilians seem more pleased that we've arrived than sorry about the damage. On seeing the lines of destroyed German transport one could feel sorry for them if one didn't think of the suffering they've caused. Everywhere one goes the sentiment is unanimous that every German should be killed. The people have compared our transport with Jerry's, and laughed as he's attempted to escape on all sorts of conveyances – bicycles, broken-down cars, horse-drawn vehicles and even donkeys. What a come-down for them after their victories in 1940! I've seen dead Germans, with just a twinge of pity and no more, because I've also seen the other side and think of the misery these same Germans have caused. You know I'm not hard, darling, and this doesn't make any difference. I think of myself and the other millions who could have been happy at home, but for these people. I don't hate them all, but I'm glad to know that they're no longer having things all their own way. These civilians have a better idea than we do what Jerry is like, and it's quite common to see them drawing a finger across their throats when they see prisoners. The S.S. are their special "favourites".

All my love to you and Paul,
God bless you,
Leslie

Thursday 28th September 1944 – No. 48

My darling Gracie,

We moved again last Friday evening. It rained and I slept most of the time. When I woke, we were passing through a town, and I was struck by the cleanliness of it – apart from considerable bomb and shell damage. The language of the local people is unintelligible to us.

Just as it was becoming dark we developed engine trouble and had to drop out of the convoy. We pulled in to the side of the road, but the driver couldn't put things right in the dark, so we decided to stay the night. Norman was with me, and there was the driver and his mate. We learned that there was a school a hundred yards away where some troops were sleeping, so we went there. There was plenty of straw about and we made ourselves comfortable. I took my boots off for the first time for three days. We slept very well. In the morning we managed to scrounge half a slice of bread and half a cup of tea from some troops who had stayed the night at the roadside.

The driver got the engine going and drove into the village to put the finishing touches to the job. There we were invited into a house where the lady, who spoke terrible English, gave us a cup each of "ersatz" tea, without milk. We moved off, and made good progress. We were famished and were delighted when some apples were thrown to us. I think I ate five without stopping! We were continually waving, as usual. There were several showers of rain.

Eventually, after crossing a couple of bridges, we skirted a town and found our party at our immediate destination. We slept in the truck again and I took my trousers off for the first time for four nights. Next morning it was fine. We were, and still are, without bread and the food wasn't at all plentiful. Soon after dinner we moved again, but only a short distance. Norman, Alf and I were left behind in order to tell a sergeant that we'd moved and we would all be picked up later. We didn't know why we were staying until it was too late to make preparations for a long wait. We parked ourselves in a tent and waited. I happened to have a book in my pocket and Norman had his writing pad, so it wasn't too bad at first. We hadn't our coats or anything to eat, and we were soon very cold.

We waited and waited, until at about eight o'clock some food was brought and the truck took us back, leaving someone else to wait. The sergeant didn't turn up until one a.m. The trucks were parked in a lane, and some of the lads had already accepted invitations into nearby houses. We learnt that food isn't at all plentiful and he black market doesn't flourish as in France and Belgium, being, I gathered, somewhat on the same lines as our own – hard to find. We slept in the trucks again.

Next morning we went along to inspect our "place of business" and Norman and I went on duty until dinner-time. After tea we moved under a roof and felt quite strange. At about 7.30 Norman and I had to do duty for the rest of the night until 8.30 next morning (yesterday) There's nothing else to say except that I'm missing you terribly and could eat a good helping of chips and fish!

God bless you,
Leslie.

Sunday 1st October 1944 – No. 49

My darling,

In my last letter I told you that I was in Belgium, and as it's now over a fortnight since I left the city I can tell you we stayed in Brussels for almost a week. You may have guessed where I was. It's a lovely place, and I wish you could have been here with me. Maybe we'll go there one day – I'm sure you'd like the place, even when they have recovered from the joy of being liberated. It's a clean town – even if there are plenty of prostitutes! The Belgians are a clean people and feel the lack of soap very keenly. There are some lovely shops and the "cafés" are magnificent. There are hundreds of lovely, well-dressed women. It's a funny place – necessities are very short, although there are plenty of luxury goods to be had, even if they are dear. I've told you of the abundance and cheapness of tomatoes, plums, peaches, grapes, apples and pears. Mr Honinckz told us that the reason they're so plentiful and cheap is because they're usually exported, but now they have no outside market of course.

Although I didn't spend an enormous amount of money, I spent more, much more, in those six days, than I'd spent in any such a period since leaving England. (I'm making up for that now, having spent about ten shillings, at the most, during the past two weeks).

Our billet needed much cleaning, after its German occupiers – we're getting used to cleaning up after them. We did have beds and mattresses though. On the day after our arrival, Norman and I were sitting in a park (I told you about it) in the glorious sunshine, when a Dutch lady spoke to us. We conversed in English and French and she told us she was looking forward to Holland's freedom. She said that she didn't think that Leopold would be allowed to return as king, although the ordinary people would have him back. She told us that she still had a small stock of pre-war tea and thought it would just last out until she was able to get some more. She had never missed her afternoon tea.

The evening before we left we visited Mr Honinckz, but before we found his home – he lives at Waterloo – we went the wrong way on the tram and found ourselves at the terminus at Laeken. We didn't see the castle or the palace or whatever it is, but in any case we didn't know at the time. On the way back through the city we saw them carrying wounded from an hotel where a delayed-action bomb had exploded. We spent a pleasant evening with our friend – I've already told you about that. Next morning, whilst strolling around the town, I heard "Tipperary" played on bells. One would think it to be our national anthem.

In Brussels most people speak French and Flemish and a lot know some English, and like to try it out. In some parts of Belgium Flemish only is spoken, but we wanted to stay where French is spoken.

On the Friday evening we seven left the section to go on a detachment, which, we were told, was near Brussels. We travelled in a jeep, which took four and their kit and returned for us. We went a long way, to about 8kms. beyond Louvain. When we three arrived, we found the first four still waiting alongside a camp. Not until it was dark did anyone bother about us and then we were provided with two small tents. They would only hold two each, so three of us slept in the back room of a nearby house. You know the rest of my story from there until I wrote on Thursday, with place-names omitted, of course.

On Friday afternoon, Norman and I walked into the town, which is two or three kms. away. The place had been badly damaged, all shops are closed and very few people are about. We returned for tea and were on duty at six, until eight next morning.

At the moment, and for the past few days and I don't know how much longer we are living on German rations, including milk-less "ersatz" coffee. To-day, we haven't even had coffee. There's plenty of water in the tap, of course, but what wouldn't I give for a cup of tea! The food could be worse, but I don't know what would have happened if Jerry hadn't left his rations. We've just made and eaten some "porridge" made with broken biscuits, a little oatmeal, and water, in a mess-tin on a tommy cooker, in our room. It's ten o'clock, and time I was in bed. There's a lovely moon, as there was last night – can you see it from your window?

I wonder how long it will be before we break through at Arnhem? The going seems very tough – something like Caen. When we do get through I should imagine we'll go a long way quickly.

What's it like not having to bother so much about the black-out, love? I hope you and our son are well – he'll be three months old on Friday, which is also Mother and Father's wedding anniversary.

Tell Paul I'm thinking about him. I'm thinking about you all the time, darling. I love you.

God bless you,

Leslie.

Tuesday 3rd October 1944 – No. 50

Darling Gracie,

I wrote the night before last by candlelight, and tonight we haven't even a candle, but are managing with a German (or maybe French) night-light which I found some time ago, which isn't exactly the perfect illumination. It isn't too warm and our room never sees the sun, which makes matters worse. Also, when it rains, which is often, the rain has no difficulty in coming through. We're on the top floor and there are very few slates in position.

This afternoon Norman and I went into town for a bath and walked back in time for tea. On the way up we found a shop open, which is unusual. We bought some postcards of the place, some writing paper and ink. We are very short of reading matter – we brought a few books with us but can't do any swapping, as, of course, the Airborne people didn't bring a library with them! The lady in the shop produced about a dozen English books, but there wasn't much choice being mostly Wild West tales. We bought a couple of Edgar Wallaces for a guilder each (a guilder being worth eighteen Belgian francs, or approximately 1/10). I've done more reading during the past couple of weeks than for a long time. Usually, I hardly read books at all, but there's been no point in writing when I couldn't get rid of letters.

We're still hoping to receive letters, but there are no signs yet of any turning up. George has written to Sergeant Roper, asking him to send our letters to this address. I don't know how long we'll be with this crowd. I hope you're continuing to write, in spite of the fact that, like me, you probably feel that your letters are going into space.

I suppose you've seen the details of the demobilisation plan? I've heard of it, and it seems that in the combination of age and service I'm only 43 at the moment, which doesn't seem enough. Apparently there's to be no distinction between married and single men. I only know what I've heard, as we hardly see a paper – the last one I saw was a week old.

The light won't last much longer, and as I'm also cold the only thing to do is to go to bed – on the floor.

There are signs in the town saying that "these people have suffered enough, etc., etc., don't loot," also the ones which are in all the towns which have been damaged, to the effect that the penalty for looting is death.

Kiss my son for me and ask him to kiss you for me.

I love you very much, sweetheart.

God bless you,

Leslie

> *14234557 Sigmn. Smith, L.M.*
> *2 Coy., 2 L. of C. Signals.*
> *attd. Advanced British Airborne Corps Signals.*
> *B.L.A.*

Wednesday 4th October 1944 – No. 51

My darling,

This morning was glorious and Norman and I walked into

town. We saw a fire still burning after last night's shelling or bombing. There are two large bridges across the river and they're a fine sight. It's been a very pleasant sort of town. The houses are beautifully clean and I haven't seen a dirty window – amongst those which are left. The Dutch are a very clean people and what we've seen of Holland so far is a striking contrast with the state of cleanliness of France. The people are quite friendly, even if they do invariably mix up their greetings, often saying "goodbye" on meeting and "allo" on parting! I don't think they're sure yet that Jerry won't return, and then, of course, they can't feel too happy about the bashing about their town is receiving. Very few people speak English, and Dutch is just "double-dutch" to me, except for "yes" and "no".

Another town I've passed through is Eindhoven, and that, too, is a very clean place. I saw quite a lot of windmills, but there are probably more towards the coast. There are lots of bikes about, and one of the favourite ways of transporting one's wife or girlfriend seems to be sitting side-saddle on the carrier. There are plenty of trees, and this part is probably more hilly than one's usual idea of Holland.

(Norman and Alf are just breaking biscuits preparatory to making some more "porridge". The approved method tonight seems to be to get the biscuits between two sheets of paper and hammer them with the heel of a boot!)

I'll continue tomorrow – the banging isn't compatible with writing and the letter couldn't, in any case, go sooner. Goodnight, my love.

Thursday

The "porridge" went down all right, but it wasn't quite as good as the previous effort, maybe because we'd run out of oatmeal blocks. Still, it was welcome and was at least warming.

This morning Norman and I were on duty. Although the sun was shining, we were cold, and were glad when we could go for a walk after dinner. Then we were soon warm and enjoying our outing. It was very pleasant walking through the woods. We stood on a hill amongst the trees and could see a long way across the plain. We dropped down to a road and walked along it to a village. On our way back we asked a lady for some apples and tomatoes and she gave us some. She wouldn't take money, but asked for cigarettes instead. I only had four with me, but she was very pleased. For those four cigs we had about two pounds of tomatoes and four big, lovely apples. We made our way back over the ridge and were in good time for tea.

The water is off in the building to-day, which makes washing and shaving a problem. We're still without mail, but still hoping.

I suppose you have a good idea where I was for several weeks after leaving Wimbledon? We travelled all day until we came to West Tofts Camp – a few miles from Brandon in Norfolk. We weren't a great distance from Norwich and King's Lynn, but we had very little opportunity for going out. Of course, I had a ten-day "break" when I was in hospital at Newmarket. We did quite a lot of work during the first couple of weeks – loading and unloading and waterproofing stores, but after that we didn't have a bad time – except for those banes of my life, guards. I think, on those occasions, of the times when I used to do eight hours' "guard" practically every night every other month *(in the police)*. Of course, it isn't quite the same – one usually does only two two-hour spells, but it's much more monotonous. For one thing one's beat isn't nearly so big and there are no shops to look at or people to talk to, and one can't think of going home when 7 o'clock comes!

We used to see plenty of aircraft passing over, but never so many as on "D" Day – that day we saw hundreds go over and as it grew dark they showed their lights and made a very impressive sight.

A couple of days before we left we were issued with "Mae Wests", 24hr. ration packs and various odds and ends and we had a job packing our kit. We'd handed our kitbags in at Wimbledon and into our large and small packs we had to cram all our kit and two blankets (one of them had to be strapped outside). We all had to dispense with several things – including blanco and "Silvo"! We also had to send some of our papers home, as you know.

On the 12th of June we left there and were taken in waiting trucks to London Bridge Station. We had a two-hour wait there, before going by train to Hayward's Heath, from where we went by road to camp near Bolney. We stayed the night there. Next morning we were paid and had to change notes into francs. We received two hundred francs and could also draw a little English money if we wished, but could not take English notes out of the country. After dinner we left for our place of embarkation – I don't think I can mention the name. This was 13th June. You know what happened after that, so I'll leave you there for the moment. All this time I was wondering how you were and how long it would be before I heard from you.

All my love to you and our darling son Paul is three months old tomorrow – what a lot I've missed.

God bless you, darling,

Leslie.

Friday 6th October 1944 – No. 52

My darling Gracie,

I haven't much in the way of souvenirs, not wishing to carry anything bulky, but I have a swastika arm-band, a couple of Jerry badges and a wooden bullet – you've probably read about them using those. I meant to keep a copy of the first newspaper in free France, which was published twice weekly in Bayeux, but it has gone astray. I have a copy of a Brussels paper, which, as an English soldier, almost makes me blush. I did have the honour of being the first to operate a civilian board in France – we had part of it and the "P.O." the rest, and, of course, we worked alongside my French counterparts – women during the day and men at night. There was only one civilian at a time and we were much busier than they were, as only essential civilian phones were operating. Whilst we were there the postmaster was taken away. There were lists of arrested collaborators in each issue of the paper.

At Bayeux we had air raids practically every night, but they weren't heavy and only a few bombs were dropped. There were, for a time, some field guns near the billet and they made the devil of a row. Occasionally a shell came our way. We could see the flashes of the guns at night at the front, which was four or five miles away during our early days there. We saw the bombers going over during the softening up process at Caen and occasionally a Messerschmitt would come over to be pounded at by A.A. or chased by Spitfires. Once I just missed seeing a Spitfire shot down by a ME. and on another occasion the reverse procedure. The main thing we remember about Bayeux is the dust, when the never-ending streams of tanks and supplies were moving up. We also saw thousands of prisoners, mostly in trucks. The first night in France was spent in the open, and we had a marvellous view of A.A. "fireworks"!

At first we used the baths in town, which consisted of communal showers, but then they were reserved, quite rightly, for front-line troops, who used to come into town in trucks for a bath and a rest. From then our bath was usually a biscuit tin and cold water.

All this time I was waiting anxiously for news of you, not knowing whether we were parents or not, until I received the news two days after the event – that was the first letter which didn't seem to have been delayed. The second Sunday we were there I managed to go to Mass, at the church in St. Martin. I only went to that church once, as I was soon working in Bayeux and attending the cathedral, which was near my place of business.

On the 28th August we left Bayeux. Madame Sophie and Françoise waved us "goodbye". We were very sorry to be leaving her and she was upset at our going. That was our only regret on leaving the place.

What does our son think of the three months he's spent in this world?! He won't remember the war, anyway. Give him my love, won't you?

God bless you,
Leslie.

Tuesday 10th October 1944 – No. 53

My darling,

To-day I'm back where I started from when I went on this last job. Yesterday morning breakfast was at 5.30, after which we packed. Dinner was at 11 and we moved off at 12. We hadn't gone far before our truck developed engine trouble and we were held up for about 15 minutes. After that we made good time and caught up with the rest of the convoy just in time for tea. Soon after seven we arrived here, unloaded our kit and had a cup of tea and biscuits and cheese. After having made our beds and washed, Norman and I went out at 9.30 and caught a train into town – a 15 minute journey. We hadn't much time, as the last tram was at 11, but we walked along the familiar main street and went into a café for a couple of beers. Drinks seem to have gone down since we were here before – probably they're controlled now. It was good to speak a few words of French and to see notices we could understand. We were glad to be back and hope we stay here for a time.

The trams were very crowded – the people push in and hang on to the outside and even on the buffers. Whilst waiting for the tram we spoke to a man who expressed the desire to go to Berlin and give them a piece of his mind. He had been in prison in 1942 and was badly treated and said he was very lucky and was only there six months. We found in the café that our 100 fr. notes are now no good, and we'll have to change them. Fortunately, Norman had others. We still have most of the pay we drew before leaving. We managed to get inside the last tram and arrived safely back at the billet, which is a fine house. There are three stories and we are on the top one. It's something like the Princes Road type, but probably better, although of course, at the moment, it is bare.

Love to all,
All my love to you and Paul,
God bless you,
Leslie.

Wednesday 11th October 1944 – No. 54

My darling Gracie,

I'll continue with my effort to fill in some of the blanks of the last few months – I took you up to where we left Bayeux, and have told you that we passed through Caen and Falaise to stay at Monteaux-Couliboeuf and remained there five days. We were in a cheese factory where production was temporarily at a standstill. We used to wash in the mill stream. There was a dammed-up pool where some of the lads bathed. There I watched the women of the village doing their washing in special sheds constructed by the side of the stream. They trail the garment, blanket or whatever it is, in the running water, perhaps rub on a little soap, perhaps give it a little scrub, beat it with a wooden beater, and rinse. Rather chilly in winter, I should think.

Several of us were at that time suffering in different degrees with diarrhoea. I had a dose of it which lasted at intervals for quite a long time and it was most uncomfortable, especially when travelling and at places where sanitary arrangements weren't of the best. I had one dose at Bayeux and then it started and continued until some time after we arrived in Brussels.

After leaving Bernay, we eventually had our first view of the Seine. As you know, it bends a lot, and we travelled along its banks for some time. It is very lovely, with little islands here and there, and wooded banks. All the bridges had been destroyed and we saw lots of barges which Jerry had probably used for crossing and which maybe were intended for the invasion of England. We crossed at Elbeuf and again at Rouen by pontoon bridges...

All my love to you
Leslie.

Monday 23rd October 1944 – No. 59

Darling Gracie,

It seems people are more used to our presence now, but they're still most pleasant – it's just that the initial "madness" has died down a little. We hear that even the end of the war won't surpass the rejoicing of this city on 3rd September when the first Allied troops entered. There's still plenty of entertainment by the people, but I've been put off by being mostly on my own, since Norman and I are on different shifts...

Norman has been visiting a house where only French is spoken, which is what we want, and is going to take me with him.

Several shops are re-opening under the lawful owners, after having been requisitioned by Jerry. There's a W.H. Smith which recently re-opened. As you say, I don't think they're really used to the idea that Jerry has gone, after all that time. I wish you could be here with me to share in the expressions of gratitude. There are notices in English, French and Flemish thanking us for the "speedy deliverance of our own dearest Belgium", notices of welcome and chalked on walls one sees "England and America for ever". People who speak English wear white stars.

Yesterday evening Norman and I went to a café-cum-dance hall, which is rather a pleasant place. We found ourselves a small table where we could drink our beer and watch the dancing. We hadn't been there long before there sat down at the next table a soldier with a very charming young Belgian girl. What she saw in him I don't know, as he was most boorish and rude. He knew no French and she knew very few words of English so they hardly spoke. He started to talk to us in a

Scottish accent which we found great difficulty in understanding. Eventually we found ourselves talking to the girl, and there ensued a French and English lesson! We taught her quite a few words and she pulled us up a few times. She had a few dances with her companion on whom she was completely wasted. Finally we left there, walked around for a short time and went in to bed.

My love to all
To you and our darling son, all my love,
Leslie.

Wednesday 25th October 1944 – No. 60

My darling Gracie,

We have been having the same miserable weather as you, darling, so I can sympathise with you. As regards the "Yanks and silly girls making eyes at them" I can say that my impression is that here British soldiers are more popular.

My French hasn't improved much since the first couple of months, but I can carry on an ordinary conversation. I can't talk fluently, nor can I understand people if they talk very quickly. I could probably speak quicker if I didn't bother about grammar – some of the lads can gabble away and make themselves understood, but even I can notice their mistakes. I don't want to do that. I hope to improve shortly. I lack "cheek", for one thing, and so probably lose opportunities of speaking to people, although sometimes they insist on speaking English, which isn't very helpful. I hope to go with Norman to a house where they know no English – probably tomorrow night. We've heard of some French classes and intend going tonight to find out whether they're suitable…

I suppose Germany could make it very tough for us, but once we can break through, say, at Arnhem, I don't think they'll have much chance of house-to-house fighting. It will understandably be harder for us than it was in France, but if we can overrun the country as we did there it won't make much difference if some of the towns fight from house to house. Then, as Norman says, there's our bombing, which must become heavier on Germany as the necessity of bombing occupied countries decreases. I saw in the day before yesterday's paper that we started offensives in Holland. The papers were talking of the "plains of Westphalia" and of how we'll roll over them with tanks when we pass Arnhem. The part of Germany I saw was certainly very flat.

As you say, it's only to be expected that, with terms of "unconditional surrender", Jerry will fight to the last. It's only natural. As the "Universe" or the "Herald" said, if we told them now what we proposed doing with them, perhaps they'd change their minds. Of course, the fact that their bosses' lives depend on it makes a difference.

I've no doubt the people in Brussels are agitating against the Black Market, as I hear that things are in a pretty bad way. I've heard of some people saying that they "did at least have something to eat when Jerry was there". It looks as though "someone has blundered" over the food supplies question.

Here are a few more places I've seen – Louvain, Diest, Houthalen, Nijmsel, Eindhoven, Grave, Nijmegen, Beek, Berg-en-dal, and lots of other places whose names I can't remember or never knew.

After we seven left the section we learnt that the airborne invasion was to take place and that we were to be part of its "seaborne tail". It was two or three days before we actually joined them and started up the corridor, which was then only an arrow on the map. The first day of our journey we stopped for lunch just short of the Dutch border and stayed there the rest of the day. We saw lots of transport planes going over as well as plenty of stuff passing us along the road. That night Norman and I were on guard – we were parked at the roadside. During the night we spoke to several Dutchmen in khaki who were about to re-enter their own country.

Next morning we moved off, but only went a few hundred yards before stopping for the day. In the vicinity there was evidence that there'd been a bit of a "do". I picked up a torn "swastika" armband in a wood just off the road. I also saw several dead Germans – and the results of one of our own trucks going over a mine. It was cleared up by then, but there was still enough to be seen – enough to stifle any pity I might have felt for the dead Jerries. That day we heard that Brest had at last surrendered.

We moved off that night and I slept most of the time. We crossed the Escaut and Wilhelmine canals and stopped at about seven in the morning. There were plenty of American paratroops about and some of them were guarding a "collection" of nearly three thousand prisoners. They were herded together in an open space. At intervals other batches were brought in, and some were taken away in trucks. They were, on the whole, a miserable looking crowd, and there were oldish men, and boys who looked no more than fifteen or sixteen years of age. One batch left the camp and was taken along the road, and as they passed us one of the American guards said to us "Some of them won't come back".

One small party came in escorted by two British soldiers on motor-bikes. The prisoners were being made to run, and "encouraged" by the motorcyclists and jeered at by bystanders in our convoy, they did their best. I didn't think it necessary and *I've* no sympathy for them.

We saw lots of gliders in the fields and examined one of them. The weather was lovely. We were just settling down in the trucks when we were ordered to turn around and go back the way we'd come, as Jerry had cut the road ahead of us. My truck was one of the first away and we were soon retreating as quickly as possible. There was nothing I could do so I went asleep. I woke up a few times and found that we were still travelling, although at one time I heard an altercation in progress between our officer and another. The latter was complaining because we were mixed up in his convoy! I thought it rather ridiculous, to say the least.

When I finally wakened, we were stationary and it was pouring with rain. I got out of the truck and walked along the rest of them. Everyone else was asleep. The cooks didn't take long to produce breakfast, which was welcome. It was discovered that one of the trucks had had to be "ditched" – of course it was the one containing Norman's bedding and some of his kit. It was subsequently recovered, but minus Norman's blankets, groundsheet and several articles of kit.

Eventually all our convoy was complete, but we stayed there till the evening. During the day we saw a lot more gliders going over. The weather was good and I took the opportunity and washed a towel. Whilst on the journey rations weren't too plentiful considering that we were living in the open, and we seven used to get some potatoes, boil them in a biscuit tin and eat them – just potatoes with salt – and we enjoyed them.

At about six that evening we turned around again and made our way back the way we'd retreated, the German attack on the road having been beaten off. We made good progress until about eight o'clock when the truck Norman and I were in developed petrol trouble and we had to drop out of the convoy. There was another convoy parked on the cyclepath and we drew in as close as we could on the grass verge. Norman and I were sitting in the wireless cabin listening to the wireless, while the driver and his mate attended to the stoppage, which was only a few-minutes job. Suddenly there was a shaking of the truck and we thought perhaps a bomb or a shell had landed close to us. The sets moved towards us and we were considerably shaken.

We clambered out and found that another truck had run into the back of ours, tearing out the back and one side. It had then continued, knocked a smaller truck into the ditch and injured four soldiers who had been standing by it, one of them very badly. Norman was cut a little on the cheek and was very lucky to have escaped with that. Neither the driver of the truck which hit us, nor any of us, was otherwise injured. Our vehicle had been pushed about fifteen yards and a sapling was bent down underneath. An ambulance was soon there and took the injured away. The truck was in a bad state and we decided we'd have to stay until morning, so we went to a school a few hundred yards away and slept on some straw. We were glad to be able to take our boots off at last, and slept well in spite of the guns which were banging away all night.

Next morning we returned to the truck – the driver was of the opinion that it would go when we'd cleared up the mess. We tried to get breakfast from the convoy parked there, but the best we could do was half a cup of tea and half a slice of bread. Then we started on the truck. One of the girders under the body was pressing against one of the tyres and we had to lever it away. One side of the body was open and we had to tie it up with wire, and also improvise a mudguard. Eventually we started off, but had to pull off the main road to complete the tidying up. While we were doing it a Dutch lady invited us in for a cup of tea. There was no milk in it but it was welcome. It was difficult talking to her, as her English was terrible, and of course our French was no use to us. At about ten we really got going. We were objects of great interest and no wonder. The body was shaking about and Norman and I were kept busy holding the thing together and re-tying here and there. We were very hungry, but we had several welcome apples thrown to us, which we ate ravenously.

I'll have to leave you now. All my love to you and Paul.

God bless you,

Leslie.

Saturday 28th October 1944 – No. 61

My darling,

When Norman and I came off our last night duty we heard of some French classes at a Methodist canteen, so we decided to go along that evening to see whether they were suitable for us. After tea, Norman and I went by tram to "Wesley House" where we had a cup – or rather several cups – of tea and biscuits. We made enquiries about the French lessons and found that that night (Wed.) the advanced class was held and they had elementary on Fridays. At 7.45 we went to the vestry for the lesson. There were fifteen or sixteen of us seated around a table and a lady who knew no English took the class. We were each issued with a huge writing pad as an exercise book. We found the lesson not at all "advanced" and were consequently a little disappointed, but, as we could see that a lot of what the lady said wasn't understood by many, we think that the class will "shake down" and that we'll have something harder. She gave us a dictation test at the end of the lesson and advised some to go to the Friday classes, which are taken by a man who knows

English. It was easy for us – so easy that we made a couple of silly mistakes! After the lesson we returned to the canteen and had more tea and biscuits. Norman's cold was still bothering him – and still is – so we went in early and to bed.

Yesterday morning we went to the Berlitz school of languages to make enquiries regarding French lessons. The school is alongside the Church of St. Gudule, which is not technically the cathedral but is regarded as such, there being no cathedral. We found that we could have lessons for two of us at 26 francs each. There are no classes but tuition is usually for small groups – the smaller the better. Individual tuition is 33 francs and I suppose is best, but we preferred to go together. The school has a good reputation – you may have heard of it. We arranged for a lesson at five o'clock on Tuesday and if we like it will go as often as we can.

We were on duty in the afternoon. For the evening, Norman had an invitation to supper which was extended to me. We arrived there between 7.30 and 8. The people are M. and Mme. Gortz and have two young sons and a daughter of three – the latter was in bed. He is a "professeur" at a big school in the city. Neither he nor his wife knows any English, which suits us down to the ground.

As soon as we arrived we had some Benedictine. Mme. G. insisted on making pancakes for us, and soon we were tucking into them. We ate quite a lot of them and enjoyed them, in spite of the fact that they were different from peacetime ones because of the lack of proper ingredients. We had couple of cups of tea, followed by two glasses of vin rouge. We arranged to go for supper next Friday, and before leaving had another glass of Benedictine. M. G. walked to the tram stop with us at 10.30, and we were soon "home".

To continue my story –

We eventually rejoined the rest of the convoy, which had reached our destination. We were given dinner and received some mail. Norman and I had to sleep in the damaged truck, but before going to bed had to dig a slit-trench. During the night there was quite a lot of artillery fire. Next morning we were up at 8 and had breakfast. During the morning we saw about ten MEs going over with plenty of AA to speed them. In the afternoon we moved about a mile, but three of us had to stay behind in a tent to await a sergeant and tell him that the party had moved. We waited and waited and grew colder and colder. During our vigil we saw some air activity, which included five MEs coming down for good. One of the pilots baled out from a great height and took a long time to reach the ground, falling about a mile from us.

Earlier on we'd heard that British troops were fighting on German soil for the first time for a hundred years – four miles from Nijmegen. We were on the outskirts of Nijmegen! Just before it went dark we watched a party burying eight bodies. The service was conducted by a Catholic Padre, and then he and three German prisoners started filling in the graves. We were cold so we borrowed the spade from the padre and helped fill in the graves – that's one of the seven corporal works of Mercy, isn't it? Actually, of course, our motives were selfish, as, as I've said, we were cold and that warmed us somewhat. That's another on the list of jobs I've done while in the Army. The Padre told us that there were six Germans and two British dead.

At about eight some food was sent to us – we'd been there since 1.30 – and we were relieved and rejoined the convoy, which was parked under the trees in a road. We slept in the trucks again. Next morning Norman and I were on duty with the

Airborne Sigs. After tea we moved into a block of flats which had been hit several times by shells. The roof was badly damaged and we were on the top floor so that when it rained, which it subsequently did frequently, the rain had no difficulty in coming through the ceiling. We managed to find enough space on the floor in which to sleep, but the room was always damp and chilly – apart from the dampness, the room had a northern aspect and the sun – when it shone – didn't shine into it at all. The building was heaped with debris and there was a most unpleasant smell.

At 7.30 Norman and I were on duty again – on our way we saw a wonderful "firework" display of AA shells bursting and thousands of "tracers". The AA fire continued all night. During the morning six MEs came over, machine-gunning, and I saw three of them very low and swooping down. We heard later that, amongst other things, they'd shot up a couple of ambulances. We were on duty until 8.30 a.m.

After dinner we went for a walk through the woods until tea-time, after which we went for a shower. (Two of the lads had made friends at a nearby house and we were offered this facility). During our walk in the afternoon we spoke to a man and although the conversation was carried on with difficulty, our Dutch not being what it might be, we learned that we could see part of Germany from where we were standing, and he told us the names of the nearest German places. We didn't recognise any of the names except Cleve, which brought to our minds Anne of --. We could see Arnhem too.

We were living on awful German rations. The worst part for me was the absence of tea. Next morning we were awakened early by the noise of shells coming over and our artillery replying. Before dinner Norman and I walked partly into the town – Nijmegen. One day we walked into the town, which was being knocked about at intervals and there weren't many people about and no shops open. We saw the river – the Waal, which becomes the Rhine when it enters Germany – and the two fine bridges. Every day we were shelled and sometimes bombed and often saw Jerry planes and saw and heard dive-bombing.

One day, Norman and I went for a walk, and hearing that we were only a couple of kms from the border, we walked along in that direction. There was no indication of the frontier except a notice in a field which we were later told meant "German border". A Dutchman pointed out to us which was Holland and which Germany. The border wasn't across the road, but alongside it. We walked about a hundred yards into Germany before returning. The front – if one can call it such these days – was only a km or so away and we could hear mortar and machine-gun fire. When we were returning through the woods our artillery opened up and shells were continually whining over. Before we reached the billet, a plane came over and shrapnel from the guns was falling around us like hailstones. We had to sleep fully dressed that night, as trouble was expected, but we weren't called out.

Occasionally a C.A. came and we bought a few cigs. One morning when we were going on duty we saw two houses which had been burnt out during the night by incendiary bombs. The residents were standing outside amongst what furniture they'd been able to rescue, watching their houses smouldering. There were lots of fires in town too. Another day, Norman and I walked into Beek, just beyond which is the frontier post, complete with customs office, money-changing office and souvenir kiosks. They'd all been knocked about. We made another trip into Germany and saw a "Kleve" tram. Just inside the German border was a burnt-out German armoured car.

Almost always, when out walking, we saw German planes being chased and fired at by ours. We saw hundreds of heavy bombers going and returning – a most impressive sight. One day a man was killed by an anti-personnel bomb just outside the billet – that was our only casualty. The shelling used to shake the building and some were very close. Our guns made a terrible din and shook the place even worse. The day before we left we were told we were to leave for England with Airborne, but at night the order was cancelled.

It's now dinner-time. I hope there'll be a letter to-day, but in the meantime I'll say *au revoir*. My love to all.

God bless you,
Leslie.

Monday 6ᵗʰ November 1944 – No. 67

My darling Gracie,

When we were with Airborne Sigs. it was unusual for L. of C. personnel to be so near the front, but, for some unknown reason, they were short of someone to do that job and we were called upon. It seems strange to me that they didn't take our equivalent with them – it wasn't as though they were killed and we were reinforcements, because we were sent for before they left England. Anyway, I'm glad I had the experience, but also glad it's behind me. It wasn't very pleasant or "healthy".

When we returned we were welcomed very effusively by the section and understood why when we learned that after we'd gone they'd been told to be prepared for casualties! We didn't know that when we went, and I doubt whether the unit did, as everyone was under the impression that we had "clicked" for a "cushy" detachment just outside the town. Still, as I said, 'twas an interesting experience and we're all right and I can at least say I wasn't always soldiering well behind the lines. I have seen Germany, too. Actually, when we were first in Bayeux we weren't so far behind.

I suppose it seems queer to be taking French lessons in a largely French-speaking place, but we think it necessary. We find that we are continually using the same expressions and phrases, but hope that with the lessons and practice we shall widen our range. It's also astonishing how little French one uses in the ordinary run of things – it isn't even as necessary here as it was in Bayeux. The people take a pride in their English, even though sometimes it's harder to understand than when they speak French.

Talking about drink, you must remember that in these countries wines and liqueurs are a normal drink and I don't suppose they're anything like as dear as in England. Even the Sophies used to draw their ration of wine every month. It was rationed there, being considered a necessity I suppose.

Regarding the dead Germans and the truck that I mentioned, what I meant was this – apart from the truck, I would have perhaps felt a little pity for them, until I thought of the trouble they'd caused. But, I saw the truck – or what was left of it – first. The area had been cleared of the (probably) bits of bodies, but there were still a couple of feet (which we buried), pieces of clothing hanging from the trees, broken rifles, unposted letters (one from a sigm. describing to his mother how much he'd enjoyed his short stay in Brussels) and across the road were his and his companion's graves. Incidentally, the one I mentioned was a Catholic. I wondered whether his mother knew he was dead – that's always my first thought when I see British graves –

whether or not their wives and mothers know that they won't see them again. Seeing all this just intensified my non-pity for the dead Germans.

Of course we use mines although I don't suppose we've used a great number on the Continent as they're a defensive weapon. I see your point about the possibility of the position being

La famille Remi — friends in Brussels

reversed, but they started it, and if it hadn't been for the millions of Germans like the ones we saw we should still be at home. Maybe those in the ditches were anti-Nazi, but they represent the nation which is taking a slice out of our lives.

You've read of the "smell of death" – we smelled it often on that trip, even where there were no bodies. I told you once before I saw several tanks near Falaise and that one – with a Polish crew, by the way – had been burned out. The driver had been unable to get out and had been burned to death in his seat. It's different from reading about it in the papers. Sorry, darling, but I like you to understand what I mean. It's not a matter of fighting and one side or the other being unlucky – it shouldn't have been necessary, and who's to blame?

On Sunday afternoon I went with Norman to the Belgian Red Cross canteen, and we were given the address of some people who wished to entertain British soldiers as their expression of gratitude for their liberation, so we decided to try it. We arranged to go there yesterday. It wasn't far and we were soon there. The family Remi consists of a woman and two no-longer-young daughters. They made us very welcome. They gave us some very hard biscuits with jam, and some very good tea. One of the daughters knows a few words of English and was very anxious to learn. We did a lot of listening and and heard a lot of what they thought of us and Jerry and so on. They had taken a great interest in the war, the affairs of their country and their king. We left at 11.30, with an apple and some grapes, saying we'd ring up when we were free to go again...

Every word of this letter sends my love to you.

God bless you,

Leslie xxxxxxxxxx

(From now on life settles into a routine, and my father's letters are full of humdrum doings: duty, French lessons at the Berlitz school, visits to the homes of the various hospitable Belgians they encountered – the Gortz family, the Montoisys, the Godderés and the Remis (Henriette and Berthilde and their mother). They are also filled with questions and answers about

the everyday doings of friends and family, comments on the doings of the day as reported in the newspapers, and occasional requests for items to be sent from home.

Only anecdotes of general interest are included.)

Friday 17th November 1944 – No. 71

Darling Gracie,

On Wednesday we went to the Gortzes. During supper a colleague of Mr Gortz arrived, a school-teacher. We spent a pleasant evening talking and drinking wine and Benedictine. Our fellow-guest was a prisoner near Berlin for ten months. He worked twelve hours a day – or night, most of the time at a sugar factory. He said the civilians with whom he worked were too scared to talk, and he didn't have the chance of mixing with them outside, of course.

He said he and his fellow-prisoners were glad when there was an air-raid because no work was done then. His job was shovelling coal. They were mixed Belgians and French, and in the prison camp the latter were treated worse than they were. They all slept on unchanged straw, which had previously been used by Russians and Poles. The food was bad.

He knew a few words of English and we taught him a few more. One thing they find impossible to pronounce is "th" – on the ticket which one has to give to the "professeur" at each Berlitz lesson my name was written "Smits" yesterday.

They told us that our planes were very considerate and never bombed them during the night. Even so they thought it pretty bad, although from what we we've seen the damage is nothing compared with ours. We couldn't resist giving them a description of what air raids are really like. We left them near

11.30 and walked home…

I like warmth and comfort when I'm writing – it's anything but warm sitting on the edge of one's bed in this gloomy, unheated, stone-floored apology for a room…

The house situation is bad and will be worse, I suppose, but I do hope we'll be able to get one – I'm looking forward to having a home of our own, and so, I suppose, are you. Perhaps we'll have to have a "Portal" or some such thing…

All my love,

God bless you both,

Leslie

P.S. I enclose a "Swastika" armband which I found in Holland. I don't know how it was torn – maybe the owner couldn't get it off quick enough, or more probably he didn't know anything about it.

L.

Tuesday 28th November 1944 – No 76

My darling,

When the Germans first came here they were very polite and used to lift children from trams and so on, and couldn't understand why people rejected their advances. It didn't last long. I've told you of the ban on smoking on trams because they used to find their uniforms burned by cigarettes. People then started carrying razor-blades instead, so the Germans set apart one end of the trams for themselves, but found they made too easy a target for a gun in a passing car and stopped that.

Belgians had to carry cards, similar to our identity cards, showing they had a job, and if they couldn't produce it on the spot were sent to Germany. They would hold up trams to check them, and to search for other things. The Montoisys told us that one day a friend of theirs was on a tram which was stopped. As he got off the tram with his hands up he remarked that he had nothing in his hands and nothing in his pockets. Now the French for pockets is "poches", and he was accused of saying "Boche". He got off lightly with five days in prison.

They consider it an honour to have been imprisoned here, as, I suppose, it usually implies that they have done something to displease their "protectors".

I suppose you saw in the papers that Germany definitely did attempt to invade us and was stopped by the RAF setting the sea on fire? We've heard from several sources of the large numbers of badly-burned Germans who were seen, in the hospitals and passing through.

Have you seen the news film of the strike in Denmark, when the Germans had to give in to the people? There you see the Germans pushing people about in the streets, patrolling with tanks and riding motor-cycles along the pavements. The people just "downed tools" and refused to do anything until their demands were met.

I wish I could remember all the things I've been told – here and in France – about the people's lives during the occupation. It's been a nightmare for the great majority of them. They could hardly believe it when they found that the place would no longer be filled with those grey uniforms – no wonder they were mad at first when their beloved "Tommies" came.

Some, of course, are disappointed that all their troubles are not yet over, and there's no doubt that they are in some respects worse off than when Jerry was here. There's very little milk and coal, and no butter – outside the "black market". The Govt. is blamed and it certainly doesn't seem to be doing much about it. The people want to work for us as they had to for Jerry, only more so, and to eat. The stuff must be here because Germany used to take it. Belgium is a big coal producing country, and the people used to see the fires the German troops had, and most of the rest went to Germany and to German-controlled industry. The people had to work in the factories, helping Germany's war effort, and now want to help ours, but, they say, those factories are lying idle.

I hear that a lot of the agitation from the Resistance people is from a lot who joined on the 3rd Sept. when the danger was over, and are seizing the opportunity to gain their own ends ...

I think I've gone on long enough for now, don't you? It all boils down to the fact that we're welcome here. If anyone says anything to the contrary when I get home there'll be trouble. Also for those who said "propaganda" to the stories of the occupied countries – send 'em over here to talk to the people who know ...

Love to all,
God bless you, darling,
Leslie.

Tuesday 26th December 1944 – No 88

Gracie, my darling,

On Christmas Eve I was on duty. As soon as we came off duty we had a wash, missing tea, and then left for the Godderés. We arrived there at about 6.30 and it was lovely to be indoors and warm. There were there, besides our host and hostess, their mothers and Mr Godderé's sister and her husband and their two sons. The first thing we had to do was to admire the children's presents, of which there were plenty. The boys weren't a bit shy, but very well-behaved. One is nearly nine and the other I should say about four. They both speak French and English and speak the latter like well-bred English children. All present could speak English – the two mothers with a very slight accent and the younger people with no accent.

They'd made a fine job of the flat, and except for the absence of glass in the doors, and cuts in the furniture and ceiling one wouldn't notice it had been damaged. There was a Christmas tree in front of the french windows and it looked very nice, covered with "snow" which is really fine glass. The first thing I noticed was an array of bottles! We were soon drinking a whisky and Martini, followed by a gin and ditto. The candles on the tree were lit and the younger boy insisted on the lights being out for quite a time.

Eventually we moved over to the salle à manger for dinner. There was soup, hors d'oeuvres and potatoes and rabbit, followed by Christmas pudding and custard. The meal was accompanied by warm vin rouge. We enjoyed dinner very much – I don't know what was done with the rabbit, but it was the nicest I've ever tasted, just like chicken. Norman beat me by having two helpings of pudding.

After dinner the children went to bed, after kissing everyone, and Norman and I had to go in and say "goodnight" to them when they were in bed. We returned to the "salon" for coffee, before which we were photographed several times – I forgot to mention that a neighbour and his wife and son arrived before dinner and it was he who took the photographs. They didn't speak English, so our French had a little airing. We chatted over the coffee and later returned to the dining table to play roulette. We only played for low stakes, although it looked as though a lot of money was changing hands. There were stacks of coins, the usual stake being ten centimes, which is worth about a tenth of a penny. It was a little confusing for us but we soon were used to the game.

We started off with a whisky and soda and continued with gin and cognac. The latter was some which had been saved since before the occupation to be drunk at the first Christmas after the Liberation. A very pleasant time was had by all. We played until five o'clock, the time passing quickly. Norman won about fifty francs, and I lost about twenty.

The neighbours left, also M's sister and her husband, leaving the children asleep – they were in the only bed. We were provided with a mattress, a couple of blankets and pillows on the floor of the dining room and our hosts had the same in the salon. We had another cognac before retiring at five-thirty. We didn't undress, of course, but just took off our blouses and boots. We were very comfortable and slept a little until 7.15 when we were called. They gave us an omelette and a little bacon and a cup of tea in a hurry, and we left at 7.45 with a parcel of cake and an apple.

We'd had a most enjoyable time and everyone was very kind. We walked for about ten minutes before a tram came. On the way down we could see khaki figures asleep in the cafes which had been open all night. We left the tram at 8.15 and just had time for a quick wash before duty at 8.30. No-one felt like work, of course, but fortunately there wasn't a great deal of it. When we went off duty at one the Remis were waiting outside with two parcels each for us. We had each one of their lovely tarts and a writing pad, a sample of which you have in your hand now. We promised to see them sometime this week and after a few minutes left them to go for dinner.

We were provided with plates, and had pork, and turkey and chicken, potatoes (roast), cabbage (no sprouts!) and plenty of stuffing, followed by pudding and sauce. It was quite nice and just enough. There were also two pint bottles of beer, an apple, an orange (very small), a cigar and a bag of sweets. We'd received five cigars with our free cigarette issue and from the German on the bands it would appear that they were intended for the Wehrmacht.

After dinner we went to bed and died until five o'clock, when we staggered round for a taste of tinned plums, before arriving on duty at five-thirty – half an hour late. Everything was under control and there wasn't much doing. We did an unheard-of thing – smoked on duty during the day, as we had been doing in the morning when the colonel walked in with his Christmas greeting. He must have known we'd been smoking although we'd put them out, but he didn't say anything.

Norman and I were due off at 7.30 and were released at 7.15. We dashed to the billet for our coats and hurried to the Palais des Beaux Arts to hear the Hallé orchestra. We were unwashed and unshaven, but we'd made up our minds to go if off in time. We felt terribly "scruffy", of course. We were just handing in our coats as they played "The King", and had no difficulty in finding seats upstairs. It's a fine big place. Unfortunately we didn't get a programme, as there weren't many. John Barbirolli was conducting and the orchestra started off with an overture by Rossini. Then Solomon appeared and we heard Tchaikowsky's Concerto in B flat minor. I missed you lovey.

Solomon got a marvellous ovation and played something else. After the interval it was all Strauss. First was the overture "Gypsy Baron", then "Radetzky" (by Josef Strauss) followed by "Tales from the Vienna Woods", finishing with the overture

Home on leave — 1945

"Die Fledermaus" – how well known that is, and yet I, for one, had no idea it was "Fledermaus". As an encore they played Londonderry Air. It seems the Hallé will be here for a week or two yet. On Thursday there's a celebrity concert, with Joan Hammond and Nancy Evans amongst others I don't know. One day the latter is singing with the Hallé and included in the programme are two arias from Carmen.

When we left the concert it was a lovely night, moon and star-lit and frosty. We slept well that night and got up just in time for breakfast. It's colder still and freezing hard, but we welcome it as long as the sky is clear, even though shaving is an ordeal – I can't feel my razor in my fingers. Actually, at the moment, the sky isn't too clear and we've heard no "music" of aircraft. I believe we're doing quite well and opinion seems fairly general that this attack of Jerry's might be a good thing for us. The Belgians have had the wind up, some of them, and one can hardly blame them...

All my love to you and our darling.

God bless you,

Leslie

Saturday 30th December 1944 – No. 90

My darling,

I expect to see you in about a week's time. Yes, my love, unless something goes wrong, I will be with you on the 9th! For the first time, I have been lucky in the draw and am the first of the section to go, the next one going a week later. I thought my leg was being pulled at first, but it's true, and needless to say, this week will be one of the longest I've known ...

Yesterday I made a trip to my "tailor's" for a new suit. It doesn't fit too well, and I look like a "rookie" because he had no flashes or shoulder-titles. Perhaps I'll treat myself to some while I'm home.

Yesterday evening we visited the Remis and received a very warm welcome. They gave us a couple of fried eggs and chips, followed by pancakes. My eyes nearly popped out of my head when I saw the eggs, which were the first I'd had since Valenciennes. That makes six in more than as many months and spread over only two meals!

I hope I can remember how to fasten a collar and tie – I'm a little weary of these clothes...

Every bit of my love to you and Paul.

God bless you,

Leslie.

(After returning from his leave in the bitter January of 1945, my father settled again into life in Brussels. A routine of work, guard duty, French lessons, visits to the Remis, the Gortzes and the Godderés, and occasional excursions to places like Waterloo. As the excitement died down, there was a sense of ant-climax, which persisted through the rest of that winter, and into the spring. Even the news, in May, of the end of the war did little to cheer him. The surrender of Germany had become inevitable, but that in itself was no longer the longed-for moment. Instead, returning home was the real goal, and that began to seem a long way off; further removed, indeed, than in the optimistic days immediately following the Normandy Landings.)

> *14234557 Sigmn. Smith, L.M.*
> *19 T.S.B.O. Section*
> *Royal Signals*
> *H.Q. 11 L. of C. Area*
> *B.L.A.*

Tuesday 8th May 1945 – No. 50

My darling,

So it's happened at last! I wonder what you feel like? I don't know really how I feel – terribly pleased, of course, but one can hardly realise it's over after all this time. I suppose I'd feel more about it if I knew I'd be rejoining you soon, for good, although a big step in that direction has been taken. I don't feel like celebrating in the usual way – I just want to be with you and feel glad about it all.

At tea-time yesterday we heard that the Belgian radio had announced that the war was over, and we thought it would probably be true although they always seem to be a little in advance with news, and in this instance were basing their announcement on the German report of their capitulation. We wanted, however, to hear it from the BBC. Looking from our dormitory window we could see one of the priests telling a crowd of boys something and they broke away cheering and dancing about. All day long bombers were going over, probably carrying ex-prisoners.

After ten we went to the baths. On the way we could hear our National Anthem in the cafes, and people gave us the "V" sign and so on. We enjoyed our shower and swim and returned to the billet. During the afternoon the other section left us – you may have gathered that we've finished our job here. We thought of going along to the Gortzes, but decided against it as we were both feeling rather tired and knew if we went there we'd be late going to bed.

By this time it was taken for granted that the war was over and papers were selling like hot cakes. We bought one each and went to have a look at the town. The main streets were crowded and we thought it would be difficult to find a seat in a café – we didn't feel like celebrating, but were thirsty and wanted a quiet glass of beer. We walked away from the crowds, across the canal and found a quiet café, where we had four glasses of beer and read our papers, and talked.

We were both thinking of home and wondering what our respective wives were doing – then we thought that, not hearing the Belgian news, you wouldn't be quite so sure, although I suppose everyone knew it was just a matter of hours. We wanted to hear the 9 o'clock News, so we left the café about 8.30 to walk to the C.W.L. Everyone seemed to be in town and it was flags, flags, flags, the women in holiday attire and some wearing skirts of the national colours.

A few truck-loads of German prisoners passed and they were greeted with jeers and catcalls, especially from the women – one I noticed shaking her fist and shouting "sales Boches" (dirty Boches). I couldn't help a slight feeling of pity for them – prisoners in a rejoicing capital, but these people know them better than we do.

There was a dance on at the C.W.L with the "Desert Rats" band, but they had an interval for the News. Then we heard that the war with Germany is definitely over and that Mr Churchill will speak at three and the King at nine.

Later

When the News had finished, the chaplain announced that there would be a Mass of Thanksgiving at 10 o'clock next morning at the Church of the Sablon. Norman and I left the canteen and walked to the main boulevards, where one could hardly move for people. Although it wasn't dark, the first thing I noticed was that the street lighting was in operation – probably not up to normal standards, but still a wonderful sight. I suppose you're quite used to it by now. The neon signs were working, too, and were loudly greeted. Planes were flying over, very low, and throwing out a few flares. Traffic was practically at a standstill and people were standing on the tops of trams and crowding onto lorries and jeeps. Lots of people were wearing paper hats and carrying flags. We made our way through the crowds, feeling rather detached – I was wondering what you were doing – and thought maybe you'd be changing a nappy or something like that!

Actually, although everyone was excited and happy it was

quite orderly – as orderly as such dense crowds can be. Occasional fireworks were let off, and some people were dancing about in and out of the crowd. When we'd seen enough of crowds we returned to the billet. It was just after ten and we were the only people in. Soon after we went to bed, two "All clears" were sounded.

This morning we had a few jobs to do and at 9.45 left the billet. I noticed that every tram had a flag or flags fastened to the trolley. I took a tram as far as the palace and from there walked the short distance to the Church of Notre Dame des Victoires du Sablon – aptly named in the circumstances. I expected it to be crowded and was surprised to find very few people present. It was a military Mass, said by the Chaplain-General. We were all seated at the front. When I left I walked back to the palace, and noticed lots of chalked notices announcing a "manifestation" there at five o'clock, and "Vive le roi", "Vive Leopold III" and even "Vive Albert"! This, apparently, is a reply to the Socialist resolution to ask for the King's abdication on his return.

I bought a couple of papers as souvenirs – I wonder whether you've kept any, love? – and went to the C.W.L. for my "elevenses". Then I walked to a tiny park I wot of, read one of the papers, and then started this epistle. I had to stop in order to return for dinner. We have civilian cooks now, and after a bad start they're doing all right!

The weather is very warm. At three o'clock we listened to Mr Churchill and I blancoed my belt and gaiters! We felt too hot to do much and just lazed about. I didn't hear the bells ringing, but someone said they heard one lot. Town is still very crowded. The trams stopped running soon after three, which is just as well, as they haven't a great deal of room to move, although it means that the crowds of people who came into town will have to walk home. Planes are still going over and throwing out flares and one I saw was trailing a huge Union Jack behind it. I'm in the C.W.L now, of course, and I'll go down to listen to the King.

<u>Later</u>

I've heard him, and now there's not much more to say. I heard that Japan had protested to Germany for making a separate peace!! I wonder whether Japan will carry on to the same extent as Germany did, or whether she'll realise that there's no hope?

I haven't had a letter from you to-day and don't think there'll be any mail at all. The situation is rather confused, as we're sort of spare parts now. I hope my letters arrive in good time – we just hand them in when we can and trust to luck. I hope it won't be too long before I hear from you, my love, and hope that at least I'll get another one before we move, which will probably be any day now.

Tomorrow we go to the Remis and are dreading it!

I hope you and my son are well and happy – I do so much want to be with you. Kiss him for me, my darling, and ask him to kiss you for me.

Love to your mother and Nina and George. My wonderful darling, my lovely darling, I adore you.

God bless you,

Leslie xxxxxxxxxxx

P.S. – Wed. – Received your letters of 2nd and 5th. Probably moving tomorrow.

L.

Chapter Seven

Hamburg: May 1945

The 8th of May 1945 was VE day, the end of the War in Europe. In Trafalgar Square, they were dancing in the fountains and flags were waving from almost every building. For civilians, life could at last get back to normal, although the effects of the war would be felt for many years in rationing and economy measures. Troops began to be demobilised and to return home. In the Far East however, the war against Japan ground on, while in Europe, British soldiers, the erstwhile liberators of occupied lands, adopted a new role. Instead of going home and rejoining their loved ones, they found themselves wearily climbing back into their trucks and moving deep into the heart of Germany as an Army of Occupation.

No longer cheered by grateful crowds, no longer part of a fighting machine, they began to lose their feeling of doing an essential job. The euphoria, the sustaining excitement were gone, and the months became a grey succession of days spent on routine jobs and longing to be home. They made few lasting contacts with local people – understandably, the Germans were not so keen to socialise, and British troops were actively discouraged from fraternisation.

Germany itself had been devastated by the war. City streets were filled with rubble, gas and electricity supplies had broken down, and even water and sewage systems were destroyed in many places. Communications and transport were almost at a standstill, and strict rationing was in force; within this chaos, epidemics and famine were rife. 2,500,000 German men were still absent, held in camps by the Allies, and for at least another year, seventy per cent of the population was made up of women and children. Perhaps because of this, acts of violence inflicted by the victorious British and American armies on the defeated nation were comparatively few. Instead, the soldiers who had fought for six long years to bring about the downfall of Nazi Germany were now to become instrumental in the reconstruction of the post-war country.

Hamburg had suffered 187 air attacks in the years between 1940 and 1945, and in July and August 1943 repeated bombing raids caused a firestorm in which 50,000 people died. So great was the devastation that Albert Speer, Hitler's Minister of War Production, predicted that it would only take a few more raids like that to bring Germany to her knees.

Into this city of blank-faced, shell-shocked people, the British transports rolled, carrying, among others, men of the Royal Signals who would carry out essential communications work while attempts were made to salvage something from the ruins and begin the painful process of rebuilding. Hamburg was to be their home for longer than they believed possible, as 1945 dragged on and spilled into the dull months of the following year. Yet, given the relationship between conquerors and defeated, the men of the British Army established fewer friendships during their long stay in Germany than in the heady weeks in Normandy and Belgium.

Saturday 12th May 1945 – No. 51

My darling,

I'm starting this letter without an address at its head, as I don't yet know which will be the best to use, having at the moment "no settled address". This is my first letter from Germany, although, of course, you'll remember I've been in the country before!!

On Wednesday it seemed certain we'd move next morning. I received your letters but couldn't answer them as we were due at the Remis, and were fairly certain it would be our last visit. We walked there, through the still-crowded streets, arriving before eight. They had visitors in the shape of cousins with a daughter of eight months, who was very good. The "third degree" we expected wasn't as severe as it might have been, maybe in view of the fact that they were more sad about our impending departure. We had a very good supper, as usual. We promised to write and to see them if ever we returned to Brussels. I let them choose three snaps and they were very pleased. When we left Madame kissed us on both cheeks. We did our best to thank them for their kindness. They wished us "bon voyage et bon retour" and we left about 11.30. Usually when we leave the streets are practically deserted, but this night there were still crowds about and great excitement. Most people seemed to be taking the two days off, and next day being Ascension Day would make it three.

Thursday morning we were awakened and told we had to leave at ten o'clock, so everyone rose immediately and started packing. I've never been in such an "unpacked" state before, having taken advantage of the drawers in the cubicle. It was 11.30 before we eventually moved. It was very warm and as usual we were crowded together in the truck. We skirted

Louvain and passed through Diest, stopping at Bourg Leopold for half an hour. We passed through part of Holland and crossed the Meuse at Venlo, eventually arriving in Germany.

Here, there were no flags or waving people to welcome us. We passed through some small places, badly damaged, where the people were mostly expressionless, although a few seemed to glare – it's hard to tell really – and one or two children waved. At six we reached our stopping place for the night – Suchteln, never heard of it! – where we had a meal and were allotted tents. It was pleasant to be in the country again, in such lovely weather, and I wouldn't have minded staying a few days. Some of the fellows went into the village, or town, or whatever it was, and reported a hostile attitude on the part of the "natives".

I slept very well. At 8.50 next morning we were on the road again. The weather continued glorious, and the most notable event of the day was our crossing of the Rhine at Xanten. I can't say much about it except that it's certainly a fine river and the engineers have done a marvellous job bridging it. We didn't pass through any big towns and our geography was rather hazy as to our proximity to them, but I thought we were somewhere North of the Ruhr collection. The small towns we passed through had been badly smashed, by bombing mainly. And some of them were dead places, with just a few people wandering about. In some places the church was ruined, and in others it had come off better than the surroundings. We saw several collections of gliders in the fields. In some places there were still a few white flags out.

The countryside was lovely – why they want anyone else's I don't know, but imagine the people in places like those we passed through would have been satisfied with it – like some of the nicest parts of England, well-wooded, with little valleys and streams and green grass. At one point we passed along a road where for several kilometres it was bordered with trees bearing white blossom – a beautiful sight.

It's hard, as I said, to tell what people's attitude was, but the general impression seemed more of curiosity without friendliness. We by-passed Munster and eventually arrived in Osnabrück. There, the town is finished, although the outskirts aren't badly damaged. Having seen Falaise, it's hard to use superlatives, as nowhere could be worse than that, but from what I've seen so far England escaped very lightly.

We went about four kms. beyond Osnabrück and stopped at a guest house, or beer garden or road house – or whatever they call them. We didn't know how long we'd be there, but we unloaded and moved in, and had some tea. The view from the house was good and just across the road was a small lake, mostly full of rushes and so on, whilst along the side of the house grounds ran a large stream. One thing I've noticed here is that there seem to be plenty of streams and rivers suitable for bathing, and the people take advantage of them.

Next day our money was changed into Marks – one Mark is worth sixpence, which makes things easy – or at least, it will be easier when we get used to talking about, say, ten marks instead of about fifty francs for the equivalent of 5/-. There are one hundred pfennigs in 1 mark.

In the morning we did fatigues and in the afternoon kicked a football about – in spite of the heat. It was terribly hot for me. In the afternoon we were told we would leave next morning for here. After supper Norman and I sat on a seat by the side of the lake, and I started this. The frogs kick up an awful row all night.

Yesterday – Sunday – morning we were up at six and were away before nine, the weather again being hot. We made good progress, in spite of the bad state of some of the roads, when we were shaken up somethin' 'orrible. Some bridges had gone and had been replaced. We crossed the Weser – further South on this river is Hamelin – and arrived in Bremen. I was pleasantly surprised at seeing the river – I don't know why I should have been, as I had no idea what it was like. People were swimming and sunbathing and boats were on it. One bank was sandy and the other green and it was a very pleasant sight. The bridge was of our construction – pontoon. The town is not a pleasant sight, having been very badly battered. German policemen were on point duty. We didn't go right into the centre of the city and soon left it, stopping for dinner – one sandwich and a cup of tea – soon after.

When we restarted we were soon on one of Hitler's famous "autobahnen" – you know the motor roads he had constructed. There's nothing extra-ordinary about it, except perhaps its length and the fact that there were only two or three cross-roads in the seventy-odd miles we travelled on it. Most of the crossings are by means of bridges, many of which had been blown – incidentally, that was the only sign of fighting we saw on the whole stretch and in fact we hardly saw any on the journey, in the country. The road is just an ordinary dual-roadway with a good surface, but not as good as, say, the East Lancs Road or the Kingston By-pass.

We passed a convoy of returning French prisoners. Quite a lot of girls appeared friendly as we passed – some were on bridges under which we passed and others just at the roadside. We crossed, I think, the Elbe and came to Hamburg. The bridges, or most of them, are intact. We skirted the city and stopped in a – suburb, I suppose, where we made tea, while someone went ahead to find out exactly where to go. We got some water from a house and the people seemed quite friendly. Some children asked us for chocolate, but didn't get any, as we hadn't got any. Even around there there was plenty of damage and craters galore, but the city itself has had a h– of a hammering. I think I'm right in saying it is Germany's second city.

We were brought to this house in a street which has escaped comparatively lightly. We went out and strolled around the town. We're not allowed out unarmed or alone and the penalties for fraternisation are heavy. There were plenty of people about, queues at bakeries and offices, but very few soldiers – except German.

I don't feel like writing any more, but I'm sure you'll excuse me if I have a nap before tea. I feel I could write more, but the flesh is weak and I didn't have much sleep last night, especially after travelling in the sun all day.

All my love to you and Paul,

God bless you,

Leslie.

> *14234557 Sigmn. Smith, L.M.*
> *19 T.S.B.O. Section*
> *Royal Signals*
> *H.Q. 11 L. of C. Area*
> *B.L.A.*

Tuesday 15th May 195 – No. 52

My darling Gracie,

Yesterday we went to a place re-named "Taffy's Bar" and drank some beer. There was a civilian orchestra and it played, amongst other things, "Lili Marlene". I wonder what they and the waiters were thinking.

Fraternisation is still frowned upon, but non-frat isn't going to work. The general attitude of the people seems to be more of curiosity than anything else, here and there one sees a look or attitude which could be construed as arrogance or defiance. Some people say "good morning" and seem to want to be friendly. Being such a big port, I suppose there are lots of people who speak English and are really friendly to us. On the other hand there must be those who, apart from being at least technically enemies, have lost someone either in fighting or air raids and who will be feeling anything but friendly. We're not allowed out unarmed or alone.

There are quite a lot of soldiers – it's rather hard to distinguish between them and policemen, unless they're the same thing at the moment – and a lot of them salute us. In view of the reputed German passion for uniforms I can't understand why they didn't have a smarter one and to fit, unless it's just the officers who have that privilege. In comparison, a British battledress is the essence of smartness. And those awful long-peaked, ill-fitting caps they wear!

The people all seem well-fed and healthy, especially the women – unless it's just the natural tendency of the women to appear well-upholstered. The women are well – if not smartly – dressed. One thing I noticed, especially in the country districts, was that a lot of children and some women were barefooted, but on the whole they're better shod than the Belgians. By that I mean they don't appear to have had to resort to those heavy-looking wooden-soled shoes so common in Brussels. This is probably the result of the looting of leather stocks from other countries.

On the journey here we saw lots of people on the roads with carts bearing their possessions – reminiscent of the pictures of the people of other countries some years ago.

A new word seems to be in process of manufacture – the verb "to frat", also used as a noun, and usually in connection with young women, of course. It would be interesting to talk to the right people, but I'll have to wait for that until maybe this regulation is relaxed. I wish my German was as good as my French.

Next door there are troops billetted and they have in the front garden a bust of Hitler, with a noose around his neck. A German woman was seen laughing at it.

There are proclamations in English and German posted up – "We come as conquerors, but not oppressors, etc." and notices about curfew, currency, bank accounts, communications, suppression of Nazi organisations, etc. and a German language newspaper is published.

I'm dying to hear from you, sweetheart – that's the worst part of these moves. I'm loving you and missing you and longing to be with you, my darling.

God bless you,

Leslie.

Thursday 17th May 1945 – No. 53

My darling,

The most interesting thing to happen yesterday was that I had to give particulars of my police service, the memo. being headed "Police for Occupied Territory" – or something to that effect. That's all I know about it, and I'm not particularly interested unless it's something to prevent my going further from home.

I suppose you've seen in the papers about the de-mob, or rather, release, plans? According to what we've read, Norman and several others should be out before Christmas. This doesn't concern me, and I'm more interested in whether there'll be any more leave in the near future. It's four months since I came back and I think it's time they started doing something about it.

We have quite a comfortable room here, six of us sharing it. We have a wooden bed each – very hard, but still a bed. We're on the top floor and have access to the flat roof from which we have a view of a stretch of water and lots of roofs.

We seem to be cut off here – hardly any papers and no mail worth mentioning, no-one to talk to except each other and nowhere to go. The last point doesn't bother me much, so long as I have time to write, read, and perhaps study, but some people are missing the distractions of Brussels. I'd like very much to be back there, of course, because I like the place and could at least understand what people were talking about.

All my love to you and our darling,
God bless you,
Leslie.

14234557 Sigmn. Smith, L.M.
19 T.S.B.O. Section
2 Coy., 2 L. of C. Signals
attd. 8 B.S.A.
B.L.A.

Sunday 20th May 1945 – No. 54

My darling,

I meant to write yesterday evening, but there weren't any lights in the billet. Last time you wrote you were awaiting the official announcement of the end of the war. Like you, the ending of the war "just doesn't seem to register" and won't until I'm back with you for good. We didn't feel exactly thrilled at the news – it was more a quiet satisfaction that such a great step towards "civvy street" had been made. We knew that it didn't make any immediate difference to us, especially those of us with high de-mob numbers, for whom the prospect is "occupation" or a journey East.

I don't know whether you're just being optimistic or whether you don't realise that it's more than a "threat" of further service which is hanging over me – there's no doubt about it love. I'm group 38 and must be prepared for some time in Germany or... The papers say that up to group 25 will be out by Christmas, but no mention is made of further releases, and my immediate hope is that I'll stay in Germany as the lesser of two evils and that I'll get frequent leaves, or that decent quarters will be found so that you could join me. I don't suppose you're any more keen on the idea of coming to Germany, in its present state, than I am, but there's probably plenty of time for that.

I dare say you've seen Hamburg mentioned a lot in the papers. It was supposed to be not very Nazi and that Hitler didn't get a very warm welcome when he visited and didn't come again. Some of the people go out of their way to be friendly, even lighting cigarettes for soldiers. If I ever see Paris, I'll probably think it the most marvellous city I've seen, but until then my choice is Brussels, with London a close second. Of course, none of them can compare with Liverpool – you're there!

I'm wondering whether I'll have leave for one of our anniversaries – there's one in June, one in July and one in August. I wonder how far Paul will have progressed with his walking when I see him. I do hope it won't be long now – perhaps it depends on how soon the port of Hamburg is ready, which, according to the papers, shouldn't be long now. There's no mention of leave yet.

We were told to-day that letters will not be censored in future, although I suppose they'll still be liable to examination at Base. It'll give me great pleasure to stick this envelope down myself!

Kiss my son, my darling son, and tell him I love him too.

God bless you both,

Leslie.

Tuesday 22nd May 1945 – No. 55

Darling Gracie,

I wonder what you're doing now, my love – writing to me perhaps? I can imagine you sitting at the table typing, but you've no idea of my surroundings, have you? I'm in the billet, on the top floor of a largish house. We have a table in the middle of the room and Norman and I are busy writing at it. Three are out and the other is sitting on his bed writing. There is a rest room on the ground floor and someone is playing the grand piano we carried across the road the other day. He's just played "I'm in the mood for Love" – does that remind you of anything? I suppose eventually he'll play "Warsaw Concerto" – it's almost inevitable. The music comes by way of the open windows. Through the window I can see our stretch of water – a backwater of the Elbe. We've been forbidden to bathe because of the danger of typhus and so on.

We hear that the next leave – whenever that may be – will be of eleven days' duration, but whether that means eleven days at home or eleven days in the UK …The mail has just arrived and there's nothing for me. I'm very disappointed.

We've had pork for dinner for several days now and it looks as though it'll be the same tomorrow. Also we've had spam for breakfast every day since we arrived here.

I can't say much about the people because I don't see much of them and even so can only judge from appearances and little incidents one hears about. Three of the boys went to a hair-dressers to-day. There were three Germans awaiting attention, but one of our lads was bowed to a chair before them. He put his cigarette out when he sat down, but the barber rushed out, brought in an ashtray, lit his lighter with a flourish and gestured for him to continue smoking!

One sees oldish fellows picking up cigarette ends outside the billet, even early in the morning. They seem to be terribly short of cigs. I think most of the people would be friendly enough if allowed to be, whether genuinely or not, but one occasionally sees an unfriendly glare. Most of the women are blonde and the great majority of the children of both sexes also, but the men don't seem "typically German" in that respect. I've seen very few women worth a second look and such a lot of them are ungainly and well-upholstered – typical fraus and fraüleins of the imagination.

I'll leave you for now love, and hope there'll be something from you tomorrow. All my love to you and Paul.

God bless you,
Leslie.

Wednesday 23rd May 1945 – No. 56

Darling Gracie,

The weather has been dull again to-day and we've had some rain. This morning we were on duty and this afternoon just lazed about – I slept until tea-time. After tea, Norman and I went for a walk. We suggested trying to walk around the lake – it isn't really a lake, but as that's what it looks like that's what it is. There were some sailing boats on it – it would be very nice there in peacetime, I should imagine. We passed our H.Q. where a piper was marching up and down in front of the guard, complete with kilt, and he attracted some interest. We saw several "Heil Hitlers" and Swastikas painted on walls.

We followed the "lake" round – it's really lovely, or would be but for the damage round about. Once again I say that Hamburg certainly had a "hammering" – apparently the bulk of the damage was caused by one raid in the summer of 1943. We walked through a residential part where there were some fine houses. The view across the water was lovely – plenty of trees at the water's edge. There are several offshoots and we passed over a few bridges. We kept as close to the water as we could but occasionally had to make little detours. Eventually we came to a place where the water narrowed and there was a new-looking stone bridge spanning it, so we crossed there and started back along the other side. It didn't take us so long along this side and we were soon "home", feeling better for our outing, which had lasted an hour and a half.

It was 7.15 when we returned, so we were in good time for supper at 7.30. We'd heard that Mr Churchill had resigned, so we listened to the 9 o'clock News and heard what had happened – I wonder whether I'll be home for the Election?

I'd better stop this for now. Goodnight sweetheart – I love you.

Thurs. evening

This morning I didn't go to bed, but darned some socks instead. Whilst I was having my "elevenses" your letter of 13th arrived – still in sequence. After dinner, Norman and I went for a walk, during which we had a haircut. We went to a civilian hairdresser's and didn't have to wait, although we were glad no one else was waiting. I heard Norman's man tell him he was

Czechoslovakian. Mine said a few things in "English" but I couldn't understand him. He gave me a good haircut which cost one mark (sixpence).

On the way we saw a couple of truckloads of Russians – men and women and children – who waved to us. They were complete with red flag. Some of the lads have seen lots of them, and also columns of prisoners with their womenfolk trailing along with them.

We walked around the town, which is rather a depressing experience – destruction everywhere. We were both struck by the scarcity of churches – of course, some of the heaps of bricks and stones might have been churches, but we can't recognise any. The few we have seen have been Protestant ones, although one or two of the shells have no indication. We haven't seen a Catholic church yet. Probably this isn't a Catholic part of Germany, but one would expect to see some sign of a church.

We saw a crowd of people queuing to buy the newspaper which is published by us – the "Hamburger Zeitung" I think it's called – and which is probably their only source of information except for the notices plastered about. Two German soldiers stopped us and one of them – an elderly man – asked in good English for the English for "stamp", showing us his identity card and pointing to it. They were on their way to a military office to have them stamped. It's hard to say really what people are thinking – I suppose there's a mixture, some servile, friendly, indifferent, hostile. Some soldiers salute us – did you see in the paper where a "blimpish" officer ordered his men to salute German officers and it was subsequently stopped?

We returned to the billet and eventually had tea. At five we came on duty and it's now 7.30.

As you gather, the A.T.S took over from us at Brussels, having arrived in the country only a few days before. One of their sergeants was from Liverpool Trunks. Another girl – from Eire – was most indignant when one of the men expressed his preference for Belgian, as opposed to English girls. Most of the girls, from my short experience amongst them, confirmed my view that, generally speaking, Signals attracts a good class of girl.

I spent the last few days before we handed over to them just helping them from my longer experience on switchboards over here. Some of them were P.O. operators, but most of them hadn't operated for months, and even so, knowing the "mechanics" of operating is only a small part of the job, especially in a different theatre. They were appreciative of my efforts, as they were taking over a "difficult" board at too short notice. I felt rather sorry for them and hope they're doing all right.

Some of the fellows used to "canteen crawl", buying cigarettes at each one, selling or bartering in the Black Market – that's why the canteens stopped selling cigarettes. I could have bought jewellery for you that way, but I'm sure you'd rather do without, wouldn't you, love? No one could have a surplus out of rations unless he didn't smoke. Again, some would have cigs sent them from home for disposal in the same way.

Our son must be a big boy now and I wish I was there to "cart him around". I'd love to see him. I want to be with you both and live a normal life with no one to say "do this" or "do that".

Give my love to all. It's nearly ten now and we'll be relieved shortly.

God bless you,
Leslie.

Friday 25th May 1945 – No 56

Gracie my love,

This morning we were awakened by Sergeant Roper, who was guard commander – incidentally his first during his Army career, which shows how some people get away with it. He offered me what he said was tea, but I saw it was whisky and refused it. That's his idea of a joke. We did some cleaning up after breakfast and did nothing more until dinner-time. During the morning we heard that Himmler had committed suicide.

After tea, Norman and I went for a short walk before returning for supper at 7.30. We walked around the Botanic Gardens. At the entrance to the park is the grave of a Tank Regiment man who died of wounds. He is a Catholic and there is some poetry in German and English on the grave, and lots of people seem very interested in it. We saw a few Italians in the park. Coming out, we walked alongside the "GPO" where a lot of decrepit-looking vans were standing. Above the "Deutsches Reichspost" on the sides of the vans was the eagle and swastika although it had been painted out on some of them

The women here don't seem to bother much about makeup, but whether or not it's because it's difficult to get I don't know.

You say some people don't believe we'd bombed houses intentionally. I don't know about that, but there are plenty of houses and flats destroyed – in the places which resisted I suppose some of it would be by shelling. The damage here seems just the same as at home, only more so – very very much more so. Some of our fellows were cheered up on seeing the damage in Germany – particularly the ones with wives and families in London. My feelings are more of sorrow that it should be necessary. If it wasn't for the fact of innocent people being killed, I would feel glad that Germany has felt the war, but I would have liked to have seen the country before it was knocked about.

Norman and I aren't so pleased with ourselves now that we're in a German speaking area – we understand how some of the fellows must have felt in France and Belgium. Incidentally, I think I can safely ask you to send my "Teach yourself German" now! It certainly is baffling, but we're not yet allowed to talk to people so it doesn't matter so much. If anyone comes on the line I can say "I don't understand" or ask them if they speak English!

Regarding looting – there seems to be looting and looting, if you see what I mean. It depends on who does it and what is looted. The other day it was published in orders that it had to stop, and that a certain latitude had been allowed during fighting, but now it must stop.

I'm going to bed now – I wish I could dream about you. I'm glad Paul isn't old enough to really miss me and that I can slip into his life without his knowing I haven't always been there.

Je t'aime, chérie. I love you very much, sweetheart. Kiss my son for me, won't you.

God bless you,
Leslie.

Saturday 26th May 1945 – No 58

My darling Gracie,

After dinner yesterday, about a dozen of us had a game of football until tea-time. I enjoyed it very much, although we had no proper kit, and it's tiring playing in army boots. I'm already feeling achey and tired and will probably feel worse tomorrow – I'm not as young as I used to be!

We are working now at our usual job, but aren't very busy yet. The present job is only temporary and they're fixing up something bigger for us to handle – still in Hamburg though. There's some talk of us working a sort of enquiry bureau, but we don't know any details. I'd like a change from what I've been doing.

I've only had two samples of German beer – at the beer garden near Osnabrück, which I enjoyed, and a pint at "Taffy's Bar" which I didn't like and left a nasty taste in my mouth. I've read about soldiers dying after drinking stuff.

I do feel desolate here, and both Norman and I will be glad when the no frat is lifted, as I think it will have to be soon. We want to talk to people, but in any case it won't be so easy as in France and Belgium. It's not very nice for us here, and I hope people realise we're ordered not to speak to them, except on business. Some of the chaps don't want to have anything to do with Germans – they're all "bastards" – pardon the word, but that's the usual description by fellows who feel that way – some are only interested in women, and others of us would like to find out what the people think and thought. It'll probably be difficult to get at the truth, but we hope to be able to try.

It was much nicer being a "liberator" than a "conqueror", but how much nicer it would be to resume being a husband and father!

It's 2 a.m. and I suppose you and my other darling are asleep. Sleep well, sweetheart, and remember that each night and day brings us nearer that time when our separation will end and we'll be together without the thought that in a few days the army will claim me again. I thank God for you and our baby and may He bless you both and keep you well and happy,

Leslie.

Monday 28th May 1945 – No 59

My darling Gracie,

I'm aching from my waist down, as a result of the football. After coming off duty at about 8.15 I had my breakfast and then had to put a move on to get to church. On the way I saw another convoy of "Displaced Persons" – there must have been at least fifty trucks before I lost sight of them, and they were still coming. I don't know whether they were all Russians, but most of the trucks carried Red Flags. There were man, women and children and an occasional green uniform – does the Red Army wear green?!

This morning it was pouring with rain when we "paraded" at 8.30 for fatigues. Some of us had to load a lot of heavy boxes of equipment on to a truck and then went with it for unloading. After about two hours' searching for the place without success, and having had a good look at Hamburg – some parts of it two or three times – we had to return for further directions. Someone was found who knew where the place was, but it was too late for Norman and I to go out again because we had to be on duty at one o'clock. During our "tour" we saw another large convoy of "D.P.s".

Tomorrow we open two new exchanges, further away from our billet and on a type of board all operators detest. Norman and I will still be together.

I believe there are some A.T.S in town, and there's a rumour that they won't be allowed out without escorts – quite understandable, considering we aren't supposed to go out alone or without arms. I wonder what the procedure will be?! Not that there's likely to be any lack of volunteers

I wonder whether I'll get leave in July? It'd be nice to have leave in the Summer for a change – my last two were Winter ones, and not even the same winter.

My special love to you and Paul,

God bless you both.

Leslie.

(My father settled into life in Hamburg, and his letters become filled with routine doings. He had lost much of the feeling of being a soldier doing a worthwhile job, trained to fight for his country if necessary, and became simply a telephone operator in a shabby uniform. He had good friends, of course, amongst men of his unit, and at Hamburg Trunks, the switchboard where he was employed.

He was eventually promoted to Lance-Corporal, and although the Royal Signals is known as a "corporals' Corps" because

The workplace – far from home

NCOs and Signalmen have a relatively high level of responsibility, he valued this promotion not for the status, such as it was, but because it meant fewer turns on guard. His son was growing up without him, which was a constant source of

286

resentment, and his chance to get back to Liverpool and set up a home of his own was slowly receding.

Finally, after sixteen months in Hamburg, and over four years after he received his call-up papers, release came at last.)

Chapter Eight

Demob and Home: September 1946

Back home in England, life was returning to some sort of normality. For many, already back with their families and back at work in "civvy street", the war was in the past, and it was time to pick up the threads and to make the most of the peace which had been so bitterly fought for. For some, who because of their jobs in essential services, had never been called up, the adjustment was much easier. Even so, the post-war world, with the promise on the one hand of a better life for the British people, and on the other the everyday reality of rationing and austerity measures, was a very different place from the 1930s. Working men, returning home from war service, were less prepared to accept the class structure that was in place before the conflict, and in 1945, after Churchill had dissolved his wartime coalition, voted in the first Labour Government under Attlee.

We tend to think today that it was all over with the surrender of Germany and Japan in 1945, but for many men this was far from being the case. We hear of the "Forgotten Armies" of World War Two: the Eighth Army in Italy; the American troops fighting alongside the Chinese in Manchuria; the men in the Far East who continued the bloody struggle against the Japanese for months after the surrender of the Germans in Europe had been celebrated; even Bomber Command claim that they did not receive proper recognition.

But what of the men in Europe, the troops who had fought and travelled through Normandy, Belgium, Holland and

Germany itself? They found themselves far from home, with no choice but to go on working for an employer they had never chosen – the British Army. And nobody in England gave them a second thought, apart from their own families. Their wives struggled with day-to-day problems back home and their children grew up without them. Every day was filled with yearning for home, every hour ticked off as time bringing them closer to release. But that date, around which their lives revolved, was unknown to them until several weeks before they left.

The system for demobilisation involved a calculation which took into account a man's real age and his length of Army service. My father, on demob, was "38" although his real age was 32. He had been in the Army from the age of 28.

Soldiers had to hand in their uniform (and were charged for missing items!) and had a choice of a suit or a sports jacket and flannel trousers. As these were mass-produced, the fit was often less than perfect and the quality of the material sometimes dubious. It says much of the relative lack of prosperity of the times that men were often wearing their demob suits many years later. Men like my father were looking forward to shedding their battle dress, but agonised over whether to take a suit or jacket, whether to keep their greatcoats, and what condition their own clothes were in, not having been worn for several years. Nowadays, most men returning to civilian life in such circumstances would undoubtedly treat themselves to a completely new set of clothes.

Going home after four years in the Army, during which period the world had heaved and changed forever, was an anxious time for many. Feelings of anticlimax and disappointment were frequent. A lack of recognition for the job they had done and jealousy of men who had spent those years at home could gnaw at them; joblessness could dispirit them; and trying to adjust to households where the womenfolk had learned to cope without them could unsettle and unbalance many, leaving them unsure of their changed role.

But nothing in the world – no trepidation about their welcome home, nor fears for the future – could detract from the excitement and exhilaration, so long suppressed, of knowing that at long last, they were on their way home.

14234557 L/Cpl. Smith, L.M.
36 T.S.B.O Section
1 Coy., 12 L. of C. Signals
B.A.O.R.

Sunday 18th August 1946 – No. 21

Darling darling,

My news to-day is that I leave here for good on 2nd September – that's a fortnight tomorrow. It's come at last, my love, and you can guess how I feel! Only two more weeks in the Army – whoopee! I can't say exactly when I'll be home, as we haven't heard any details since they started using Cuxhaven for demob. All I can say, is that, leaving here on the evening of Monday the 2nd, I could be home on Wednesday evening if there was no delay anywhere, but probably that is being optimistic, especially as there's the documentation and issue of clothing to be done, but Thursday is possible. Perhaps I'll have a better idea in a few days' time. However, I should be home for the weekend, so you can kill the fatted calf, etc.!!!!!! I hope this sounds as good to you as it does to me, lovey ...

Kiss my "little" darling for me – you won't have much more opportunity of doing it for me!

What do my grey pants look like?

Ta-ta for now, my darling. All my love to you and Paul.

God bless you,

Leslie xx

Tuesday 20th August 1946 – No 22

My darling,

I'm in the guard room, with, I hope, the certainty that it's for the last time. Of course, any decent unit wouldn't put a bloke on guard after he'd had his "medical" – in fact, some units look upon one as a "guest of the army" in such cases …

You'll have had my letter with my glad news, I hope – but that doesn't mean any slackening off in writing, my love! You can stick it for another couple of weeks, can't you, lovey?!

Yesterday morning I was very busy at the office, and wasn't able to pay much attention to my new trainee – Mrs Rodgers. I had to leave at noon, as the truck to take us to the Hospital was to leave at one o'clock. We had dinner, and soon after one were on our way to 9 British General Hospital, which is some distance away – about half-an-hour's run. It's a modern hospital – they haven't finished building it yet, and work is in progress.

There were seven of us. We were weighed, measured and sight-tested by R.A.M.C. orderlies, and then had to wait a short time for the M.O. to arrive. I weighed 11st. 12lbs., which is probably less than when I came into the Army (I was 11st. 8lbs., without my clothes, then) and considerably less than my weight has been on occasions during my Army career. I seem to have shrunk in height! At least, I was 5'10" in my bare feet, and am now only 5'10 1/4" wearing my shoes! I galloped through the bottom line of the sight-test chart.

I found the M.O. quite human, and he gave me a good examination. He advised me to see about my gums again, which I've been intending for a week or so – I have a little bleeding again. He pronounced me all right, and as soon as I had dressed, we left.

On the way back – it was only 3 o'clock then – we looked at our respective sheets to see what the M.O thought of us. We were all "fit for further service". On our arrival in town, we celebrated in ice-cream, tea and cakes. We then had a look at the Gift Shop. The prices are stiff, but I wish I knew exactly what you would like – there's a fairly good variety of perfumes, for instance, ranging from 8/6 to 50/-. Sequin-covered bags, tablecloth sets, etc.

To-day I've continued busy at the office. I had to leave at 4 to prepare for guard. At 6.30 the guard was "mounted", and a fitting finish, it was done in style.

The weather continues good generally, with cool nights and warm days.

All my love to you and Paul, my darlings.

God bless you,

Leslie xx

Thursday 22nd August 1946 – No. 23

Darling Gracie,

To start where I left off – in the guard room – some time after I'd written to you, just after midnight, the guard was "turned-out" by the orderly officer, who was the Sgt. Major. So I did my last guard in style. After that I slept from about one, with a telephone interruption at some ridiculous time like 4.30 or thereabouts, until 6.15, when the bell from the sentry-box started ringing and wouldn't stop – I think one of the sentries must have fallen asleep against it!

Yesterday I continued busy at the office – my Mrs Rodgers isn't too bright, I'm afraid. In fact, she isn't bright at all, and makes me feel rather irritable. Being qualified for the "Couldn't Care Less Brigade" myself, I shouldn't worry, I suppose, but I should hate to think that after I've gone she'll say "Oh, Cpl. Smith didn't tell me about that!" which is what will happen, I'm sure, and it's not a nice thought ...

This afternoon I went to the Q stores to try to change underpants, but he's hardly anything in, and won't have anything until next month. He says I'll be able to change things in "Blighty" on my way home, but I haven't much confidence in that, apart from the fact that I'll be wearing one pair ...

Peter has had a letter from Don Booker, who repeats what we've heard so often – that this final journey is horrible, and only the thought that it's the last sustains one. The impression seems to be that the Army, having no further use for us, loses interest altogether. He says that the actual demob takes a few minutes, but he left here on Wed. and arrive home on Sunday. Going on that, I should arrive on Friday (6th). He also says he got a good sports jacket and flannels and that the suits weren't up to much. I wonder!

I can't make up my mind whether to hang on to my greatcoat or not – I have to take it to England with me, and I believe they charge 38/- if you keep it.

That's all, lovey,

Eleven more days in Hamburg!

All my love to you, my darling, and to Paul, my darling.

God bless you,

Leslie xxxxxxxx

Friday 23rd August 1946 – No. 24

My darling,

I'm glad you're excited about my homecoming, lovey. I suppose it'll take me some time to get used to the idea that I haven't to go back "to the war". Yes, love, we'll be able to take our son out and about, and live a more normal life. As usual – no, I can't say that, as I've never been demobbed before, but the feeling is the same as pre-leave, only more so – I have fits of depression and utter miserable-ness, my excitement being suppressed inside, with occasional outbursts of joyfulness and all's-right-with-the-world-ness. I seem to have thousands of things in my mind, all sorts of little jobs I want to do, letters to write, etc.

I hope my sports jacket hasn't shrunk – it wasn't too roomy before. I hope you manage a coat and shoes, lovey – don't let the prices put you off too much. I'm not demobbed every day …

All my love, my darling.

God bless you,

Leslie.

Monday 26th August 1946 – No 25

My darling,

This is my last full Monday in Hamburg! This time next week I'll be on my tortuous way.

Our demob party took place on Saturday evening, as arranged. We "38s" were toasted and replied individually. As usual, drink was plentiful, and a good time was had by all. Personally, I'm glad it's the last demob party for me, as I didn't feel too good. Next morning, which was Sunday, of course, I felt horrible, which was rather unusual, as a night's sleep normally puts me more or less all right again. I got up for breakfast – three Aspros and cup of tea – and went back to bed. If I hadn't known there was a 5.30 p.m. Mass, I suppose I'd have dragged myself to church. Thank goodness one is only demobbed once – I hope!

I still feel miserable.

All my love to you and Paul.

God bless you,

Leslie.

Wednesday 28th August 1946 – No 26

My darling,

Oh, first I must mention that I'm in a bad temper and labouring with a sense of being badly done unto. I'd been told to make Thursday my last day at Trunks, which was bad enough, as most people get about five days off, but I didn't mind that so much, as I wanted to make sure that my successor at least half understands what she's doing, but tonight I read in "Orders" that I'm Orderly N.C.O. on Friday, which is really rubbing it in. In effect, it means that all the time off – extra – I get is Saturday morning…

I'll just wait and see what offers in the way of clothes, lovey. I'm not too optimistic, but it doesn't worry me very much – it's not as though I'd nothing to wear and dependent on what I get. As I mentioned before, I was wondering if it wouldn't be better to take flannels and sports coat instead of a suit. Anyway, I'll see what they've got…

Yesterday, we – 38s – paraded at H.Q. at 9.15, and at 10 the O.C. condescended to receive us, one by one. The "interview" took less than a minute. We returned to the billet, and at 11 I was at the M.I. room for Typhus inoc., and from there went on to Trunks, where I had to do a little "pulling out of coals" for my deputy…

I hope we do manage to have a few days somewhere when I

get back, lovey.
    Ta-ta for now.
    All my love,
    God bless you,
    Leslie.

Friday 30th August 1946 – No. 27

My dear darling,
    Your letter of 27th came to-day, and first of all I must say I'm
pleased to hear you've managed to fix up at least one week off (I
hope!) A week seems terribly short – except when one is waiting
to go home, of course – and I hope we'll be able to extend it.
After all, if Paul says I'm going to take him "all over the place",
we'll have to do something to justify his statement, n'est-ce pas?

I suppose a suit is more sensible, but on the other hand I think
it time I had some new flannels. From what I've seen of the suits
they're "all right" and no more – still, they're probably good
enough for a poor old married man with a family!! I hadn't really
any definite ideas about my greatcoat, but thought that, as I've to
carry it to England in any case, someone (coalman, etc.) at the
worst would be glad of it for a couple of quid, even if it were no
use to me. I wouldn't take an overcoat instead of a mac...

Yesterday morning I went to Trunks for the last time – to
work, anyway, as I'll probably pop in on Monday to say goodbye
to some who weren't there – and asked if, in view of the fact that
I'd to do Orderly N.C.O on Friday, I could finish at lunch-time
instead of waiting until 5. It was all right, of course, but I'm afraid
that I'd have stayed away in the afternoon in any case...

At 2 I attended my last pay parade, and shortly after that we
went to the Stores to hand in our kit, arms, etc., being parted

from it all after four years – I shed no tears though!

I suppose you've mended my grey pants, love – and did you mend the moth-hole on the shoulder of my grey suit?

I'll finish now, lovey – when you get this I'll be nearly on my way. It seems northerners go to York and others go to Guildford – they seem to have cut out places like Ashton-under-Lyne, where I expected to go.

Love to all,

God bless you,

Leslie.

Sunday 1ˢᵗ September 1946 – No. 28

Darling Gracie,

I suppose this will be my last from Hamburg and it'll have to be a quick one. It's 10 o'clock and I've slipped out for a bite to eat after a busy evening – packing and making up a parcel. It's amazing how much there is to do, and I'll be glad when it's all over...

Yesterday I went for a shower to Standard House, and on my return to the billet was "invited" by a couple of our corporals to help move some stores. I told them where to get off and went out again to the Naafi...

I've broken the back of packing my kitbag. I have to do this more carefully than normally, as our kitbags are taken from us during the journey.

They've put most of the lights out.

Goodnight, lovey.

All my love to you and Paul,

God bless you,

Leslie xx

Epilogue

"Je suis un simple soldat anglais. Je suis blessé. Pouvez-vous m'aider?"

I repeated the words to myself under my breath, handling the small book with care, as if it were a priceless document. In a sense it was. My father's French phrase book, distributed to soldiers landing in Normandy in 1944, encapsulated so much about the war. Young men who had been uprooted from home and sent to fight abroad, learned their first words of the language this way. Not the usual conversational openers, but straight in with the essentials: "I am an English Private. I am wounded. Can you help me?"

The musty scent of the phrase book placed it firmly in the past, but I rehearsed the words as if they were vital to myself. How old was I? I don't really remember, but these were some of the first French words I ever learned, along with the phrases with which my father larded his speech. When I started to learn French at secondary school, my father's enthusiasm and, I must admit, his help with my homework, swept me along, and I made good progress. But even he may have been surprised when I continued with the language to A level, adding Spanish and Latin along the way, then carried on to University and finally a career as a teacher of modern languages.

Returning to France with pupils on French exchanges, and lodging with a variety of staff from the twin school, I would sit often on the first evening, attuning my ear again to the rhythms of the language and imagining how it would feel to be a young British soldier sharing a meal with the first French people to be met in war-torn Normandy. How different my experiences of travelling abroad from those of my father!

When he returned to Liverpool, it was to the house in Smithdown Road where my mother was living with their son Paul, her parents, her sister Nina and brother George. My grandparents were frail; my grandfather was soon to die and my grandmother to become bedridden with diabetes. There was no possibility in the circumstances of leaving the house, as my mother had become established as the housekeeper who looked after everyone while Nina still went out to work in the Cunard Building at the Pierhead, and George was still working on the trams. And so the time went by. My grandmother died, George married and left to set up his own home, and my father remained in Smithdown Road with his wife and, by now, two sons. He nearly had his own home, but not quite, for Nina still shared the house.

Meanwhile, having returned from the war to the Civil Service, my father, found himself working at the Ministry of Social Security, later to become the DHSS. He worked in Princes Road in Toxteth, Hamilton Square in Birkenhead, and finally in Garston. He was promoted to Executive Officer, and retired in 1979. He was then able to fulfil his dream of living in a house of his own. Tan y Llyn, nestling in the hills between Mold and Wrexham, was the house which he had bought some years previously, close to the cottage where we had holidayed for 10/- a week during the 50s and 60s.

"A house of his own..." The phrase, in the end, had a bitter irony. The dream, which sustained my father through the war years, of setting up home with his wife and children, had evaporated over time. When he finally moved into his own house, his much-loved wife had been dead for several years, his sons had long since left, and he was, indeed, alone.

My father loved Tan-y-Llyn and the quiet hills and fields, and the lake cupped in the heather-clad slopes rising behind the cottage. His retirement here was happy – he had friends, he was involved with the Catholic church in Mold, and he had his garden, which was another dream from the early Liverpool days. But the war had stolen four years of his youth, years which could never be recaptured, and which, in an undramatic way common to millions of soldiers, had altered the course of his life forever.

Our Stolen Years